Dawn of Eden

*Love sustains Rachel when
tragedy shatters her dreams*

by

Barbara Michel

About the Author

Barbara Michel is thankful for her Christian heritage, a part of which can be traced back to Mennonite ancestors. The insight and understanding of people that she gleaned during the years she and her husband were in the pastorate is portrayed in the lives of her characters.

Barbara has won short-fiction contests, writes a how-to column for a small national writer's magazine, speaks at numerous writer's workshops and gives inspirational talks.

Copyright© 1997
BARBARA MICHEL

Son-Rise Publications
143 Greenfield Road
New Wilmington, PA 16142
1-800-358-0777
ISBN 0-936369-96-5
Printed in the USA

Dedication

To my grandchildren, Tiffany Lynn, Jonathan Christopher, Elizabeth Paige, and Trisha Renae who bring great joy to my life. May you continue to learn of Jesus and steadfastly follow in His footsteps.

Acknowledgments

Thanks to my husband, Rev. Gerald Michel, for his continued encouragement and for assisting me when I do my research.

To Evelyn Minshull, in appreciation for her friendship, her expertise, and her continuing support.

Appreciation to the Mennonite Information Center in Holmes County, Ohio.

Particular thanks to Martha Schlavach, an Old Order Amish young lady from near Millersburg, Ohio who answered numerous questions about Amish life in her district.

Gross Dank to Amos and Nora Hoover for translating the English words and phrases in Dawn Of Eden into Pennsylvania Dutch.

Blessings to my Mennonite cousins, Eli, Lizzie, and Ella for their friendship and inspiration.

To Donna and Jim Jackson for doing the layout and design for the Amish Eden series.

To Patricia Dunn for the cover painting.

To Florence Biros, my publisher and friend.

Title Page

Chapter 1	page 11
Chapter 2	page 25
Chapter 3	page 41
Chapter 4	page 53
Chapter 5	page 65
Chapter 6	page 79
Chapter 7	page 89
Chapter 8	page 101
Chapter 9	page 117
Chapter 10	page 129
Chapter 11	page 139
Chapter 12	page 151
Chapter 13	page 161
Chapter 14	page 173
Chapter 15	page 187
Chapter 16	page 199
Chapter 17	page 211
Chapter 18	page 225
Chapter 19	page 233
Chapter 20	page 245

Introduction

The books in the EDEN series give the reader a view into Amish culture. Evangelical Christians, Amish or *Englischer*, embrace most of the same basic Biblical beliefs. One such truth, the Lord loves obedience, is vividly portrayed in DAWN OF EDEN. We do not always understand the Lord's ways; but the Scriptures encourage us to remain faithful and to trust our heavenly Creator.

In DAWN OF EDEN, Rachel is confronted with traumatic events and perplexing decisions. She asks her heavenly Father for guidance; even though she does not doubt, she searches for answers and finds herself wrestling with indecision. One Scripture that is dear to her heart is Proverbs 3:5-6, "Trust in the Lord with all thine heart and lean not unto thine own understanding. In all thy ways acknowledge him and he shall direct thy paths." Rachel struggles to remain faithful, even when life seems to throw her a curve ball. She reminds herself to trust *der gut* Man rather than her own judgement. When calamity strikes, she is devastated, but wrestles to practice faith and patience.

In the Eden series, Old Order Amish and Mennonite are portrayed as they believe, peaceful, moral, ethical, compassionate, and Biblically sound followers of Jesus Christ who strive to remain faithful to God and separate from what they consider worldliness.

CHAPTER 1

Holmes County, Ohio

Gusts of November wind seized snow from the pine boughs, whipped it into frosty swirls, and hurled it onto Rachel Kay Lapp's porch. Sitting in a wooden rocker by the kitchen window, she watched the white fluff pile up on the sill. She adjusted the blue smocked pillow behind her back and rocked slowly as she pondered. Her fingers tightened on a letter from Liz Ann Lapp, her favorite cousin from Lancaster County, Pennsylvania.

Again, she peered at the neat handwriting and her heart cramped. Liz was helping two friends prepare for their weddings. Closing her eyes, Rachel sighed. Weddings were a time of joy, but they always made her feel more alone. At thirty-three she'd had but one caller and he had married someone else. *I might not have lost him—if it hadn't been for the accident.*

"*Es het nix aus mache sette* (It shouldn't have mattered)," she whispered. But it had to Jonas.

Howling wind slapped the windows as though intent on breaking in, and long icy fingers forced themselves between tiny cracks to investigate the kitchen. Touching her fingertips against the frigid glass, Rachel peered across the meadow through the dancing cloud of flakes to the farmhouse where she had been born. The pipes of the well that the gas company had drilled on the family property a few years back were barely visible. She thanked the Lord for the conveniences the fuel had made possible.

Wayne, her brother a year younger than herself, had taken over the farm when he had married. He and his wife still looked after her. So did Henry, her brother two years younger. They sometimes treated her like a maiden aunt.

"*Vell . . . sell is was ich bin* (Well that's what I am)." The words created painful reverberations deep in her heart. She peered to her left at the house on the neighboring farm. The stark front porch created bleakness within her. How many times a day had she looked at the house and pictured Jonas? How often since his wife's death had she wondered what it would be like to be married to him? She frowned. What would she say if he asked her to marry, now?

He turned his back on me when I most needed him, she thought, but harbored no resentment. Why did her memories of him lie like dead leaves? If he showed renewed interest, would her feelings for him revive?

Her mind scrolled back sixteen years to the July she had been seventeen. She had donned a new deep-rose dress, brushed her black curly hair, rolled it neatly and put on her prayer cap. She knew that going to town always put a shimmer in her gray eyes. Donning her black bonnet, she pinched her dimpled cheeks to make them pink and climbed into the black family buggy with her mother.

Gripping the braided reins, Fannie flipped them against Muddy Foot's flank to signal to the frisky three-year-old carriage horse that they were ready to go. Turning to Rachel, she smiled. "Let's stop in and see Mary Kate? " she said in the German dialect of the Amish.

"*Ja,*" Rachel said. "*Sie grickt net viel Besuch* (She doesn't get many visitors)." The old lady was sort of funny, but Rachel liked her.

Mary Kate didn't answer her door, so Rachel assumed she wasn't home. She bounded down the porch steps ahead of Fanny and skipped to their carriage. A strange brown dog raced from the barn. Rachel stared at it from her buggy seat. "*Dummel Dich, Mem* (Hurry, Mama). That dog doesn't look friendly."

Fannie bustled through the gate, but the mangy canine positioned himself between her and the carriage. Growling deep in his throat, he bared his teeth. Gripping the gate post, Fanny stared at him.

Muddy Foot snorted and shook her mane. When the dog's attention turned to the horse, Fannie moved quickly.

Her foot was precariously on the small metal step when the dog snarled and bit one of Muddy Foot's hind legs. The horse whinnied wildly and reared, kicking at the offending canine. The carriage jolted, then jerked forward, throwing Fannie off balance. She cried out as she tumbled and struck her spine on the carriage frame.

Rachel Kay screamed. Heedless of the barking dog, she leaped to the ground. "*Mem!*"

Fannie sprawled on her back in the dirt, her black bonnet askew and her fingers clutching the gate post. "*Ich kann net muhfe* (I can't move)!" Her blue-gray eyes were wide from fear and pain. "My back! Rachel Kay, *Ich kann net muhfe!*"

"Oh, *Mem*." Rachel Kay knelt in the rutty lane in the scorching July sun. "*Wass* (what) can I do? "

Anguish twisted her mother's features. "Go for help."

Fright bubbled into Rachel's throat. "I can't leave you here alone!"

"You can't lift me, and I can't help myself." She stared at the scruffy brown dog that continued to snarl at them and chewed her lower lip.

Stretching to her full height, Rachel barely reached four-foot-ten and weighed ninety-five pounds, but she hoped the spark in her silver-gray eyes looked threatening. She glared at the dog. "*Geh Heem* (Go home)!"

The dog's raised hackles and the growls that issued from deep in his throat underscored his intention. Remembering the broom in the carriage, Rachel eased her way to the back to retrieve it. Fear seized her with paralyzing clutches, then determination to help her mother forced the talons of fright to release her. Gripping the broom, she swung it at the offending canine. He didn't back away. Neither did Rachel. She hated to strike any animal, but what choice did she have with this demented creature? "*Geh heem*!" She used her weapon in a chopping motion, striking the dog's shoulder. With a vicious snarl he sank his fangs into the bristles. Jerking them free, Rachel swung again. This time the broom whacked the dog's back. Another blow struck his hip. She continued to trounce him. Finally, the dog howled and raced to the barn, its tail between its legs.

"You're a brave girl," Fannie said, her voice tremulous.

Although she maintained an outward calm, Rachel didn't feel brave. Her nerves seemed like a tangled mass of quivering spaghetti. She had to get help, yet she couldn't leave her mother defenseless.

Muddy Foot blew and stomped as though she could not understand the hold-up. Shaking her mane, she turned her head, apparently trying to peer around her blinders at Rachel and the woman who lay sprawled in a rut in the lane.

The dinner bell! It could also be used to sound an alarm. Mary Kate had had no family, nor had she had an emergency, so the bell probably hadn't been rung in years. Running across the lawn, Rachel seized the frayed rope and yanked. The bell swung wildly, but there was no sound. She peered upward under the bell. The clapper was missing, and lacy spider webs with trapped insects crisscrossed the insides.

"How can this be happening? " She prayed the dog would not return as she raced to the shed for something with which to make a racket. Spotting a two-foot piece of pipe, she seized it, hurried to the bell, and whacked it furiously.

Seconds seemed like minutes. Her arm stung from the vibration of striking metal against metal, yet she continued to beat the bell.

Jonas Yoder, the young man who had been calling on her, appeared at the rise. Vigorously waving one arm, he raced across the cornfield through the thirty-inch-high plants. As he stopped out of breath near her, he swiped off his straw hat. The sun shimmered on his raven hair, and perspiration made his shaven face shiny. "*Was is letz* (What's wrong)? "

She had managed to remain collected, but now that Jonas was here, tears streamed down her heart-shaped face. "Mama's been hurt." She pointed toward Fannie.

"*Ach!*" His indigo eyes widened, then he hurried to the prostrate woman. "*Wass* can I do to help? "

"Stay with her," Rachel said, not waiting for her mother to answer the man. "There's a mad dog in the barn. I couldn't leave *Mem* unprotected."

"*Ich bleib do. Du geh fe Hilf* (I'll stay. You go for help)." Concern and admiration played across his handsome suntanned face.

Leaping into the carriage, Rachel tossed the broom to him. "If that beast returns, you'll need a weapon." She slapped Muddy Foot's rump with the reins and took off for the phone shack.

The following days collided with one another in a blur of chaotic activity. Rachel felt swept away in a whirlwind of confusion and anxiety. Fannie remained in the hospital for a month. When she came home, she was in a wheelchair. Her back had been fractured, leaving her paralyzed from the waist down. Rachel, being the oldest of the *Kinder*, had taken over the household duties as well as the raising of her eleven younger siblings. Her father had done his best for the family and tried to help his disabled wife, but the traumatic change had altered the plans for Rachel's marriage and a home of her own. Her mother died two years after the accident, and she lost her father to a heart attack a year later. This left the entire responsibility for the family on Rachel's nineteen-year-old shoulders.

A shrill whistle shocked Rachel from her reverie. *"Ach!"* She jumped to her feet. Her long gray skirt swished around her legs as she hurried across her flowered kitchen vinyl to her stove. The kettle she had put on to heat and forgotten vibrated with wildly boiling water. Turning off the gas burner, she sighed. The deluge of memories had stolen her desire for a cup of peppermint tea. She peered at the coffee she had made earlier for her brother. Retrieving a brown mug from the cupboard, she clunked it onto the white counter top. Instead of pouring the brew, she sauntered to her maple table, slumped to a chair, and propped her elbows on the blue-plaid cloth. The table had several boards, but now it was without any, making it look small and lonely.

"Like me," she murmured, not in a habit of permitting herself to wallow in thoughts of what might have been. She loved the Lord and wished to serve Him, and being pessimistic was against all she believed in. *Had I planned my life and lived it the way I wanted to, things would be different now.* She looked at the spray of dried flowers on her wall and felt similar.

Proverbs 3:5, one of her favorite passages, came to her mind and she recited the familiar words. "Trust in the Lord with all thine heart; and lean not unto thine own understanding." The verse reminded her that the Lord knew what was best.

An image of Susan, her youngest sister, drifted into her thoughts and nestled there. Her heart had felt empty three years ago when Susan had married and left home, although she'd had her two youngest brothers with her at the time. As of a year ago, they, also, moved out to begin lives of their own. A sigh escaped from deep within her.

Was she destined to spend the rest of her life alone? *Is that what der gut Man wants?*

She planned to travel to Lancaster County in the spring to visit relatives. Nostalgia gripped her as she pictured Liz Ann Lapp. *Why wait?*

As though challenging her, a sudden gust of wind howled through the pine beside the gate and flung snow against the window.

Someone stomped on the porch, making her jump. She assumed it was Sara Kate, Wayne's oldest daughter, for she'd been teaching the ten-year-old how to knit. Crossing the kitchen, she opened the door. Her eyes widened as Jonas Yoder's six-foot-two frame filled the opening.

Stepping into the room, he closed the portal. "*Sis am Kaelter warre* (It's getting colder)." He shucked out of his jacket and tossed it to the wooden bench. Removing his black felt hat, he faced her, his expression enigmatic. "I want to speak to you, Rachel."

Her hands fluttered. "*Nem doch an Sitz* (Take a seat)." She motioned to the table, not bold enough to invite him into the living room. After all, he was a widower and they were not courting. Should they be alone in the house? On the verge of asking him, she bit her tongue. Lack of experience sometimes made her seem prudish, although she was far from it. "Would you like a cup of coffee? "

"*Ja. Gross Dank* (Many thanks)."

Even though he had practically jilted her years ago, having him near made her nervous. But then, maybe his past rejection was what made her jittery. Going to the counter, she heaped a plate with still-warm raisin-filled cookies and placed them in front of Jonas. She took a seat across from him, but instead of meeting his gaze, she stared at the bowl of red apples between them. "What do you want to talk about? "

"*Vell* . . ." He took a bite of cookie, chewed methodically, then swallowed. "You make the best cookies in the county."

"*Gross Dank.*" She laughed softly. "I've had a lot of experience."

"*Ja.*" Sipping his coffee, he looked at her over the rim of his cup. "I've been alone for two years."

She had felt alone for a lot longer than that, due to his changing his mind about marrying her, but she had no intention of dredging up that bucket of slime. After all, with her mother's *Kinder* under foot, she would not have been able to put enough emphasis on being his wife. She sat quietly stirring her coffee. To cover for her shyness, she smiled.

"Your dimples are still the sweetest ever."

"Oh." The single syllable hung between them as heat cruised across her cheeks.

He cleared his throat. "*Ich deet gleiche mit dir gehe* (I would like to go with you)."

She smothered a gasp. Was it being near Jonas that made her heart pound—or was it the fear of making a mistake? Would dating him mean ecstasy or another disaster?

"*Was is letz* (What's wrong)?

"I . . . need time to think."

His indigo eyes widened. "Think about . . . *wass*? "

Had no woman ever turned him down? She studied his face. His nose was a bit too large, but he was a good-looking man. Although he was only thirty-eight, silver threads shimmered in the black waves of his hair and beard. Remembering she still clutched a spoon, she placed it in her saucer and picked up her cup. Maybe a drink of hot coffee would thaw out her tongue. But was her tongue the problem? Was it her heart that questioned this man's intentions?

"*Vell*? " He retrieved his black hat from a nearby chair and shoved it onto his head. "Maybe I caught you at a bad time."

"No. *Vell . . . ja.*"

He stood, but paused, his eyes searching her face. Then shrugging, he rammed his arms into his jacket and turned to the door.

Panic seized her. Was she letting her last chance slip out the door and vanish? She leaped to her feet. "Jonas, wait."

He turned, his expression expectant. "*Ja?* "

She felt foolish and didn't want to stutter. Taking a deep breath, she said, "I would welcome your company."

He smiled, showing even white teeth. "I thought you would."

She closed her lips on a retort that would wipe the grin from his face. Did he look smug—or was pride baring sharp fangs within her. Had she made a mistake—or was she questioning her blessings? Well, she hadn't promised this man anything, and maybe their relationship wouldn't become serious. She knew she didn't love Jonas, yet, but maybe her feelings would deepen. The thought nearly froze her fingers to the back of the kitchen chair. Did she want to love Jonas?

"I'll stop by this evening—if that's all right."

"*Ja.*" She intended to ask her ten-year-old niece to be present so she and Jonas would not be alone. "Can you come for supper? "

His smile broadened. "I'll see you about six o'clock, *Gel* (right)? "

She nodded mutely. When he left, she went to the window to watch him cross the field to his house. His steps were sure and his broad shoulders squared as though he had just won a victory. Rachel figured she should be delighted over his renewed interest. Instead, doubts assailed her, ravaging her confidence.

Lancaster County, Pennsylvania.

A harsh November wind swirled snow across the highway and blew clouds of fluff against the windshield of Peter John Lapp's green Trans Am. The first snow storm of the season was well under way. Leaning forward slightly, he peered through the arch that had been swept clean by the wipers.

Liz Ann thought about the way her brother used to keep owning a car a secret. Now he openly drove it, although he was not permitted to park it on Amish owned land. She watched him, then the road. Relaxing was difficult, for the car sped over the icy highway much faster than the horse drawn conveyance she was used to. She eyed her brother. "Mir hette am Pap sei Karritsch nemme sette (We should've taken Papa's carriage)."

Peter John chuckled. "You have your toes against my heater and seem to be enjoying the comfort."

Liz Ann drew her lips taut. Since Amish weren't permitted to have cars, she wasn't going to admit her gratitude over being warm. She had preached too many sermons to her brother to have them flung back in her face. "*Is es net zeit fe des rumspringe stappe* (Isn't it time you give up Rumspringe)? "

"*Ach*! There's too much fun out there waiting for me."

"*Druwel kann immer warte* (Trouble waits, too)."

"*Ja*? " He shrugged. "The Scriptures say not to worry about tomorrow for there's enough to be concerned about today."

"Oh, Peter. That Scripture is meant to help us increase our faith, not to use as an excuse for frivolous actions, and you know it."

He glanced at her, his green eyes sparkling. "My car gets you to Beilers' quicker than some old nag can haul a carriage."

"Jenny isn't an old nag!" She thought about how Eli Beiler had kept his Buick a secret, until recently. Now, he boldly drove it. She sighed. "It's past time for Eli to settle down, too!"

"*Ja, vell,* we will . . . someday."

Someday might be too late, Liz thought, pondering her love for Eli. She had made every excuse she could think of for his continued rebellion, but he was twenty-two. Her heart contorted. How many times had she warned him that she would not accompany him anywhere in his car, then relented?

A blue pickup passed them, then pulled in ahead too quickly. When Peter braked, the car began to slide forward. Then the back end swung to the right, and the front skidded into the oncoming lane. Gasping, Liz braced for impact. Expertly maneuvering his vehicle, her brother avoided a collision.

"Peter John! Take me home!"

"We're closer to Beilers', so we might as well continue. Sarah and Elizabeth are expecting you to help them prepare the house for their weddings."

"*Ja.*" Hiding her trembling fingers under her navy cape, Liz stared out her side window. Her eyes were identical to Peter's green ones and they both had curly black hair. His face was round and boyish; hers was heart-shaped with delicate features. She had been dating Eli for almost a year and had been praying for him to settle down. He would make a wonderful lifetime partner—if only he'd get rid of his car and give up *Rumspringe,* the time a young man spends running around before he joins the Amish church.

"Did Elizabeth ask you to be an assistant at her wedding? "

"I'm assisting Sarah and Joseph. You are assisting Elizabeth and Elam." The wedding was only two weeks away and Liz Ann was getting anxious. Sarah Beiler had waited for two years for Joseph King to return to the Amish community and join the church. He had left, gotten a job in a florist shop, and dressed like and lived like an *Englischer.* Eli wasn't as bad as Joseph had been—yet...

Peter John slowed the car to turn into Beilers' lane. As they passed under the spreading limbs of the old oak, Liz watched the few brown leaves that still clung to the icy branches jerk spasmodically in the wind.

Peter gave her a playful poke. "Since Elizabeth and Sarah are having a double wedding, why don't you and Eli make it a threesome? "

"For the same reason Leah Miller won't get serious with you." Her eyes accused him. "If you don't settle down, soon, you might lose her."

"*Neh*. She understands."

"*Ja*, but a girl can only stand so much, then she is forced to take action!"

"Like you? " He laughed. "Your eyes look like misty green moons every time someone mentions Eli's name."

"That isn't true."

"*Ja* it is. Hang on." He swerved from the tracks in the lane and pulled into deeper snow. The vehicle slid sideways.

"Peter!"

The sedan came to a stop inches from Beilers' mailbox. Her brother turned off the engine and grinned. "You're delivered in one piece."

"*Ja, vell*, it's due to *der* grace of *der gut* Man (God)." Wind tore at her cape and threatened to rip off her bonnet as she climbed out of the car and headed for the porch. Hearing voices, she paused to look around. The Beiler farm seemed frosted with a three-inch layer of whipped cream. The small bushes appeared as though they had been rolled in confectioner's sugar. The whiteness made the scene appear pristine. Her eyes widened as she noticed Isaac Beiler, Eli's father, on top of the one-story chicken house roof. Eli clambered up a ladder at the other end of the building. Clinging to the bail of a bucket of warm tar, he headed toward the older man. Isaac clutched a six-foot strip of roofing. The slant of the roof was slight, but he seemed to be struggling to maintain his balance as the wind seized the roofing and flipped it.

The kitchen door swung open and nineteen-year-old Sara stepped outside. She wasn't wearing a cape, and concern brimmed in her light-blue eyes. Instead of her usual glow, her lovely face was shadowed with foreboding. Her prayer cap was slightly askew, showing more blond hair than was customary. Her peach skirt billowed in the wind as she peered at her father and wrung her hands.

Liz Ann hurried to the porch. "*Was is letz* (What's wrong)?"

"Papa wanted to patch the chicken house roof before winter and insisted on doing the repair before the storm got bad."

"It's already bad!" Liz Ann turned to peer at the man. He was in his mid-fifties, but looked older. He grappled to seize a flapping corner of the roofing that the wind had jerked from his grasp. "*Dank der gut Man* that Eli's helping."

"*Ja*, but . . ." Sarah shivered and wrapped her arms around her slender body as though endeavoring to hold in the warmth.

Eli looked concerned as he headed toward his father. Esther, Eli and Sarah's mother, stood on the ground, holding her cape tightly against her body and staring upward at her husband. Peter John came to the porch, but his eyes were on the men on the roof. Isaac seemed to slip, then regain his balance.

"*Ach*. I'm going up to help," Peter said, running across the yard toward the ladder.

Before he reached the top rung, a fierce gust of wind seized the roofing, yanking Isaac sideways. His feet flew from under him.

Esther screamed as he toppled.

Sarah clutched Liz's arm as her father's body slid toward the edge of the roof. "No! Oh, no!"

CHAPTER TWO

Slipping and sliding, Eli and Peter hurried across the roof toward the older man. Before they could reach him, he careened over the edge and landed with a sickening whoosh in the snow.

With a cry, Sarah raced to him. Esther knelt, clutched his gloved hand, and called. There was no response.

"*Pap!*" Shivering, Sarah bent to examine her father.

Whisking off her cape, Liz Ann wrapped it around Sarah and was immediately assaulted by the frigid air. Eli clambered down the ladder and raced around the chicken house with Peter, his blue eyes filled with anxiety.

"*Er is ummechtig* (he's unconscious)," Esther said.

"Oh, *Mem.*" Sarah's voice caught.

"*Kom ann*, Eli," Peter called. "I'll drive you to the phone shack to call an ambulance."

Icy gusts of wind tore at Liz Ann's pink skirt, and she shivered uncontrollably.

Eli called over his shoulder, "Go inside before you get pneumonia."

Her teeth chattering, she hurried to the kitchen. Elizabeth Stoltzfus, the eldest Beiler daughter, came from the parlor. A white apron covered most of her light-green dress. Her face was radiant, her brown eyes warm with joy. Liz Ann knew her happiness was because of Elam Miller. Elizabeth, a widow with an infant daughter, and Elam, a widower with two young sons, planned to marry this month. Elizabeth and Sarah, her younger sister, were having a double wedding.

Excess moisture collected in Liz Ann's eyes as she crossed the room to hug Elizabeth. "Your *Pap* has had an accident."

"*Ach!*" Shock crossed the woman's pretty features.

Liz Ann quickly explained.

Seizing her cape, Elizabeth yanked the kitchen door open. "You'll watch Priscilla for me, *gel* (right)?"

Liz Ann nodded.

The nine-month-old girl crawled into the kitchen from the parlor. Her blue eyes peered at the closed door, then she looked at Liz Ann. "*Mem?*"

"She'll be back." Liz Ann removed her navy bonnet, hung it on a peg and adjusted her prayer cap. "Let's rock a bit." Sweeping Priscilla into her arms, she kissed her golden ringlets and pondered as she rocked and hummed. *How badly is Isaac hurt? How will this effect Sarah and Elizabeth's weddings?*

An ambulance siren wailed in the distance, came closer, then passed the house. The wail died with a sickening moan near the chicken coop. Closing her eyes, Liz prayed.

Minutes later, Sarah entered the kitchen. "*Hertzlich Dank* (hearty thanks) for the loan of your cape."

"How's Isaac?"

"He's still unconscious."

Elizabeth whisked into the room.

"Where's Esther? " Liz Ann asked.

Sarah hung up the borrowed cape. "She went to the hospital with Papa."

Flipping the snow from her cape, Elizabeth said, "Peter and Eli returned, but they're following the ambulance to the hospital."

Priscilla wiggled to get down. Liz Ann set her on the floor. "Everything's going to be all right."

Sara clasped her hands. "Oh, I feel so guilty!"

Liz Ann peered curiously at her. "About *wass* (what)?"

"*Ich bin bang wehig dem Pap* (I'm worried about

Papa)—yet, I keep thinking about the possibility of my wedding being ruined."

Elizabeth smiled, although concern shadowed her eyes. "*Pap* will be fine, and our weddings will be *un wonderbar*."

Liz Ann watched Priscilla crawl into the parlor to Ruth, Elizabeth and Sarah's thirteen-year-old sister. The girl was watching the two younger Beiler boys, ages three and five.

"*Vell*," Elizabeth said, "we'd better get some work done."

As Liz Ann considered the extra work of a double wedding, she pictured Elam Miller's two sons. Daniel was in first grade and seemed quiet. Jesse Mark, however, was a four-year-old dynamo. The trouble the boys got into was usually instigated by this curly-headed blond ball of activity, although innocence shimmered in his light-blue eyes.

"We'd better start upstairs," Elizabeth said, dumping cleaning liquid into a pail of scrub water.

"The windows are all to do." Sarah retrieved cleaning rags. "Yesterday, Susanna and I scrubbed the walls in two bedrooms."

Liz Ann remembered how Susanna Yoder, Elam's pretty blond sister-in-law, had schemed to marry Elam after his first wife had died. Realizing her wrongdoing, she asked for and received Elizabeth's forgiveness. The two became good friends.

"I'll shine the windows." Liz Ann reached for a roll of paper towels. "Where is Susanna?"

"She's watching Michael Zook's youngest two *Kinder*," Elizabeth said. "He went to an auction this afternoon."

Sarah retrieved a can of scouring powder from under the sink. "Michael's such a little man, but his heart is as big as a mountain."

Liz Ann reached for the window cleaner. "He takes care of his four *Kinder* as good as any woman."

Elizabeth picked up her filled pail. "*Ja*, but he needs a wife."

Sarah turned to look at her. "He's so short! Most ladies are several inches taller!"

Elizabeth quirked one brow. "That wouldn't make any difference if they loved each other."

"But he's still grieving the loss of his first wife."

"She's been dead five years, Sarah. One must pick up the pieces and go on with life. *Der gut* Man gives us strength to adjust and accept new blessings."

"*Ja*," Sarah said. "Just like Susanna."

Liz Ann thought about Susanna's anguish when she had fallen in love with John Zimmerman. He was Beachy Amish; she was Old Order. She had been faced with the decision of giving him up or suffering *Meidung* (shunning) by her Amish family and community. Either situation would have devastated her. She had come to stay with the Beilers to think and pray. John solved the dilemma by joining the Old Order Amish church. "When are Susanna and John being married?"

Elizabeth smiled. "The last Thursday of November."

"*Ja*," Sarah said. "They'll be going to Mercer County to live with Susanna's mother. I'll miss her." She sighed. "And now, Papa..." She wiped a hand across her brow. "I can't concentrate on cleaning."

Elizabeth gave her a pat. "We must keep trusting *der gut* Man for Papa's recovery."

Sarah glanced at Liz Ann, the shadow of a smile curving her soft-pink lips. "We couldn't get along without our Elizabeth's encouragement, *gel*?"

The women had nearly finished one bedroom when Peter John's car sped up the lane and stopped with a crunch of snow. Sarah dropped her cloth in her bucket and headed for the stairs. Still clutching a roll of paper towels, Elizabeth hurried after her, but Liz Ann remained long enough to finish shining a window. As she skipped downstairs, Peter John and Eli were on the porch, stomping the snow from their boots. The door swung inward and they tromped into the kitchen.

"How's *Pap*?" Sarah asked.

Eli plopped onto the bench and sighed. "He's conscious, but the doctor wants to keep him over night for observation."

Elizabeth moved closer to him. "Did he break any bones?"

"He cracked three ribs. He must have hit the side of the roof as he went over. *Dank der gut* Man it wasn't worse. He fell between two cement blocks." A grin brightened his countenance. "I had shoved the snow from the roof so we could see where to put the patch. He plowed into the pile. It softened his landing."

Elizabeth frowned. "Then why was he unconscious?"

"I figure his head must have grazed the cement block."

"*Dank der gut Man a hundret muhl* that he didn't hit it squarely."

The serious expression on Eli's face was unlike him. "*Pap* could've been killed."

"Is *Mem* staying with him?" Elizabeth asked.

"*Ja.*" Shucking out of his jacket, Eli hung it on a peg by the door. "Peter and I will go back for her tonight."

Sarah propped her hands on her slender hips. "I can't concentrate on festivities when *Pap* is in the hospital!"

Peter shrugged. "I'll be glad to drive you to the hospital."

She glanced at her sister. "Why don't we go? Ruth is here to watch Reuben and Little John."

Elizabeth looked pensive. "*Vell, Pap* isn't hurt badly. *Mem* will be all right alone with him, but she may get upset if we don't get more of the work done, *gel*?"

Sighing, Sarah headed for the stairs. "If we keep working, we can finish the upstairs before dark."

Elizabeth followed, lugging a pail of clean soapy water. "Maybe we can go to the hospital with Peter John when he goes back for Mama."

Sarah's face brightened. "*Ja!*"

Skipping up the stairs to Sarah's room, Liz Ann thought about the amount of preparations for an Amish wedding. They would have to clean the entire house. "How many guests do you expect, Sarah?"

"Four hundred." The girl paused to look at her purple wedding dress. "Elizabeth's is the same color."

Liz Ann touched the material. "It will make a nice Sunday dress for all winter."

"Ja."

Looking at the new prayer cap and apron, Liz Ann thought about how Sarah would wear it for her wedding, then put it away. The next time she would wear it would be in her coffin. *That's our way.*

Three days later, Liz Ann went to her bedroom to change into a light-blue dress. She pinned her cape and apron, then brushed her hair until it shone. Rolling it up, she put on her prayer cap and smiled. Eli was coming for her, and he had promised to come in his carriage. The roads were clear, but the first November snow still covered the fields. Glancing out a window, she listened for the clop-clop of horse's hooves and the rumble of carriage wheels. At the sound of a car, she curled her fingers into fists. She had told Eli she would not go with him in his car anymore. Had he ignored her warning, again? *Fer wass* (Why)?

From the second-story window, she watched the blue sedan come up the lane and stop by the gate. When Eli climbed out of the car, he glanced up and grinned. Taking off his black felt hat, he waved it. Whirling away, she crossed the room and plopped onto a wooden chair, refusing to acknowledge his greeting.

A soft snowball struck the window. Some of the snow stuck and melted pieces trailed down the glass. Her lips drew taut. Tears were close, but she battled them.

"Liz Ann," Naomi called.

"*Ja, Mem.*" Her parents didn't approve of Eli's continued *Rumspringe*, but usually didn't say much about her accompanying him. It was nice to be trusted by your family, but she was disgusted with herself for being so lenient.

"Eli's here, Liz Ann," a younger sister sang.

"I'm *koming.*" She slowly made her way down the stairs. This time, she wasn't going with him. He had to know that she meant business. As she crossed the pink-and-gray vinyl kitchen floor, her eyes met his. She rounded the large oblong table, keeping the piece of furniture between them.

Martha, her sixteen-year-old sister, stood by the sink. Gold highlights played in the light-brown hair at the front of her prayer cap. Her green eyes traveled from Liz's face to Eli's. Apparently sensing trouble, she vanished into the parlor. Where had her mother gone? Where were her other siblings? Even Peter John had deserted her. Nevertheless, Liz Ann squared her slender shoulders. "I'm not going with you this morning."

Eli's blond brows rose nearly to the black felt hat he had neglected to take off. "*Fer wass?*"

She propped her fists on her hips. "You promised to come for me in the carriage."

He leaned against the maple cupboard. "*Vell, Ja,* but..."

"There's no excuse, Eli Beiler."

Apparently striving to look innocent, he made a helpless gesture with his hands. "I was late, and Sarah wanted me to hurry."

Gripping the back of a kitchen chair, Liz narrowed her eyes. "Don't you dare blame your rebellion on your sister!"

He chuckled. "You look cute when you're irritated." Rounding the table, he touched her cheek.

Fighting tears, she turned away. "I warned you about your driving that car."

"I know, but Sarah and Elizabeth are counting on you to help with the final details of the weddings."

Cornered again! Liz sighed, but eyed him sternly. "This is the last time, Eli." She went to the line of hooks to the right of the door, grabbed her bonnet and tied it with more zest than necessary, then rammed her arms into a heavy black sweater. Clutching her cape, she flipped it around her shoulders. Not looking at Eli, she opened the door and made her way to his car.

He gave her a cautious side-glance as he opened her door, then rushing around the vehicle, he slid behind the wheel. "I'll get you there in a hurry."

"Never mind hurrying. Just get me there in one piece."

He laughed. "Limber up, Liz Ann. We could have a lot of fun."

Her fingers curled into fists, but her heart ached. "It's time you settle down." It was a worn-out refrain, and she figured he wasn't listening.

"Papa came home yesterday."

"Oh? How is he?"

Eli shrugged. "His ribs are taped, and he complains of not being able to take a deep breath, but other than that he seems all right." He grinned. "He had the ladies waiting on him, catering to his every whim."

"That doesn't sound like Isaac."

"That was yesterday. I think he was enjoying all the attention. This morning he said he was going to tackle the barn work."

Liz gasped. "You stopped him, *gel*?"

"*Ja*."

When they arrived, Sarah was waiting at the door. Her blue eyes, the same shade as her dress, displayed her joy. "Joseph is here to help with the planning. So is Elam."

Liz glanced across the room to where Elizabeth and Elam sat on the padded bench. Elam had recovered from the buggy accident that had injured his legs, although he still sometimes used crutches for added balance.

Nine-month-old Priscilla sat on his lap. She gazed lovingly up at him, then giggling, she reached up and clutched his light-brown beard. *"Pap."*

"I pray *Mammi* Hazel will be able to attend the service," Sarah said, a slight frown shadowing her brow.

"Ja." Elizabeth's word was encouraging, but she looked doubtful.

Liz Ann pictured Elizabeth and Sarah's paternal grandmother. The sweet elderly lady had been living in the *Dawdy Haus* for several years, taking her meals with the family, and helping with simple chores. Her health had gradually declined. Now, she was bedfast.

Sarah placed a pile of plain paper and several pencils on the table. "Let's get to work, *Mem*."

Esther smiled, her hazel eyes twinkling. The woman was in her early fifties and had only a few gray hairs. She had put on a few extra pounds. Isaac's not being badly hurt had put a glow in her rosy cheeks. "I have my duties under control, including the cooks lined up. You asked your sidesitters, but have you girls decided on which are going to be for each of you?"

Elizabeth took a place at the table and picked up a piece of paper and a pencil. "Our *sidesitters* are mostly dating couples, and since dating couples can't be *sidesitters* for the same bride, we'll each have to take one of the couples." She eyed Sarah. "If you wish to have Liz Ann, I'll choose Eli."

"All right." Sarah took her chair. "Leah can be my second girl, and Peter John can be with you and Elam."

Elizabeth smiled. "I'd like Susanna Yoder as one of my *sidesitters*."

Sarah nodded. "John Zimmerman can be with us. Samuel Miller will be Joseph's second attendant." She glanced at Liz. "Is Martha willing to sit for Elizabeth?"

Liz nodded. "She feels honored to be asked."

Joseph took a seat beside Sarah; his straight black hair shone from wetting it. Love emanated from his dark-brown eyes as he gazed at his bride-to-be. Drumming his fingers on the tabletop, he looked pensive. Suggestions began to fly between the couples, and before dinner all the details had been discussed.

Sarah turned to Liz Ann. "Can you stay here the night before the wedding?"

"*Ja*. That way Eli won't have to come for me at dawn."

Michael Zook gripped the handle of a bucket as he peered out a frosted window of the barn. Silvery moonlight slanted across the snowscape, making the trees along the fence row sharp silhouettes. He thought about the double wedding that would take place the next morning. "I don't like weddings. He supposed it was because he'd had such hope on his wedding day. Then, eight years after the ceremony, his dream had exploded into shards of sorrow and grief.

"She's been gone for almost five years," he said to the wind that howled around the corner of the barn. Loneliness wrapped him in an icy cocoon. He pulled his jacket collar tighter around his neck as he thought about his four *Kinder*. How blest he was to have them. His frown deepened. Something was bothering his seven-year-old Moses, though. If only the boy would talk to him about it.

Hearing footsteps, he looked toward the door. His oldest, twelve-year-old Lydia, stood watching him.

"You okay *Pap*?"

He forced a smile. "I'm hungry."

Her blue-green eyes brightened. "Supper's ready, and we're waiting for you."

Clinking the bucket handle over a nail, he joined her. "It gets dark so early these days."

"*Ja*."

Snow crunched under his feet as he walked to the

house. He permitted his thoughts to dwell on his misfortunes. However, by the time he climbed the two porch steps, he had regained control of his galloping thoughts. *The Lord is good and His mercies everlasting. He has sustained me*, he thought. *I will trust Him.*

Sitting on the bench inside the door, he removed his barn shoes. He stared at a small clump of manure on the vinyl, then his eyes traveled across the room to his youngest son. Moses had light-brown hair and warm-brown eyes, duplicates of his own. "Moses," he summoned softly. "Please pick up what you dropped on the floor and remove your barn shoes."

The boy shrugged, then quietly did as he'd been told. Michael wondered why Moses had to be reminded so often to do things he knew he should do. Sighing, he took his place at the table.

Lydia set a steaming chicken casserole in the center of the table. At twelve, she was five-foot-three, an inch taller than Michael. Her eyes, much like her mother's, glistened.

As she poured his coffee, she sighed. "I can hardly wait for the weddings tomorrow."

"Tomorrow will come," Michael said, wrestling to sound cheerful. "Tomorrow will come."

Liz jumped awake and sat up. Faint rays of light filtered into the room. Susanna was asleep, but Sarah's bed was empty. Liz squinted at the clock. It was ten after four a.m. *This is Sarah and Elizabeth's wedding day*, she thought. Joseph and Elam would be arriving soon.

The leg of a chair scraped the kitchen floor, telling Liz that her friend was already at work. Getting up, she dressed and groggily hurried downstairs. Sarah was carrying the last kitchen chair to the porch. When the appointed couples had the bench wagon unloaded, they would put the smaller furniture on it. The larger pieces would be taken to the wagon shed to leave the downstairs free for the service and meals.

Sarah smiled. "Help yourself to breakfast. The men have eaten and gone to do the barn work."

"*Haw ich mich verschlofe* (Did I over sleep)?"

"Not really. I was too excited to stay in bed." Sarah set the skillet on the stove.

Liz Ann helped herself to the freshly brewed coffee, then glanced out a window at Joseph King's teenage brother. "Is Jesse the lead *Hustler?*"

"*Ja.* There will be a lot of horses to care for. I hope they keep the three apart who have the tendency to scrap. Do you want an egg? "

"*Ach.*" Liz Ann reached for a slice of bread. "I'll make a ham sandwich, then get busy."

Susanna skipped down the stairs. "You should have awakened me, Sarah." Her blue eyes sparkled, and her face was aglow. Poking a truant straw-colored curl back under her prayer cap, she laughed. "I might have slept through your wedding."

Sarah giggled. "Not with all the commotion."

Doors banged as workers arrived. Voices of excited ladies hummed, and the clanging of many pots and pans reverberated from the summer kitchen. The sound of scraping and bumping told Liz Ann that the men were moving the portable partitions that separated the first-floor rooms. Legs clicked as other men unfolded the benches and clattered them into place. Time sped by as many hands completed myriads of chores.

Sarah glanced at the clock. "It's almost seven. Liz Ann, tell my sidesitters that it's time to dress for my wedding." Beaming, she skipped upstairs.

When Liz Ann came into the bedroom with the girls in the wedding parties, Elizabeth was with Sarah. Both brides were radiant, which added to Liz's excitement. "Joseph and Elam and their attendants are changing in Eli's room."

Liz Ann pictured the grooms in their new black frock

coats and black bow ties and grinned. About the only time an Amish man wears a bow tie is at his wedding. She pursed her lips. Do grooms keep them after the ceremony or throw them away?

When the bridal parties were dressed, they returned to the kitchen to greet the guests. Liz Ann took her place on the bench beside Sarah, struggling not to appear giddy. Joseph sat between his attendants; Elizabeth and Elam were seated likewise. Relatives, friends and church members arrived and shook hands with the bridal parties. The ladies went upstairs to deposit their heavy winter capes, and the men congregated around the barn. Liz Ann continued to sneak glances out the window.

The *Hustlers* were kept busy tying horses. Numerous gray carriages lined up against the fence. Old-Order Mennonites arrived in black buggies. Mennonite guests began to arrive in black cars with black bumpers. Hired vans with *Englischer* drivers purred up the lane. They stopped at the gate to let off passengers, then moved to park near the barn.

Near eight o'clock, Aaron King, one of the ushers, went to the barn to round up the men. The women *Forgeher* (ushers) were responsible for getting the ladies. The procession into the house was very orderly. The ministers took their places first, followed by the parents of the brides and grooms. Isaac and Esther, parents of Sarah and Elizabeth, came in. Noah and Anna King, Joseph King's parents, were present, but Elam's mother and father were too sickly to make the trip from Mercer County in the winter. Elizabeth said that she and Elam planned to visit them before the end of the year.

Liz Ann watched as grandparents came in, then other relatives and friends. As in regular church services, men and women took seats in separate sections. Several relatives and friends of the brides who were helping with the cooking sat in the kitchen so they could attend the service and keep an eye on the cooking food.

The grooms' unmarried siblings were the first of the young people to enter and take their places. They were followed by the couples who had just been published (couples whose wedding plans had been announced at a church service). Young relatives and friends entered last and took their places.

When all were present, the men simultaneously removed their hats, signifying that the dwelling place had become a place of worship. In accordance with an old custom, the ministers present kept their hats on until after the first song.

Anxiety bubbled into Liz Ann's throat. During the singing, she watched the eight ministers get up and go upstairs. Her heart began to pound as she watched Sarah and Joseph ascend the steps after the ministers. She knew the destination was the *Abroth* (the room established as the council room). Elizabeth and Elam followed. Liz Ann knew this was the time when the ministers asked if the couple had remained pure. She knew Sarah had, and after Moses death, Elizabeth would have refrained from impure acts.

Liz Ann's mouth went dry as she pictured herself sitting in front of the Bishop and deacons to answer the question at the time of her own wedding. She was thankful that the Lord had given her the grace to remain untarnished. Still, with men eyeing her . . .

Shuffling overhead drew Liz Ann from her reverie. A chair leg squeaked on the vinyl, signaling that the couples were being dismissed. She knew the ministers would remain to decide which part of the service each would take. The silence encouraged her to pray for her friends. She closed her eyes. In the distance a dog barked and a cow lowed. The serenity encouraged contentment.

A wild scream pierced the air. Women gasped. Men leaped to their feet. Liz Ann grasped her throat, her eyes wide. What horrid thing was happening? Not on Sarah's wedding day!

CHAPTER THREE

Another scream rent the air. Now Liz Ann recognized the cries were of frightened or infuriated horses.

"*Stopp!Geh zurick* (Stop!Get back)!" called Jesse King, the sixteen-year-old head *Hustler*.

Not wanting to leave her seat, Liz Ann wrestled with curiosity. Some of the guests moved to the windows, apparently hoping to discover the origin of the commotion— or to gauge what they could do to help. Aaron King, Jesse's older brother, hurried through the kitchen and out the door.

"*Sel's mei Gaul* (That's my horse)!"Michael Zook excused himself and rushed from the room.

"And mine." Jacob Zook followed his brother.

Within minutes the animals were separated and the barnyard settled down. The men returned, quietly apologized and took their seats. Soon, the hushed whispers quieted. Liz Ann prayed there would be no more interruptions.

Sarah and Joseph descended the stairs. Liz Ann's pulse quickened as she and the other attendants joined them. The members of the church began to sing the *Lob Lied*, the second song at most Amish church services. Since Liz Ann and Eli were dating, she had been coupled with Samuel Miller, Elam's younger brother. When she glanced at him, his azure eyes held depth and mystery. He winked, causing her to nearly miss a step. They were leading the procession, and she prayed no one would notice how nervous she was. Sarah and Joseph were second; Leah and John

Zimmerman completed the first bridal party.

Entering the room, each took a seat on the six caned chairs arranged for them, the young ladies facing the young men.

As Elizabeth and Elam entered with their attendants and seated themselves in like manner, Liz Ann's trembling fingers dipped in and out of the holes in her cane chair. Realizing what she was doing, she folded her hands in her lap.

As the congregation sang another song, the ministers entered. Bishop John Zimmerman and Deacon Benjamin Zook took two of the three chairs placed at the head of the bridal parties. Liz Ann smiled as her father, minister Christopher Lapp, took the third chair. The other five ministers who were present sat together in the congregation.

Joy and admiration created excess moisture in Liz Ann's eyes as Christopher Lapp rose to present the *Anfang* (opening). He preached about creation and how God had created Eve for Adam. He then encouraged Sarah and Elizabeth not to fall into temptation as Eve had done. He spoke to the grooms, telling how the church believed in taking only one wife. He looked at Joseph, at Elam, then called for silent prayer.

The members of the congregation knelt at their benches, their backs to the front of the room. Liz Ann's knee rolled over a crack in the floor and she cringed. When the prayer ended, the people stood, but still faced the back of the room.

Deacon Benjamin Zook read Scripture. He ended by saying *"Was Gott zusammen gefuget hat, das soll der Mensch nicht scheiden* (What God hath joined together, let no man put asunder)."

The congregation sat for the remainder of the reading. Liz Ann rubbed her knee, hoping no one noticed.

Bishop John stood to deliver the main sermon. His jacket hung a bit loose on his tall lean body. He stood straight and proclaimed the beliefs of the church with earnestness. The main part of his sermon contained comments about the married couples in the Bible. He ended his sermon in the traditional way of weddings with the story of Ruth and Boaz. He then read more Scripture.

When he finished, he looked around the room. "Sarah Beiler and Joseph King have consented to marry. Does anyone here have any reason to object?" He paused a moment, then addressed Sarah and Joseph. "If you are still of like mind, you may now come forth in the name of the Lord."

Liz Ann blinked back tears. Smiling, Sarah and Joseph clasped hands, walked forward, and stopped in front of Bishop John.

The Bishop looked at Joseph. "Can you profess, Brother, that you accept this our sister as your wife and that you will not leave her until death separates you? And do you believe that this is from the Lord, and that you have come thus far by your faith and prayers?"

"Yes." Joseph smiled at Sarah.

The Bishop addressed Sarah. "Can you confess, Sister, that you accept this brother as your husband, and that you will not leave him until death separates you, and do you believe that this is from the Lord and that you have come thus far by your faith and prayers?"

"Oh, *Ja*," Sarah said, almost reverently.

Bishop John turned back to Joseph. "Because you have confessed, Brother, that you want to take this our sister for your wife, do you promise to be loyal to her and care for her if she may have adversity, affliction, sickness, weakness, or faint-heartedness, which are many infirmities that are among poor mankind, as appropriate for a God-fearing husband?"

Joseph answered in the affirmative.

Liz Ann took a deep calming breath as Bishop John asked Sarah the same question.

"Yes," Sarah whispered.

The Bishop took their right hands, put them together, and held them between his. "May the God of Abraham, the God of Isaac, and the God of Jacob be with you together and give His rich blessing upon you and be merciful to you. To this I wish you the blessing of God for a good beginning, and a steadfast middle, and may you hold out until the blessed end. This all in and through Jesus Christ. Amen. Go forth in the name of the Lord. You are now man and wife."

Heart racing, Liz Ann watched her friends return to their chairs. Sarah was radiant; Joseph beamed.

Elizabeth and Elam stood. She handed him one crutch, and they moved forward to repeat the procedure. Brilliant rays of sun streamed through the windows as though the Lord were pouring a special blessing on the marriages. When the second couple returned to their seats, the room seemed it might burst with pure delight.

Bishop John asked one of the ordained men to give a testimony. Two other ministers spoke briefly and added their blessings to the two married couples.

Isaac Beiler, Sarah and Elizabeth's father, was asked to speak. Moving to the front of the room, he testified of how the Lord had spared his life when he had fallen from the chicken house roof. His eyes traveled over the congregation and he glanced toward the kitchen as he spoke of his appreciation for all the help their relatives, friends, and church district were offering this day. Tears shimmered in his eyes as he spoke of marital joy. He smiled at Elizabeth, then at Sarah and thanked the Lord for his wonderful family.

Noah King, Joseph's father, said a few words of encouragement. The Bishop rose, made his closing comments, then asked the congregation to kneel. He read the prayer on page 55 of the *Christenpflicht* (the prayer book read at the close of most Amish Church services).

The congregation stood for the benediction. Liz Ann longed to race to hug Sarah and Elizabeth. As Samuel stood, his knee cracked, the sound seeming loud in the silence. Liz Ann repressed a giggle. His eyes met hers, and he grinned.

The service closed with a song. Merriment danced in Samuel's azure eyes. As he leaned toward Liz, a beam of sunlight shimmered on his blond hair. "So much for that. Now the festivities begin."

She grinned. "Elam said you were a rascal. He was right, *gel*?"

His spontaneous laugh rippled around them. "*Ja*. "His eyes sparkled with more good-natured fun than Eli's, although Samuel had settled down and become a member of the church.

The young people exited rapidly, followed by both bridal parties. The young men went outside. Liz Ann was glad the day wasn't too cold. She went upstairs with the young women as some of the men moved the benches for the noon meal. Each table was made up of five benches. Three formed a table. A trestle made them the right height. Two benches, one on each side, served for seating. As soon as the tables were put together, women covered them with tablecloths.

Picturing the *Eck*, the seats of honor for the bridal couples, Liz Ann smiled. Tables in the living room would be placed end-to-end to form a large U. Usually, one corner of the table is reserved for the bridal party. *Today, both corners are going to be occupied by a bride and groom.*

Liz stopped at the table in the upstairs room where both brides displayed their wedding gifts, most of which had arrived days before. Liz Ann reached to touch an ornate oil lamp.

"Joseph said he bought me a special present. "Her smile brightened Sarah's face. "You know what it is, *gel*?"

"*Vell...ja,* but you'll have to wait until he gives it to you."

"*Ach!*Give me a hint."

Liz Ann laughed. "And spoil your surprise?" Joseph had purchased her a set of stainless steel pans. He had also bought a set of glasses with matching candlesticks.

The scraping of benches, noisy chatter, and the din of banging and clanking kettles drifted up the stairs. Liz Ann had seen men carrying in large chests of unbreakable dishes that the Beilers had rented from the district. Friends and relatives rapidly set the tables. The main dish was what the Amish call "roast," a bread filling mixed with shredded chicken. There was also creamed celery, a customary fare. In the tradition of Amish weddings, ladies arranged celery in containers so that the leafy tops looked like pretty plants.

The Beilers were serving about 400 people, so there were mountains of mashed potatoes and quarts of gravy. Huge containers of coleslaw and gallon jars of applesauce waited in the cellar. Four ladies had each baked ten cherry pies, and Joseph's Aunt Nan had made over four-hundred doughnuts. Large pans of fruit salad and bowls of tapioca pudding sat on the sideboards.

Elizabeth came into the room. "Sarah, the ladies want your new tablecloth for your *Eck*."

Sarah gasped. "I forgot. "She headed out of the room, then whirled to gaze at her sister. "*Wass* about your table?"

Elizabeth's smile broadened. "Elam gave me a pretty new tablecloth this morning."

Fancy dishes filled with nuts, mints, other candy, and special bowls of fruit were placed on the *Eck*. There were also crackers and dip, along with slices of cold meats.

The bridal parties went to the living room tables. Liz Ann took her place beside Samuel. Long tables had been placed in the kitchen for the bride and groom's parents as well as the older guests. When all the places were taken, all bowed their heads for silent grace. A second after the

"Amen," Liz Ann noticed Samuel pop a mint into his mouth. She smiled.

At the end of the meal, they bowed their heads again for silent grace. As they left the table, workers rapidly cleared the dishes. They would be washed and placed back on the table for the second seating. The *Eck Leit* (corner waiters and waitresses) took places at the *Eck* to eat. The young people would have free time during the second and third seatings. Liz Ann accompanied the young ladies and the brides upstairs to be away from the bustling cooks and waiters. Glancing out a window, she watched Eli make his way to the barn with the young men. *What will they be talking about?* she wondered. Michael Zook stood with a group of men by the barn. Liz Ann thought he looked dejected. Saying a quick prayer for him, she turned back to Sarah.

Both brides passed out treats to friends who had congregated upstairs. Liz Ann knew Joseph and Elam would be treating their friends as well.

After everyone had eaten the main meal, the tables were cleared and set with potato chips, cookies, puddings, and assorted fruits.

Elizabeth smiled. "It's three o'clock. We'd better collect the young people and go to the tables in the living room for the singing."

Taking a seat beside Samuel, Liz Ann watched the brides and grooms return to their places at the *Eck*. The *Porcorer* distributed copies of the *Ausbund* (the Amish hymnal in German with only words, no music). Since brides and grooms don't join in the singing, they passed dishes of candy around the big table, then platters of cheese and sliced meat. Joseph opened a window and they tossed candy to the children.

They sang for two hours. Then, while the young people socialized, the tables were reset for the evening meal. Those who had eaten last at dinner would be served first at supper. Couples who were dating would be permitted to sit together for the meal and evening singing, so it would be the first time that day that Liz Ann would sit with Eli. She waited anxiously in an upstairs room with the other young women. Eli waited with the young men in another.

As one of the *Eck Leit* read their names, a couple stepped into the hall, clasped hands, and descended the stairs. Another *Eck Leit* showed them where to sit.

The menu for the evening meal varied from the one at noon. A dozen other cooks had prepared the food. Bowls of fried sweet potatoes and containers of creamed chicken to be eaten over home-made biscuits sat on the tables. There were platters of sliced ham and cheese as well as bowls of green beans and peas. More pies and cookies waited on the counter.

The brides and grooms took their places at the *Eck*. The living room was illuminated by brightly glowing mantel lamps that hung from wires stretched across the room. The wedding cakes were cut for the evening meal.

Couples who had been married this season—or planned to do so—were seated on the bride's side of the *Eck*. Couples who had no definite plans were seated on the groom's side. Liz Ann and Eli were in the latter group. She watched the continued bustling and wondered how a bride could ever show her gratitude for the work her family and friends did on her wedding day. Of course, married women would begin helping with other weddings. Liz Ann supposed that justified a bride's special day.

At the end of supper, the young people were served ice cream. Each couple shared a dish. Most of the couples peered hesitantly at the last bite, none of them wanting to seem selfish.

Eli glanced at Liz Ann and grinned. "You go ahead."

The other young men did likewise to their partners. Still the ladies were reluctant. Then laughing, Liz Ann dipped her spoon into the dish, scooped up the last bite, held it up, then put the spoon to Eli's lips. He chuckled, then accepted it. The other young ladies did likewise.

After the meal, instead of the black *Ausbund*, the *Unpartheyisches* passed out the *Gesangbuch* (the brown hymnal used in Sunday night meetings). The songs had many verses. Peter John led several songs with a tune of his choice; Eli led several more verses, but changed the tune and tempo; Samuel finished the song with yet another tune. After the traditional songs were sung, the young people began making their own choices.

The moon climbed higher as the cooks placed leftovers on the table called the *Fress*, the word meaning to eat gluttonously. About ten o'clock, weary guests began to collect their coats and their cranky *Kinder*. Carriages rumbled down the lane. Drivers stopped vans at the gate to collect passengers; doors slammed and the vehicles hummed into the distance, but the young people continued to sing until nearly midnight. Both brides and grooms looked exhausted.

Liz Ann yawned. "Today was *un wonderbar!*" She intended to stay over night and help with the clean-up in the morning.

Sarah and Joseph would occupy one bedroom, Elizabeth and Elam another. Peter John was to sleep in Eli's room.

In many cases, the newly married couple would remain in the bride's parents' home until spring, but since Joseph was taking over the King farm, he and Sarah planned to go there tomorrow. Joseph's parents, Noah and Anna, had already moved into the *Dawdy Haus*. Elizabeth had her small farm, so she and Elam would be living there. Liz Ann fought another yawn as she climbed the stairs.

Ohio. Rachel Kay set an African violet in the center of her kitchen table and smiled. The blue blossoms matched the blue in the tablecloth. Susan and her family were coming for supper and the blue was Susan's favorite shade. Turning to the stove, she checked to see how the baked salmon was doing. She was having candied acorn squash and fried potatoes. She had baked an upside-down pineapple cake with cherries. That was one of Susan's favorite desserts. Just before serving it, she would whip cream for topping.

She had baked a caramel cake for little Annie, her sister's oldest daughter, iced it with fluffy marshmallow icing, and decorated it. She straightened the light-blue skirt on the doll she had made for the little girl's second birthday, then bustled around the kitchen, setting the table and checking it twice.

As footsteps resounded on the porch, Rachel glanced at her purple dress and remembered that she hadn't changed into the deep-rose one she had planned to wear for the occasion. Hoping she was presentable, she swiped a hand across her pristine apron.

The door swung inward. A gust of wind seemed to blow Susan into the room with baby Susan in her arms. Matthew Yoder, Susan's husband, followed with bundled Annie cradled in his arms. She wiggled to get down. He shut the door and bent his tall frame to set the little girl on the floor. Rachel rushed to hug them. Then kneeling, she helped Annie out of her coat.

"Supper smells *un wonderbar!*" Removing his black hat, Matthew combed long fingers through his chestnut-colored hair. His deep-blue eyes twinkled as he helped Susan unwrap their infant. Rachel knew his dimples would be showing, if his beard hadn't hidden them.

Susan's soft-blue eyes glistened as she handed Rachel her baby. Rachel thought about the infection her sister had had when baby Susan was born. Because of it, Susan had been unable to nurse. *The baby is doing well, though, in spite of man-made formulas*, Rachel thought.

Susan glanced around the kitchen. "*Wass* can I do to help?"

"Everything's under control. Supper will be ready in a jiffy. "Rachel sat on the bench so that Annie could climb up beside her. "How's my big two-year-old?" she asked the delicate little girl.

"Annie big." The child's black hair shone in the late afternoon sun that streamed through the window. Her gray eyes, duplicates of Rachel's, reflected the color of her dress and shone like blue pearls.

"Ummmm." Susan eyed the pineapple upside-down cake. "You always remember our favorites, Rachel. How do you do it?"

"How could I forget!"Rachel laughed softly. "You eleven all asked for your likes at least twice a day." She brushed a smudge of powdered sugar from her skirt. "I forgot to change my dress, though."

Susan laughed. "With you it's always everyone else first. "Her expression turned serious. "It's about time you get around to yourself, dear Sister."

"*Ach.* There's plenty of time for that. "Rachel's smile felt plastic. But, maybe with Jonas's renewed interest..."

Annie looked at the table, then at the fluffy white icing on her birthday cake. "Eat?"

"*Ja.*" Surrendering the baby to Susan, Rachel went to the oven to remove the baked salmon. Registering the delight in Matthew's eyes when he spied the fish was payment enough for the fussing she had done to make this meal perfect. She loved all her siblings—as well as their chosen mates—but somehow, Susan had been special. Maybe because she had been an infant when Rachel had taken over the household duties. Her youngest sister was more like her own child. She smothered a gasp. *If Susan had been my child, I would be a grandmother! I haven't even been a wife yet!*

Susan handed the baby to Matthew and filled the water glasses. Then she chose the vegetable dish Rachel had planned to use. That's the way it had always been with Susan. The two sisters often seemed to converse without words.

A knock on the door startled Rachel. Wayne and Rosy had said they couldn't come tonight; Henry had had plans to go elsewhere, and none of her other siblings had been able to accept her invitation.

Matthew opened the door, glanced over his shoulder at Rachel, and grinned. "It's my cousin."

Stepping inside, Jonas Yoder closed the door. His eyes followed the platter of steaming salmon as Susan carried it to the table; then his gaze met Rachel's. "I noticed Matthew and Susan were here and decided to stop in to visit with them. It's all right, *gel*?"

"*Ja*, Jonas." What had he expected her to say? She figured she knew what else he wanted, too. "You'll stay for supper?"

He grinned. "*Hertzlich Dank*."

Susan went to the silverware drawer as Rachel turned to the cupboard to get a plate. Her hands were busy, but so was her mind. Had Jonas come to visit Matthew—or had he smelled the baked salmon?

Lancaster County

After slipping into a nightgown, Liz Ann sprawled across her bed. Taking one long breath, she drifted into peaceful oblivion.

A loud clatter jolted her awake. Bolting to a sitting position, she blinked in the darkness. Had she been dreaming? Her tired body dropped back to the bed; she closed her eyes.

Crash! Bang! Thump. Liz Ann's feet hit the floor. She stood, but staggered and grasped the bed post.

Susanna leaped out of bed, her eyes wide in the moonlight. "*Wass* was that?"

CHAPTER FOUR

Quickly donning a robe, Liz Ann rushed into the hall. Elizabeth and Elam opened their door. Wearing broadfalls over their pajamas, Eli and Peter John raced down the stairs. Joseph opened the remaining bedroom door; his hair was disheveled and his suspender fastened to his broadfalls at an odd angle. He eyed Liz Ann. "*Huscht Du ebbis gehoert* (Did you hear something)?"

"*Ja!*"

He hurried after Peter John. Liz Ann followed, hoping the racket had been made by friends planning to surprise them by removing the benches and replacing the furniture, but nothing inside the house had been touched.

Eli yanked the kitchen door open. "*Hey dir Kalls kommet do zurick* (Hey! You rascals come back here)!"

Joseph joined him at the door. "So that was it!"

Peering around them, Liz Ann saw the washing machine leaning against the porch railing. The first duty of the bride and groom is to wash the wedding tablecloths and other items soiled from the wedding. Sometimes the groom hid the washing machine from would-be pranksters, but Joseph and Elam had failed to do so. Liz Ann turned to grin at Susanna. "Some naughty boys tried to foil the newlyweds, but no harm has been done."

Susanna answered with a sleepy smile, then went back upstairs. Peter John stepped onto the porch and helped Eli to upright the machine.

Joseph went to assist his friends. "Let's bring it into the house."

"*Ja, gut (good)*."

When the job was finished, the young men followed Liz Ann back upstairs. Eli and Peter John were laughing, probably remembering how they had pulled tricks on other newlyweds.

Joseph rubbed his hands across his face. "It's two o'clock! We only have two more hours to sleep."

"*Ja, vell*," Eli grinned. "*Gute nacht. Schlof gut* (Good night. Sleep good)."

Liz Ann entered her bedroom. A small battery lamp produced a soft glow. Thirteen-year-old Ruth Beiler lay on her back, a hand resting near her rounded cheek. Her dark hair formed a shadow around her face. Liz Ann expected her to blink and look up with sparkling dark-brown eyes, but she didn't stir. "Did Ruth sleep through that racket?"

"*Ja*." Susanna rolled over. "That young lady would sleep through a tornado, even if the house was swept away, *gel*?"

Chuckling, Liz Ann turned off the lamp and crawled back into bed. Hopefully, she would get a little more sleep. "*Gute naught*."

The alarm resounded the instant Liz Ann's head had hit the pillow—or so it seemed. Groggily, she sat up. Susanna was already dressing. "Where do you get your energy?"

"*Ach*, I'm still asleep." She chuckled. "John and I will be getting married in a couple of weeks, and so many will be helping us. The least I can do is help Sarah and Elizabeth."

Liz Ann nodded. She wanted to aid her friends, too, although she didn't plan to marry this season. *Or maybe ever*, she thought, envisioning Eli's blue Buick.

Breakfast was over and the benches cleared from the house in fast order. Liz Ann swept the living room while Susanna mopped the kitchen vinyl. Careful not to track across the wet places, Eli and Peter John carted furniture back into the house. Elizabeth and Elam prepared the wash water while Sarah and Joseph gathered up the soiled linens. Before lunch, the house was back in order and the laundry flapped in the breeze. Farm chores drew Joseph and Sarah to the King farm. Elizabeth and Elam left for their place.

Liz Ann figured the work was finished. Until next Monday! Another friend was being married on Tuesday.

"You ready to go home, Liz Ann?" Eli asked.

Spotting his car near the gate, she narrowed her eyes. Since Amish boys weren't permitted to keep their cars on the farms, she knew Eli had made a special trip to bring it. Propping her hands on her hips, she stared at him. "You harness Stomper to your buggy, Mr. Beiler, or I'll go home with someone else."

He yawned, apparently trying to portray his fatigue. "There's no one else here who can drive you home."

She glanced around. "Where's Peter John?"

"He took Leah home. She was glad to have a ride in a car." A grin teased his lips. "And I'm too tired to bother with a horse."

Well, she was tired too. Too much so to put up with his flippancy. Turning, she put on her bonnet and wrapped her cape tightly around her. "I'll walk!"

His eyes widened. "It's three miles, and it's cold!"

Yanking the door open, she stepped onto the porch. A brisk November wind whipped her cape and lashed at her face.

"Wait." Sighing, Eli grasped her arm. "Go back in the house. I'll hitch up the carriage."

Feeling a swell of triumph, she went back inside and watched through a window. His shoulders hunched against the wind as he plodded toward the barn. Was she being harsh and unreasonable? *I'm being strong and abiding by the rules of my church.* Eli would have to learn to submit—sooner or later. She shuddered at the thought of the outcome, should he refuse to conform. Would he leave home? If he left would he ever return? Some did. Some didn't.

The next three weeks flew by. Leah Miller had been staying with Elizabeth and Elam. The couple had decided to postpone some of their after-wedding visitation because Elam was still on crutches. Besides, Daniel was in first grade and Priscilla was small. Leah shook her head. Three-year-old Jesse Mark would love to travel in the snow. The deeper the better!

Sarah and Joseph had rented a car and driver the day after the wedding and left to visit distant relatives.

Leah gazed out a kitchen window of the farmhouse. A December wind whistled through the pine at the corner of the carriage shed and flung snow against the pane, but the aroma of baking bread that wafted through the house created a cozy atmosphere.

"We must have seven inches," Leah murmured, although there was no one to hear her—except Priscilla.

Pushing aside the single white curtain, Leah tried to gauge the severity of the storm. Large flakes kissed the glass, then gracefully glided to the sill. The scene looked smothered in whipped cream—except for where the plow had humped ridges and mounds beside the lane. Even those muddy splotches were rapidly covered with a new layer of white fluff. Naked branches of the apple tree whipped spasmodically in the wind as though endeavoring to rid themselves of the thick layer of ice that blanketed them. It was Leah's twenty-second birthday, and she had been looking forward to a family gathering. This weather would probably discourage visiting.

Snow won't daunt Peter John. The thought made her heart race, then pondering his unwillingness to give up *Rumspringe,* she frowned. When she had permitted him to call on her, she had believed he would settle down. Her mental torment and aching heart told her she had made a mistake.

A chestnut carriage horse pranced into view. Puffs of frosty breath blew from the animal's nostrils and dispersed in the icy air. Jonah Stoltzfus, bundled in quilts, hunched in the sleigh. Snow sprayed upwards from the runners as he slid around the curve. Apparently noticing Leah at the window, Jonah waved a gloved hand. His red bulbus nose protruded from under his heavy knit cap and looked like it would love to burrow into his bushy black beard. Leah returned his wave and watched his conveyance vanish around a curve in the lane.

Another blast of wind seized snow and hurled it across the barnyard to deepen the already numerous drifts against the outbuildings. In a sudden lull, the laden boughs of the pine beside the gate drooped.

My spirit feels as encumbered as they look. Picturing Peter John's dark hair and sparkling green eyes, she tried to massage the frown from her usually smooth brow. Since it was Friday, even though there was a blizzard, would He go into town? Her lips drew taut. "*Ja*, he would."

Another sigh escaped from deep within her. She would have gone home to Mercer County after Elam and Elizabeth's wedding, but Emma Miller Zook, her older sister, was expecting and would need help in February when her eighth baby was born.

As Leah pondered, she absently chewed her lower lip. Deep-golden waves, parted in the center as all Amish women wore their hair, waved away from her pretty rounded face and vanished under her prayer cap. Her turquoise eyes, usually bright, were dimmed by concern.

"If it weren't for Emma, I'd go home," she murmured.

She would still be in Mercer County if Elam hadn't been severely injured in a buggy accident. After Elam had secured a position in Aaron King's cabinet-making business near Eden, He and Elizabeth had returned. Leah had accompanied them, met Peter John, and decided to stay through the winter. Now, she wrestled with her decision.

Maybe I'll go home, then return before Emma's due date, she thought. She nodded, underscoring her solution. Swiping a hand across the blue skirt of her dress, she turned from the window. Elizabeth's kitchen was roomy and cheerful. The walls were white and free of ornaments, as were all Amish homes in this district. The light-walnut cupboards matched the oval table and chairs. Unlike her parents' wood stove in Mercer County, Elizabeth's was propane. Here they were allowed bathrooms, as long as they were on the first floor and the water supply was fed by gravity. Picturing the outhouse back home and the snow, she shivered.

A happy squeal drew her attention to Priscilla; the nine-month-old baby sat on the pink-white-and beige vinyl floor, her pink skirt billowing around her legs. Blond curls poked from under her prayer cap like unruly chicks. Grasping a red block in one chubby hand, she endeavored to add it to a precariously stacked tower of one green and one yellow block. They toppled.

"Boom." Clapping her hands, she looked up with sparkling light-blue eyes.

Smiling, Leah headed toward the little girl, but the timer on the stove resounded, checking her stride. She went to the oven to remove the golden-crusted loaves. Bumping them from the pans, she placed them on racks on the counter to cool. Elizabeth's cow cookie jar sat where light from the window above the sink gleamed on the bovine's white horns. Lifting the lid, Leah took a small ginger cookie and sampled its spicy sweetness.

Muffled footsteps on the porch drew her attention to the door. It swung inward to admit Elizabeth Stoltzfus Miller. Her shoulders and the hood of her long navy cape were frosted with snow. Her smile was bright, her soft-brown eyes shining, and her cheeks as red as ripe apples. Even the end of her small straight nose was pink from the cold. Laughing, she shoved her hood back. Light streamed through the window and created red and gold highlights in the chestnut-colored waves that showed at the front of her prayer cap.

"*Sel schur is en Storm* (What a storm)!" Wiping her feet on the throw rug by the door, she shrugged out of her cape and hung it on a hook. "Animals must eat, though."

"*Mem.*" Grinning, Priscilla pulled herself to her feet by using a nearby kitchen chair.

"Hi, baby mine, *wie gehts* (How are you)?"

"*Mem.*" Releasing her grip on the chair, Priscilla took a couple of cautious tottering steps, then sat down with a plop.

Elizabeth stepped forward and swooped her up in her arms. "Mama's big girl is going to be walking, soon!" She kissed Priscilla's chubby pink cheek, then hugged her.

As Leah watched, desire for a home of her own, a good man to share it with, and children to brighten her day captured her heart.

The sound of a motor vehicle drew Elizabeth to a window. "It's Aaron. I'm so thankful he drives Elam to and from work."

Moving to the window, Leah glanced at the dark-blue van that slid to a stop near the gate. Aaron King, born Amish, but now a member of a Mennonite church, got out and trudged to the rear of the van, opened the back, and lifted Elam's wheelchair. Apparently not wishing to set the conveyance in the snow, he headed for the porch. Even though Elam was using crutches, he used the wheelchair some of the time at work to rest his legs.

Elam opened his door and grappled with his crutches.

Leah watched. "*Herzlich Dank to der gut Man* for sparing Elam's life, *gel*?"

"With a little more therapy and proper exercise he will

soon be able to put away his crutches."

"I'll see if he needs help in this snow." Seizing her long black cape, Leah flipped it over her shoulders and hurried outside. "Hi, Aaron, *wie gehts*, and how is Rebecca?"

Gripping the wheelchair with one hand, he shoved his black felt hat back. His dark-brown eyes brimmed with joy. "My wife and I are both doing *un wonderbar!*"

"How are the roads, Aaron?" Leah called over her shoulder as she tramped through the snow toward the gate.

"Bad and getting worse. I'll be glad to get home." He hurried across the porch and into the kitchen.

When Leah reached her brother, he was at the front of the van. Leaning cautiously on his crutches, he took small steps.

"Need any help?"

"*Neh, gross Dank.*" Plunging his crutches into the two-foot ridge of snow made by the plow, he gingerly placed one booted foot on the packed mound. As he shifted his weight, the crutch sank, throwing him off balance.

Leah braced herself to break his fall should he topple, but not wanting to undermine his confidence, she avoided contact. Why hadn't she shoveled a path for him? *I was too busy feeling sorry for myself over the way Peter John is acting*, she mused, vowing not to be so thoughtless in the future.

Once over the lumpy mound, Elam methodically made his way up the walk and climbed the steps. Elizabeth opened the door as he crossed the porch; a welcoming smile brightened her lovely face.

"*Dank der gut man* this is Friday," Aaron said, hurrying to his van.

"*Pap.*" Priscilla reached for Elam as he entered the room.

Slumping to the bench by the door, he propped his crutches against the wall, shrugged out of his jacket, and took the little girl in his arms. "Where are Daniel and

Jesse Mark?" He looked across the room as though he expected his six-year-old and three-year-old sons to materialize.

"Daniel is next door with *Mammi* Nancy May," Elizabeth said.

A crease appeared between Elam's eyes. "And Jesse Mark?"

"Jacob John stopped by early this afternoon, and Jesse Mark went home with him to play with Elmer."

"In this storm?"

"It wasn't snowing then."

He sighed. "Emma has enough to handle with her own seven *Kinder*."

"*Ach!*" Elizabeth laughed. "Once one has that many, another one doesn't matter, *gel*?"

"*Ja, vell . . .*" Turning, Elam stared out the window, concern in his brown eyes. He scratched his light-brown beard with long slender fingers. "I hope Jacob doesn't try to bring him home in this weather." His frown deepened. "I wish there was a way to get him a message to keep Jesse Mark until morning."

Leah figured the little boy would look forward to a trip through the snow, but Jacob John, Emma's husband, didn't have a sleigh. What if they started and had an accident? She frowned. *If we Amish were permitted phones in our homes, a problem like this could easily be solved.* Feeling a gentle rebuke for her worldly thought, she sighed and reminded herself to leave Jesse Mark in *der gut* Man's hands. Turning to the sink to peel potatoes for supper, she hoped her brother and sister-in-law hadn't read the concern in her expression.

Emma Zook finished mixing a meat loaf for supper and patted it into a casserole dish. Joyous squeals and laughter filled the living room and spilled into the kitchen. She glanced over her shoulder at the frolicking *Kinder*.

Dan and Andy, her seven-year-old and six-year-old sons, rolled across the floor, locked in a wrestling hold. Two-year-old Katy gripped the leg of a doll as she struggled to take it from four-year-old Anna May. The older girl laughed, refusing to release her grip. Katy danced and squealed. Five-year-old Elmer raced a small wooden wagon across the floor toward Elam's youngest son. Blond curls dangled on Jesse Mark's forehead and caressed his ears; his light-blue eyes twinkled as he tossed a pillow in the path of the wagon, causing it to wreck. Emma shook her head at the happy din. She thought about the new baby that would join the family in two and a half months, and smiled as she turned back to preparing the evening meal. *Dank der gut Man* for my twins, she thought glancing at eight-year-old Malinda and Amanda who were setting the table. Blond highlights danced in the chestnut-colored hair that showed at the edge of their prayer caps; their hazel eyes were usually alive with gold flecks, their coloring a duplicate of Emma's.

They don't have my dimples, though, she thought. The weight of the coming baby pulled on her back, making her feel awkward and cumbersome. For some reason, she believed the baby was a girl. "I'll call her Rose Anna."

"*Wass, Mem?*" Amanda asked.

Not realizing she had spoken aloud, Emma turned to look at her. Grinning, she shrugged. "I was just thinking about the new baby."

Malinda sighed. "I think we should quit having babies."

Amanda laughed. "I think we should have lots more."

"*Vell*, whatever *der gut Man* sends us, we'll love and care for." Opening the oven door, Emma placed the meat loaf on the top rack and arranged scrubbed potatoes around the perimeter. When she straightened she looked at the clock. "Your Papa is late getting home, so we'll start the barn work."

Amanda's hazel eyes widened. "You'll stay in the house, *Mem, gel?*"

"In this storm, your *Pap* will need all the help he can get." She peered into the living room. "Dan! *Kom ann* (come on). I need your help at the barn."

The boy appeared in the doorway, his light-brown hair tousled, and concern evident in his soft-brown eyes. "Where's *Pap?*"

"Andrew is ill, so he went to help your Uncle Michael with his milking." She propped her fists on her rounded hips. "Get your heavy coat on and *kom* with me. Amanda, you stay here and watch the *Kinder*. Malinda, get ready and *kom* with me."

Malinda wished her mother would stay in the house. She was old enough to know about the coming little one, and even though she felt weary from so many *Kinder*, she didn't want anything to happen that would endanger the new baby.

The threesome tromped through the drifting snow toward the barn, Malinda trying to place her booted feet in her mother's footsteps. Dan led the way. The boy was only seven, but was dragging his feet, apparently endeavoring to blaze a trail for his mother and sister. Bundles, the golden retriever, yipped as she bounded to them, her eyes bright and her tail wagging.

Malinda petted the dog's head. "You're a good girl."

Inside the barn, Emma pushed her hood back and turned to face her daughter. "You can give the horses their portion of grain. Dan, you go up and fork down hay for the cows."

Malinda opened the feed box and scooped grain into a measuring can as Dan vanished up the back stairway, Bundles at his heels.

Emma filled the horses' mangers with hay, tossed an armload to the mule, and frowned. "What's keeping Dan?"

Flinging the empty can into the grain box, Malinda

slammed the lid. "He's just slow."

"I'll speed him up a bit." She headed for the back stairway at a fast gait. Mounting the steps, she called to her eldest son. Near the top, her foot slipped on chaff. Screaming, she pawed the air as though she were searching frantically for something to grasp.

Malinda's throat constricted and her stomach twisted spasmodically as she helplessly watched her mother's plummeting body. She seemed to bounce and tumble down the stairs like a rag doll. Malinda reached the bottom of the stairway as her mother thudded on the straw in a crumpled heap. "*Mem!*" Kneeling, she touched Emma's shoulders. When there was no response, her horror intensified. "*Mem? Mem!*"

CHAPTER FIVE

Malinda peered at Emma's leg. It was bent at an odd angle that made her stomach cramp. A bright-red spot appeared on the front of her mother's faded light-blue dress. As she stared in horror, the blotch slowly broadened. "Dan!" Malinda yelled.

The boy appeared at the top of the stairs. His eyes widened, and he clambered down the stairs in such a hurry that he lost his footing on the bottom step and nearly sprawled beside his mother's motionless body. Bundles followed, then stood staring at the prostrate woman.

"*Geh fe de Pap* (Go for Papa)!" Malinda shouted; then thought about her brother's being younger and small for his age. "*Neh, Bleib bei die Mem* (No, you stay with Mama)."

Tying the hood of her coat tighter, Malinda yanked on her mittens and raced from the barn. Yipping, Bundles bounced after her. She headed for the pasture, for crossing it was the shortest route to her uncle's farm. Then, picturing the small creek that wound between the properties and knowing the water would be higher this time of year, she turned toward the lane. After only a few steps, she stopped. If she took the long way around, would she miss her father on his way home? "Oh Lord, help me," she prayed.

An image of Emma's prone body and the splotch that oozed across her clothing seared through her mind. "The creek will be frozen over," she mumbled. Whirling, she headed across the meadow. Wind howled through the pines and flung snow in her face, the frozen particles stinging her cheeks like bits of steel. The snow was as deep as her boots. The drifts were deeper. Snow sifted down her legs, wet her stockings, and made her shiver. Still, she trudged on.

Whining, Bundles caught the bottom of Malinda's coat and coaxed her to retreat.

She jerked free. "We can't go back!"

The dog barked annoyingly, then trudged on, the zip gone from the venture.

Clenching her teeth, Malinda tried to ignore how her legs smarted, then began to ache. Her face felt numb, yet her taut skin burned from the cold. Exertion made her pant, and the frigid air burned her lungs. "How much farther?" she asked the howling wind. Squinting, she protected her eyes with her hands and tried to estimate how far she had come. She could make out the line of trees to her right and the shadow of Michael's barn, so she was headed right, but where was the creek? Apparently the snow had drifted across the ice, making it difficult to judge its exact location. *It has to be close.*

I'd better go back! she thought, then another picture of her mother flashed before her. No! *I must get help*!

She struggled to increase her pace, but the drifts seemed to be getting deeper—as though making an effort to thwart her. A storm this severe was unusual for November, but that didn't make it less real. Suddenly, her feet flew out from under her and she landed on her back with a thud that nearly knocked the breath from her. A cloud of snow covered her. Bundles leaped forward through the veil of white to lick her face as though this were a game.

"Not now, girl." Malinda realized she had tumbled down the slope near the creek. How deep was the water beneath the frozen surface? Apparently sensing her fear, the dog whined.

"*Kom ann*, Bundles." Her mother's plight and the danger to the unborn little one filled her with determination. Clambering to her feet, she stepped gingerly but rapidly. Snapping and cracking made her heart falter. When she felt the ice give, she took several more quick steps. She was thankful when she felt solid ground.

Shielding her eyes, she tried to get her bearings. The thought of being lost in this ocean of white gripped her mind and drove her onward. Was she going to make it? "Oh, *Pap*, where are you?"

Finally she could see her uncle's house clearly. Her determination renewed, she plowed through another drift. Bundles had to take leaps to follow in Malinda's wake. The fingers of her left hand felt numb. When had she lost her glove? Choking back a sob, she rammed her hand into her coat pocket and forced one foot ahead of the other. *Only three hundred feet to go.* Stumbling, she fell again, and plunged her face into a mound of snow. This time, she didn't think she could get up. Bundles whined, then tugged at Malinda's coat sleeve.

Hearing a vehicle, she forced her head up. A green car stopped at Michael's gate. As a man climbed from the vehicle, she tried to call out, but the wind seized her breath, silencing her cry; only puffs of frosty air portrayed her feeble attempt.

The man headed for the porch. Malinda waved futilely and tears stung her eyes. *Oh, please see me.*

Bundles barked feverishly.

Hesitating, the man turned, then hurried toward Malinda. He trudged through the snow, his hood and scarf nearly covering his face.

"Peter John."

He stopped near her. "Malinda! *Was duscht Du do haus* (What are you doing out here)?"

"Mama needs help."

"*Dank der gut* Man your dog yapped." He reached for

her hand. "You look half-frozen."

"*Ja.*" Her teeth chattered.

"I'll carry you." Picking her up, he headed for the house.

Her body jerked as she fought the tears that ran down her cheeks. They felt as though they were freezing to her face. She struggled to control her convulsed shivers as Peter John tramped toward her uncle's porch.

Inside the house, Michael Zook poured himself and his brother a cup of coffee, then returned the pot to the stove. He was grateful for Jacob's help. Without it, he might have lost one of his best cows. His stomach growled. The chicken Lydia was frying smelled *un wonderbar!* His mouth watered as he eyed the golden biscuits on the counter and thought about spreading them with fresh butter and honey.

Lydia, his twelve-year-old daughter, opened the cupboard and counted plates. Hesitating, she turned. "Can you stay for supper, Uncle Jacob?"

"*Gross Dank*, but not tonight." Taking a sip of the steaming brew, Jacob wrapped his fingers around his mug. "One cup to thaw my chilled bones, then I must hurry home. Emma will be getting anxious."

Noticing a jacket flopped on the floor in the corner, Michael frowned. "Moses."

"*Ja, Pap?*" The boy in the rocker stared at the floor.

"Hang up your jacket."

Quietly, he obeyed. Michael sighed. Why did his son have to be reminded so often about the things he knew he should do?

Hearing a dog bark, Michael crossed the room to look out a window. Peter John, carrying a child, shoved the gate open with one booted foot and hurried toward the porch. Michael rushed to open the door.

As Peter John swept into the kitchen, Michael recognized Malinda.

Lydia whirled, her blue-green eyes wide. "*Ach!*"

Crossing the room, Peter placed the girl in a soft chair by the stove and turned to Michael. "Pap sent me for the chickens."

"I'll get them ready, but first . . ." The distress on Malinda's face kept him glued to the spot.

Lydia moved to her cousin. "*Was is letz*, and *wass* were you doing out there?"

"Where's *Pap*?"

At the sound of her voice, Jacob John leaped to his feet, splashing hot coffee as he thudded the mug to the table. Hurrying to her, he dropped to one knee. "*Wass is letz?*"

"*Mem* . . . in the barn." A sob racked her slight frame. "There's . . . blood!"

Michael's heart lurched; Lydia gasped.

Instantly on his feet, Jacob seized his coat. He glanced at Michael. "I'll be back later for Malinda." With an arm in one sleeve of his jacket, he yanked the door open and ran outside.

"You forgot your gloves!" Lydia waved them.

As though not hearing her, Jacob raced down the path.

Michael's concern continued to mount. "Peter John, *Kom* back and let us know if we can do anything to help."

"*Ja.*" Grabbing the gloves and thanking Lydia, Peter John hurried after Jacob. "Get in my car; I'll drive you home."

"*Viel Dank!*" Jacob leaped into the vehicle, a prayer for his wife gushing from between his lips.

Closing the door, Michael watched through the glass.

Peter John slipped behind the wheel and started the engine. The wheels spun, flinging muddy snow against the mailbox. The vehicle slid as Peter sped around a curve in the road, but he regained control before his car vanished behind a stand of trees.

Lydia stood transfixed; then she turned to her father. "Should I go over to Emma's to see what I can do?"

"*Vell...* In this storm..." He sighed. "Maybe we should wait for Peter's return." He looked at Malinda, wondering if she could further explain what had happened to her mother.

"You'll eat with us, *gel*?" Not waiting for Malinda's answer, Lydia set her a place at the table.

A tiny hand curled around Michael's finger. He looked down into Miriam's sweet face. His five-year-old was a quiet darling. Scooping her into his arms, he hugged her.

"Andrew!" Lydia called up the stairway. "Supper's ready."

The ten-year-old thudded down the steps in his stocking feet and took his place at the table. He stared at the dish of baked corn, then at the plate piled high with chicken and grinned.

Moses took his place without having to be reminded. Michael was pleased; then he noticed the boy's hands. "Moses."

"*Ja, Pap?*"

Michael pointed to the basin. Why was his youngest son's actions deliberately bordering on defiance? Michael sighed. *Will I ever get to the bottom of what's eating at him?*

Leah glanced out a window. The storm was over; the evening sun burned scarlet on the horizon and tinted the snow-scape a light-pink. Elizabeth had baked a cake and invited Abraham and Nancy Stoltzfus for a roast beef supper. Leah noticed Daniel lifting his legs high as he tramped across the yard toward the porch. She pictured Nancy, now in her seventies, struggling through the drifts on her short legs.

"I'm going to shovel a path, Elizabeth." Yanking on her boots, Leah donned a heavy dark-brown jacket with a thickly-lined hood and went outside. The shovel stood propped against the post at the bottom of the steps where she had left it.

"Hi, Aunt Leah," Daniel called as he climbed the mound of snow piled beside the gate.

Scooping a glob of snow, Leah made a ball and threw it at him.

He ducked, then slid down the slope. Losing his footing, he tumbled headlong into a drift. Instead of jumping up, he rolled over and waved his arms and swiped his legs, creating an angel indentation. "*Du bischt naus komme fe spielle mit mich, gel* (You came out to play with me, right)?"

"I need to clear the path. Why don't you build a snowman for Priscilla." Gripping the shovel handle, Leah shoved it under the snow, then tossed a scoop-full aside. It landed on the pile with a soft swoosh.

Daniel rolled a large snowball, then sat on it. "I wish Jesse Mark would come home."

"He'll be home tomorrow." She continued to work.

Daniel got a smaller shovel and began to dig at the hump made by the snowplow. He tired quickly and moved to line small snowballs up along the edge of the porch.

A cardinal lit on the corner post and peered curiously at Leah, then flew away. Leah paused to lean against the maple tree near the path. What was the strange feeling that gripped her insides? Struggling to convince herself she was being silly, she finished clearing the path through the gate and made a walkway through the ridge made by the snowplow. As she turned to go to the house, she heard a car roaring up the lane. Disliking the stares of *Englischers*, she quickly retreated to the porch.

"Wow!" Daniel jerked his head toward the road, his eyes wide.

Leah whirled to see a green Trans Am sliding sideways. The vehicle straightened, then fish-tailed toward the ditch. She gasped. The engine roared; the wheels spun, flinging snow several feet behind the car. The vehicle leaped forward, slid sideways, then came to a stop inches from the gate. It had probably been the pile of snow that had saved the post. When she saw that it was Peter John in the driver's seat, her foolish heart rejoiced; then she noticed Jesse Mark sitting wide-eyed in the passenger's seat. Tightening her lips, she thudded the shovel into the snow. The handle tha-whacked against the banister. She turned to face Peter John, but he had turned to help Jesse Mark climb out of the car.

The little boy scampered up the path, his light-blue eyes sparkling and a broad grin dimpling his chubby cheeks.

Daniel looked as though he'd missed out on something. "Was your ride fun?"

"*Ja! Un Wonderbar!*" Jesse Mark giggled. "I wanna do it again!"

Anger and dismay played hopscotch in Leah's mind. Her heart pleaded with her to excuse Peter John, but her common sense wondered how he could influence a little boy in such a worldly fashion. Ignoring her heart, she prepared to accost him, but his woeful expression halted hasty words. Again the strange feeling seized her. "Hello, Peter, *Wie mauts* (how are things)?"

"*Vell* . . . Let's go inside," he said quietly.

She hurried to the door, her heart racing. What was Peter John doing with Jesse Mark? Had he been to Emma's? *Fer wass* (Why)? She rushed ahead into the house.

Daniel and Jesse Mark came into the kitchen like another snow storm. After greeting Peter John, Elizabeth hurried to help the little boys with their jackets and boots. By the time Leah had hung up their coats, her thoughts had run amuck. Peter John's usually joyous face was shadowed with concern. Motioning to Leah, he went into the living room where Elam was romping with Priscilla.

Elam's brow furrowed. "*Was is letz* (what's wrong),

Peter?"

"It's . . . Emma," Peter said as he took a seat on the burgundy sofa beside Elam.

Leah sank to a wooden rocker and gripped the arm, her heart racing. The color drained from Elam's face. He sat motionless, staring at Peter and hugging Priscilla.

Peter quickly explained Emma's fall, Malinda's trek, and his part in taking Jacob home and calling for an ambulance. "Annie Zimmerman is watching the *Kinder*. Jacob accompanied Emma to the hospital. I thought it would help for me to bring Jesse Mark home."

"*Gross Dank*. How's Emma?" Elam asked.

"She's concerned about the coming little one. Jacob is frightened for them both."

Leah was torn between staying for the special supper Elizabeth had prepared and asking Peter to drive her to the hospital. She glanced up to see Elizabeth standing in the doorway, moisture pooling in her soft-brown eyes.

She looked at Leah. "If you and Elam want to go to see Emma, I'll explain to *Mammi* Nancy."

Elam drew a long slow breath. "Jacob will need someone, too." He looked at Leah. "We'll both go."

"I'll change my dress and be with you."

Jesse Mark's light-blue eyes sparkled. "I wanna go, too."

Daniel straightened and crossed his arms. "I'm goin' with you this time."

Elam's smile looked forced. "You boys will stay here."

Jesse Mark's dimples disappeared. "I always miss all the fun."

Daniel peered at him, disgruntled. "You don't miss nothin'."

"*Kom ann*, boys," Elizabeth said, looking appealingly at one, then the other. "With Leah gone, I'll need you to help me this evening. Then we can make farm animals out of dough."

Racing up the stairs, Leah unpinned the back of her blue dress, flipped it off over her head, and quickly donned her new peach-colored one. In the kitchen, she yanked on a pair of boots, tied the strings of her black bonnet and draped her heavy black cape around her shoulders.

Elizabeth carried Priscilla to a window. "I'm glad the storm is over." The line that creased her usually smooth forehead betrayed her concern.

"The main roads have been plowed," Peter said, "and I'm a good driver."

"So you are," Leah grumbled. His reference to driving rubbed salt in their wounded relationship. On the way to his car, she refused to meet his gaze. This wasn't the time to spar. Besides, she was grateful for the use of a car, and he knew it.

"I'll sit in the back." Elam made his way to the car, the rubber tips of his crutches making crunching sounds in the snow.

Reluctantly, Leah took the front seat. Knowing Peter's smile would disarm her, she looked out the side window. He chuckled. She tightened her lips. If only she could leave for Mercer County. *Well, as soon as Emma is stabilized . . .*

"Emma Zook has been taken to maternity," a nurse in Emergency said.

"It's too soon!" Leah whispered.

"We'll pray," Elam said, but his forehead remained furrowed.

As they made their way to a waiting room near maternity, Leah hid her trembling fingers under her cape. Peter appeared relaxed and confident, but when they were seated, Elam scratched his beard as though wondering what to do.

"Jacob must be with Emma," Peter said. "I'll see if I can find out how she is."

Leah accompanied him to the doors to the maternity wing. He hesitated. She tried to swallow, but her throat was dry. Reaching out, she gingerly rapped.

A tall, slender nurse with curly red hair pushed the door open. "May I help you?"

"Is . . . Emma Zook in delivery?"

"Are you a relative?"

"Her sister. Has the baby been born?"

"No. The doctors are hoping she doesn't deliver for several weeks."

"Is her husband with her?"

"Yes."

"Will you tell him his wife's brother and sister are in the waiting room?"

The woman smiled, changing her features from serious to affable. "You may slip in to see her, but try to keep calm. She is scheduled for surgery this evening."

Leah's eyes widened. "Surgery?"

The nurse touched her arm. "It's to set her broken leg."

"Oh!" With the complication of a broken limb, Emma would be needing even more help. Figuring her returning to Mercer County had been postponed, again, she followed the nurse to Emma's room.

Jacob sat on a straight chair in the corner, cradling his black hat. Seeing Leah, he smiled, relaxing the weary lines in his face. Getting up quickly, he strode forward.

"Hi, *Wie gehts*," Leah said softly, but her attention was already on Emma. Intravenous tubes connected her arm to a bag of solution that hung from a pole. A blanket hid her fractured leg. Leah moved noiselessly to the side of the bed. "*Wie gehts?*"

Emma's chestnut lashes fluttered, then lifted. A faint smile that didn't camouflage her pain crept across her pale face. "I've . . . been better."

"Elam and Peter John are in the waiting room." In an

effort to soothe some of her sister's agony, Leah patted her arm. "You're going to be all right."

"*Ja, vell* . . ." She caught her lower lip between her teeth. "I'm worried about the baby." She sighed, "But, I'm trying to give my concerns to *der gut* Man."

"We've all been praying."

A furrow shadowed Emma's brow. "Things seem—different this time."

Emma had had easy birthings. She had taken her pregnancies in stride, not seeing a doctor until the last month. She hadn't been to a doctor yet with this pregnancy. She planned to have a midwife—as in her last five deliveries.

Her hand rested lightly on her abdomen. "I can feel the baby kicking, so I know she's all right."

"You mean he kicks," Jacob said.

Leah laughed softly. "One of you has to be right." Hearing footsteps, she turned.

A man with graying dark hair and soft-brown eyes entered and moved to Emma's bedside. "I'm Dr. Bree. How are we doing?"

"I . . . don't know."

Lines formed between the doctor's eyebrows. "I will be examining you shortly."

Emma sighed. "My baby is in *der gut* Man's hands and I'm going to trust Him."

He nodded. "God has permitted us to develop advanced technology to help us avoid possible complications."

Emma's hazel eyes widened. "What complications?"

He rubbed his chin. "I think things are a bit different than you expect."

Frowning, Emma fumbled with the hem of the sheet.

"Don't worry, Mrs. Zook. You're in good hands."

"What about my leg?"

"We'll be taking care of that in about an hour. You're going to be fine."

"*Ja. Der gut* Man is in control."

Dr. Bree nodded. "A nurse will be in soon to prep you for surgery." Turning, he quickly left.

Her brow furrowing, Emma watched the man retreat. Leah smiled reassuringly and took her sister's hand. Two orderlies arrived, put Emma on a gurney, and wheeled her away. Jacob peered after them, concern in his eyes; then he accompanied Leah to the waiting room.

Time dragged. Leah tried to get interested in reading a magazine, but her thoughts kept returning to her older sister. What if there was something wrong with the baby? What if there was a problem with Emma? What if they lost her or the little one?

Stop it! she scolded. Tossing the magazine onto the table, she lowered her lashes and began to pray.

When a man cleared his throat, she looked up. Dr. Bree stood in the doorway, his expression a mask.

Jacob stood as though doubt had weakened his legs. "How's my wife?"

"Well . . ." The doctor took a deep breath and peered at him. "Her leg is in a cast, and she will be uncomfortable for a time. The break was clean and it will heal nicely."

"The . . . baby?"

The doctor looked pensive. "It isn't all as you assumed."

The flesh above Jacob's beard paled, and his fingers gripped his black hat tighter. Elam had stood; now he stepped closer to the doctor. Leah wanted to get up, but her legs felt weak.

Jacob's lips moved, but no sound came. He blinked and tried again. "What's wrong with Emma and our baby?"

CHAPTER SIX

Dr. Bree studied Jacob's face. "There's no need for alarm. It's just that I know you have seven children, the eldest being your eight-year-old twins, and . . ."

"*Ja*. But, what do my other *Kinder* have to do with this?"

Dr. Bree looked sympathetic. "It's just that your wife is carrying twins again."

"Are they all right? Is Emma?"

"They are fine, but your wife must have complete rest for about two months. Every week she carries the babies nearer the delivery date will be better for them."

The color came back to Jacob's face. "*Dank der gut Man!*" Tossing his black hat into the air, then catching it, he laughed.

Dr. Bree turned to Leah. "Your sister will need help until after the birth. Will you be available to help her?"

Peter rushed forward. "*Ja*. She will."

Leah agreed, but her mind whirled. If Peter thought she was going to permit him to call on her just because she had to stay, well . . . Common sense agreed, but her foolish heart rejoiced. She turned away from his round, boyish face and innocent expression to gaze out a window. It was getting dark, so all she could see were shadowy forms of vehicles in the parking lot and the small drifts of snow on the outside sill. Peter's enthusiasm was infectious, and she was drawn to him, not only because of his good looks and jovial personality, but his compassion and willingness to help anyone he could.

She steered her thoughts back to her sister and what she could do to help. *Another set of twins!* reverberated through her. They were a gift from *der gut* Man. She had helped Emma when Amanda and Malinda were born, but she and Emma had each cared for one baby. *Under the circumstances, I'll have the responsibility of caring for both new babies—as well as the rest of the Kinder.*

Michael Zook lifted a pitchfork of sweet-smelling hay, tossed it through an opening in the barn floor, and listened to it gently flop to the floor below.

"Let me try that," Charles Grayson said.

Smiling, Michael handed the fork to his *Englischer* guest. The man weighed over 250 pounds and was six-foot-three. Michael felt dwarfed in his shadow. The man had asked to stay a month and work on the farm so he could learn Amish ways. Michael was dubious, but had graciously invited him to stay.

"As smooth as this handle is, you must have forked a lot of hay." Charles stabbed the fork straight into the mound, then strained to lift it.

Michael smothered a laugh. "Put your fork in at an angle."

Doing so, but too near the surface, he lifted only a small amount of hay. "I'll get the hang of this." Laughing, he tried again, successfully completing the task. "It will be Thanksgiving Day soon. I'll get your family the biggest turkey you've ever seen."

"No thank you," Michael said softly. "We don't celebrate Thanksgiving Day."

Charles dropped a new load of hay from his fork. "Why?"

"We feel it's a political day, because President Lincoln designated it so when he was in office."

"Then you're not thankful for God's bounty?"

"Indeed!" Michael smiled indulgently. "We feel that every day should be a day of thanksgiving."

A furrow appeared between the man's brows. "I see," he said, but his tone indicated that he didn't. His last fork of hay slid through the opening with a swish. "We do the milking next?"

"*Ja*." Michael led the way, wondering if this man had been sent by God to encourage him to think more about his Amish ways. Answering Charles's questions had fixed his beliefs more firmly in his own mind. *Ja*, he thought. *God has surely sent this man.*

Ohio. Rachel Kay Lapp sat on one end of the beige-and-rose sofa in her living room. She brushed a tiny speck of lint from her purple dress. The scent of wood smoke drifted from the blazing logs in the fireplace and filled the room with a rustic essence. Due to the gas well on her brother's farm, she had a gas furnace, but she liked the homeyness of a crackling fire.

Jonas leaned against a smocked pillow on the opposite end of the sofa, his long legs stretched out in front of him, his heels resting on the multi-colored braided rug. His black felt hat, as though it had the duty of a chaperon, occupied the space between them. Ten-year-old Sara Kate, Rachel's niece, perched on a fabric-covered box on the stone hearth. Her reason for being there was to learn how to knit roses on the hot pads for a tourist gift shop—or so Rachel had told Jonas when he had questioned the child's presence. He had been a gentleman, but to still any tongues that might have a tendency to wag, she didn't want to be alone with him.

Seemingly annoyed, the man stared at Sara Kate. Rachel fought a grin when she noticed the yarn-looped knitting needles heaped on the hearth by the girl's feet. Slinking into the room, Prissy, Sara's white cat, spied the ball of pink yarn; she streaked across the hearth and gave it a bat that sent it rolling across the room, then brushed against Sara Kate's leg. Ignoring the cat, Sara Kate stared at the snapping, crackling logs. Prissy managed to wrap the loose yarn around her paws, then jerk free, leaving it a tangled mass.

Jonas scowled at the cat, then at the girl. "*Wieviel hot pads huscht Du gemacht* (How many hot pads do you have made?"

Sara Kate turned to stare blankly at him. "*Wass?*"

He nodded toward her abandoned knitting. "How many have you finished?"

"*Ach.* Just the one Aunt Rachel helped me with."

Jonas nodded as though coming to a conclusion, then turned his attention to Rachel. "I've been giving our situation a lot of thought. I wanted to speak privately with you, but it looks like I'm not going to get the chance."

Apprehensive, she lowered her gaze to her lap. Apparently Prissy was dubious, too, for she came to sit on the braided rug in front of Jonas. Switching her tail, she stared at the man with squinted green eyes.

He glared at the cat with annoyance, then turned to Rachel. "I've been alone for two years." He cleared his throat. "You're alone, too."

The impact of what he might be trying to say seized Rachel. She wasn't ready to accept a proposal of marriage from this man, but she didn't want to give up seeing him, for she might learn to care more deeply for him. When he opened his mouth to speak, she quickly said, "I think we should get to know each other better before we consider anything further."

He laughed. "We've known each other since we were *Kinder!*"

"As friends, Jonas—then you were Linda's husband. It takes time to . . . adjust to the change."

"*Vell* I didn't mean . . . I mean I meant . . ." Seeming flustered, he ran his long fingers through his black hair.

Apparently deciding that Rachel needed protection, Prissy leaped to the couch and crawled onto Rachel's lap.

Before settling, she turned so she could keep a wary eye on Jonas. Rachel watched the firelight shimmer on the silver strands in the man's dark beard and swallowed. Was she crazy for dragging her feet? Would she be sorry for not jumping at the chance to marry Jonas? In order to appear calm, she stroked Prissy, but she felt as though intoxicated butterflies were frolicking in her head.

Getting up, Jonas gripped the poker and stabbed at the crumbling logs. Sparks exploded up the chimney, causing Sara Kate to move farther away. Jonas tucked another log onto the fire. "Martha Marie is coming for a visit in two weeks. Her five *Kinder* create quite a stir."

Remembering his sister's last visit, Rachel laughed. "*Ja.*"

Jonas frowned. "She doesn't make them listen! It's unusual for an Amish mother not to teach her *Kinder* how to behave, but she hasn't been well. It's made her too lenient."

Rachel wanted to sympathize with the man, for he and Linda hadn't had *Kinder*, and he wasn't used to having little ones under foot, but she couldn't stop grinning. She supposed his being childless created his resistance, although he had more than thirty nieces and nephews. "How much damage can they do in a couple of days?"

His scowl deepened. "My sister's husband can't *kom* with her, and she's planning to stay a week!"

Rachel's smile froze on her face as she thought about the company he'd had the last two months. Each time he had asked her to come to his house to help cook the meals. Each of his siblings had several *Kinder*. Martha Marie, Jonas's oldest sister, always busied herself elsewhere during meal preparation and clean up, leaving Rachel with most of the work and supervision. Doubt squiggled within her; her fingers tapped a rhythm on her knees. "You're going to need a lot of help."

"*Ja.*"

She drew a deep breath. "Have you ever considered hiring a housekeeper?"

He sat up straight, his eyes wide. "*Wass*?"

His quick movement startled Prissy. Leaping to her feet, she hissed at him.

Rachel calmed the cat, then smiled at Jonas. "I said, maybe you should hire a housekeeper."

"*Fer wass* (why)?"

Rachel bit her lip. "Vell . . . you don't need to take a wife just because you need a woman to do your housework and take care of the offspring of your siblings."

His lips parted as he stared at her. After several seconds, he blinked. "*Vell*, I guess it's about time I head for home." He reached for his hat, plopped it onto his head and stood. Moving to Sara Kate, he picked up the knotted yarn and placed it in her lap. "You'll get more done if you grasp the needles and make your fingers move." Straightening, he grinned. "*Gute naught* (Good night) Sara Kate."

Standing, Rachel plopped Prissy to the floor and watched Jonas stride from the room. Wondering if she should try to undo the harm her suspicion had done, she followed him to the kitchen.

He stopped near the door, out of Sara's line of vision, and turned. "*Gute naught*, Rachel."

Stepping closer, she reached toward him, expecting him to shake her hand. Instead, he grasped her wrist and pulled her forward. Before she knew what was happening, she was in his arms. He was so tall, and she so tiny, her forehead was level with his shirt pocket. When she looked up to question him, his face was close. The next instant, his mouth was on hers. His kiss was warm and sweet. A moment later, he opened the door, stepped into the cold December night and closed the portal behind him.

Her mind in a flux, she went to a window and watched him trudge out the lane. Prissy jumped to the window sill and watched him vanish into the darkness. She appeared satisfied—as though she had chased him off.

Rachel moved to the center of the room. Her fingers touched her lips where Jonas's had been. Shouldn't her heart be pounding? Why wasn't her blood racing through her veins as her sisters had said it did when they were kissed? It had been nice, but she had felt nothing but kindness and friendship. She supposed she should feel empty and troubled because of the way Jonas had left. Instead, she had to fight the urge to laugh.

Is something wrong with me? she wondered. Being with Jonas was nice; she had experienced peace and comfort in his arms, and she certainly hadn't minded his kiss. If she married him would she grow to feel ecstatic over his affections? *I suppose it's possible, yet . . .*

Lancaster County. A light touch on Leah's arm drew her from her reverie. Sights and medicinal smells of the hospital brought her thoughts into focus. She turned to see Liz Ann Lapp, Peter's sister. The girl's kind green eyes were identical to his and it made Leah's heart give a sudden quick beat.

"Hi, *wie gehts?*" Liz Ann shoved an obstinate black curl back under her navy bonnet. Compassion shadowed her sweet, heart-shaped face. "How's Emma?"

Leah draped her friend's cape over a chair and took a seat on the sofa beside her as she gave a quick update, then she asked, "How'd you get here?"

A smile seemed to brighten the few light freckles that graced the bridge of Liz Ann's small nose. "Eli brought me. He's in the hall with Peter John."

Leah fought a frown. "He drive his car?"

"*Ja.*" Liz Ann thought about the pillowcases she had embroidered for Leah for her birthday. How else, other than with Eli, could she have delivered the gift? "We learned of Emma's accident when we stopped at Elizabeth's. Eli suggested we *kom*, to the hospital."

"Where is he?"

"He and Peter John strolled down the hall."

Sighing, Leah looked at her hands. "Are we encouraging them by letting them drive us places?"

Liz Ann laughed softly. "They don't need encouragement! I would stop seeing Eli, but I care so much." She straightened her lavender skirt. "And I know you care deeply for Peter."

Leah nodded. "I should've gone back to Mercer County before I got emotionally involved."

Liz Ann smiled. "I would refuse to date Eli because of the little boy that continues to dwell in his head, but I've detected the good man that's trapped inside his heart, waiting to get out."

"*Ja.* Peter John's the same way, *gel*?"

Liz Ann nodded. "All we have to do is wait them out."

"I pray so."

Peter sauntered into the room. "Eli and I are going to get a Pepsi. Can we bring you girls something?"

"I'd like a cup of hot chocolate." Liz Ann glanced at Leah. "And you?"

"Hot chocolate sounds *un wonderbar! Gross Dank*, Peter."

"*Kom* with us, Elam," Eli said.

When they had gone, Leah turned to Liz Ann. "I got a letter from Samuel yesterday," she said, referring to a brother two years her senior. "He asked about you."

Spots of heat warmed Liz Ann's cheekbones. "*Fer wass* would he ask about me?"

"You impressed him the day of the weddings."

"*Vell* . . . I sort of was impressed, too."

"He's planning to visit here in Lancaster County and asked if you'd be interested in seeing him."

"Oh, Leah! If it weren't for Eli, but . . ."

"*Vell*, maybe it would shape Eli up if another man became interested in you."

Liz Ann laughed. "That coming from you?" She shook her head. "If that were true, then why don't you give in and let Michael Zook call on you."

"He is a good man who insists he will never remarry. Even if he wanted to call on me, I wouldn't because I wouldn't want to lead him to believe I could care."

"You want *Kinder*, and he has four. Bethany's been gone for almost five years, and we all feel that he needs someone to look after the little ones."

Leah giggled. Michael's a little one, too. I'm four inches taller."

"*Vell, wass* about Susanna's brother, Amos? He's been to visit, and Sarah says he's sweet on you."

"He's kind and generous, the type of man a girl can rely on, but . . ." she sighed. "There's Peter John—if I have patience, maybe . . ."

Eli entered the room, a styrofoam cup in each hand. Smiling, he handed each girl one. They thanked him, and he returned to the hall with Peter.

Liz Ann sipped the steaming sweet liquid, then peered at Leah over the top of her cup. "You'll be staying to help Emma, *gel*?"

"*Ja*."

Excitement blossomed within Liz Ann. "I'll be glad to help you out with the new twins. I love babies."

"Me, too, but I'd like to have a few of my own."

Peter John strolled into the room. "You girls ready to leave?"

Leah's cheeks turned pink. "*Ja*."

"Eli and I are going to have a race."

"Not with me he isn't!" Liz Ann reached for her cape and eyed her brother. "And you will travel according to conditions."

"Follow us," Eli said over his shoulder. "Liz Ann wants to go to my sister's to have a piece of Leah's birthday cake."

Liz Ann poked him playfully. "You're the one who wants

cake."

Peter shrugged. "That sounds good to me, too."

A blast of icy wind slapped Liz Ann as she stepped through the outside door. She clutched at her cape and glanced at Peter John. "Where's your car?"

Flashing a white-toothed grin, he pointed across the lot to his sedan.

"We're over this way," Eli said, turning in the opposite direction. "I'll lead the way." Taking Liz Ann's hand, he bent forward, bracing against the wind.

Peter grasped Leah's hand and headed for his vehicle. Because of Elam's crutches, he and Jacob John followed more slowly.

Knocking the snow from her boots, Liz Ann climbed into the front seat. Eli started the engine and backed from the parking space. The tires gritted on the snow as they crossed the parking area. The car slid slightly as he pulled onto the highway. Liz Ann gasped; Eli grinned.

A few minutes later, Eli turned on the heater. Warm air blew across Liz Ann's legs. *This beats a cold buggy,* she mused, but immediately reprimanded herself for the worldly thought and hoped Eli hadn't interpreted her appreciation. As he picked up speed, she sat straighter and gripped her fingers. "You're going too fast."

"*Neh.* I can handle this car." He chuckled. "I have to keep far enough ahead of Peter John or he'll taunt me."

Liz Ann frowned. Her brother was probably traveling too fast, too, because he didn't want Eli to tease him.

Suddenly Eli's car shot forward, then spun around to face her brother's. Eli's foot flew to the brake. Liz Ann gasped as their vehicle slid. She could see Leah through the windshield. The girl's eyes were wide. Peter John was frantically working his steering wheel. Eli was gripping his. The two cars were heading straight for each other. A scream caught in Liz Ann's throat as she covered her face with her hands.

CHAPTER SEVEN

Liz Ann gasped. Eli worked the steering wheel. The engine roared. The wheels spun. The Buick swung one way, then another. Peter John's green sedan loomed in front of them. Knowing neither driver would be able to stop, Liz Ann braced for impact.

The two vehicles missed each other by inches before they came to a halt. Liz Ann relaxed her tense jaw and eyed Eli, her lips taut. "That was enough!

"Oh, Liz. *Es speid mich es ich sel gedu had* (I'm sorry I did that)."

"We could've all been killed!"

"*Neh*. We weren't traveling fast enough for that. We would've smashed our vehicles, that's all."

"Then maybe we should've crashed."

He grinned. "*Sis Alles alricht* (All is well)."

"You should park this thing—or better, sell it."

"I did some expert maneuvering to avoid a wreck."

"Fine." The word sounded crisp, betraying her anger. "Get us home in one piece."

Turning the car, he pulled onto the highway. Summer driving had been fun, but she'd had enough ice to do her a spell.

When they stopped in front of Miller's, Liz Ann got out of the car. A gust of wind seized her cape as though intent on ripping it off. Wrapping it tighter, she gingerly made her way to Peter John's vehicle.

Leah opened her door, put one foot out onto the snow, but paused to glance at Peter John. "You and Jacob *koming* in?"

"I'd like to get home as soon as possible," Jacob said.

Peter grinned. "I'll come back for a piece of your cake."

Elam maneuvered his crutches and started up the path; Liz Ann and Leah followed.

The front door opened, and Elizabeth hurried across the porch and down the steps, her black cape flapping in the wind.

"How's Emma?" she asked as she reached Elam's side.

Bending, he kissed her cheek. "She has a broken leg, but she's going to be fine. Both babies are doing well."

Elizabeth's eyes widened. "Both? Again?"

Elam chuckled. "*Ja.*"

"*Un wonderbar!.* Her joyous laughter bubbled around them as they bumped the snow from their boots and went inside.

Jesse Mark clapped his hands. "Now we kin eat!"

Elizabeth picked up Priscilla. The baby twisted to eye the large cake in the center of the table and giggled. The tip of her tiny tongue played across her upper lip as she rolled her light-blue eyes toward Elizabeth. "Me, *Mem*?"

"*Ja.* You get cake, too."

The baby clapped her chubby hands. Smiling, Leah went to the cupboard and began to count plates.

Liz Ann hurried forward to pull her arm down. "Birthday girls don't serve their own refreshments." Chuckling, she retrieved the plates and cups. "I'll set the table. You play with the *Kinder.*"

Raising one brow, Leah stared at her friend.

Liz Ann shook her head. "You're just like Rachel Kay."

Leah's turquoise eyes peered curiously at her. "Who?"

"A cousin of mine who lives in Holmes County, Ohio. She has been so busy helping her family, she hasn't had a chance to get one of her own." Liz Ann paused halfway to the table to study Leah's expression. "Rachel's thirty-three and has had only one boyfriend."

"*Ach!* Is something wrong with her?"

"Only that she is too compassionate." She thought of one of Rachel's neighbors in particular. "Some take advantage of her. She's my favorite cousin." She set the pile of plates on the table. "Elizabeth did a great job of decorating your cake."

Daniel stepped closer. "The white icing is snow and the light blue for a frozen pond. Mama made skaters out of marshmallows."

"I like the snowman!" Jesse Mark pushed in beside his brother. Leaning across the table, he reached into the sleigh candy dish, picked out a chocolate chip, and dropped it behind the toy horse.

"Jesse Mark!" Leah retrieved the offending bit of chocolate and glared at her nephew. "One more trick like that, young man, and you'll not get any cake."

Deep dimples formed in his rosy cheeks and his blue eyes peered at her like orbs of innocence. "*Es speid mich es ich sel gedu had,* Aunt Leah." A spontaneous giggle belied his apology. He glanced at Daniel, and both boys laughed.

Leah counted out napkins. The sound of a car drew Liz Ann to a window. "Peter John's back."

"*Un wonderbar!*" Jesse Mark raced to the table and climbed onto his chair. He glanced at the cake, then at Elizabeth. "We gonna eat, now, *Mem*?"

She smiled. "As soon as Peter gets settled."

Peter John swept through the door into the kitchen, his eyes dancing. "I brought a surprise." He handed Leah a paper bag.

Opening the top, she peeped in and returned his smile. "*Gross Dank.*" She glanced at the boys. "Peter brought ice cream."

Jesse Mark bounced on his chair. "*Un Wonderbar* two times!"

During silent grace, Eli reached for Liz Ann's hand.

Their fingers entwined behind the draped tablecloth. In spite of her inward reluctance, her heart not only had a mind of its own, it seemed to be influencing her fingers.

"Amen," Elam said.

Leah stood and sawed the knife through the fluffy icing. "What a wonderful family *der gut* Man has blessed me with."

After eating, the men migrated to the living room. Elizabeth went to the bedroom to get Priscilla ready for bed. The boys pretended to plow snow with a miniature horse. Leah took a pile of plates to the sink and began to run water.

Liz Ann gave her a playful shove. "You can't help with the clean up, birthday girl."

"*Ja* I can. We'll talk and make it fun." She set the cups into the bubbling detergent. "You spoke of a cousin named Rachel. Tell me more about her."

While Liz Ann drew rinse water, she told Leah about the accident that had paralyzed her Aunt Fannie and how Rachel had given up the chance to marry to care for her family.

Leah paused, holding a cup above the dish water. Mounds of suds decorated her hands. "Was Rachel Kay their only *Kinder*?"

"She was the oldest of twelve."

"*Ach*!" Leah bit her lip. "It would've been a wonderful family—if not for the accident."

Liz Ann nodded. Accepting the rinsed cup, she dried it. "Rachel took over in the house like a little mother. The youngest of her siblings was only two months old." Liz Ann smiled. "Rachel is a lot older than me, but we write frequently. Her oldest brother took over the farm very young. He married young, too."

"I suppose that helped."

"*Ja*. For awhile. His wife is heavy, and has a weak back, so chasing after *Kinder* has been a bit difficult for her. Rachel takes care of Rosy's little ones a lot."

Leah's eyes were wide. "Is there no end?"

"*Ja.* Susan, Rachel's youngest sister, married about three years ago. Rachel says as soon as Rosy's oldest girl, now ten, can take over watching the younger *Kinder*, she is going to make a life of her own." Liz Ann laughed. "There is a widower living nearby and Rachel says he acts interested."

Leah rolled her eyes. "More of someone else's *Kinder*?"

"No. Jonas and his first wife didn't have any." Liz Ann stacked the washed cups in a rack and reached for the plates. "I invited Rachel to our house for an extended visit. Goodness knows she needs one!"

"What's she look like?"

"She's very attractive. She's about four-foot-ten and only weighs ninety-five pounds, but she is strong and healthy. She is sweet and has a darling set of dimples. Her hair is as black as mine. Her eyes are very unusual. They are a silver gray that picks up color. Outside they mirror the sky. If she is near trees, they pick up green highlights."

"I hope I can meet her when she comes."

"I'll make sure you do." She put the last cup into the cupboard and began to dry the plates.

Eli came from the living room with a small bowl. "That was good ice cream." He handed the dirty dish to Leah. "I hope you have many more birthdays." Leaning forward, he peered out the window above the sink. "It looks like it might snow again." He looked at Liz Ann. "You about ready to leave?"

"*Ja.*" As she put away the stack of plates, she glanced at Leah. "I'll come over to Emma's tomorrow to help you."

"*Viel Dank.*"

Yanking on boots, Liz Ann thought about the ride home and prayed they wouldn't slide again. A carriage could slide, too, though, and a horse could slip. She sighed.

That wasn't a good enough excuse to warrant Eli's owning a car. Nevertheless, she climbed in and settled on the seat.

Eli jabbed his key into the ignition, the engine roared and the wheels spun. Liz Ann gave him a stern look. He laughed.

When they pulled into her parents' driveway, she turned to him. "Want to come in?"

"For a few minutes."

Most of Liz Ann's family were in the living room. Martha, her sixteen-year-old sister, shoved a pie into the oven, then skipped upstairs.

Liz Ann felt Eli's hand on her arm and turned. He had a silly grin on his handsome face.

"*Kom ann.*" He led her into the summer kitchen and closed the door.

"It's cold in here, Eli."

His grin broadened. "I'll keep you warm." He pulled her into his arms. "I want to say happy birthday."

"It's not my birthday!" She looked up, about to scold him, but his head lowered and his lips covered hers. She intended to pull away, but his mouth was so warm and inviting. Her heart raced in carefree abandon. Warmth spread through her in tiny rivulets; the room didn't feel so cold anymore.

The door swept open. "Wow!" Ella said, then whirled to face the kitchen. "Hey, Anna Ruth!"

Liz Ann had jerked free the moment her sister had entered, but the eleven-year-old had seen enough to realize what had been happening. Heat traveled up Liz Ann's neck, then fanned across her face. She hurried away, leaving Eli to explain.

Martha had returned to the kitchen. Her eyes met Liz Ann's. An expression of understanding crossed her face, and she smiled.

"I'll *kom* for you tomorrow," Eli said, seemingly unruffled by the kiss and Ella's discovering them. "You want to leave for Emma's about eleven o'clock?"

"*Vell* . . ." Her brain felt fuzzy, and she took a deep breath to clear her thinking. "That sounds all right."

"Am I invited for dinner?"

"*Ja.*"

"It's snowing, again, so I'd better get going." Moving to the bench, he grappled for his boots and yanked them on.

Liz Ann retrieved his jacket and handed it to him.

"*Gross Dank.*" Bending to her ear, he whispered. "I'll say *gute naught*, again, if you'll come to the summer kitchen."

She felt her cheeks grow hot under his gaze, and the stern expression that she tried to muster became a soft gaze. Hating to look like warm putty that he could mold, she turned away.

He chuckled. "See you tomorrow."

Ohio. Rachel Kay strolled passed the kitchen window facing Jonas Yoder's farm. She had invited him for supper, and he should have been here by now. He was usually early. Hoping her glance would appear casual, she checked to see if he was on his way. Not noticing him, she stopped at the curtain side of the window and moved the material slightly to look out. Prissy sat on the sill, peering through the glass. The cat turned to Rachel, blinked, then seemed to grin, making Rachel feel foolish.

"What are you doing, Aunt Rachel?" Sara Kate's eyes seemed more sagacious than most ten-year-old's.

"*Oh . . . vell . . .*" Swiping a hand across the skirt of her gray dress, Rachel faced the child. "I'm ready to mash the potatoes, but want to wait until Jonas starts across the field."

Sara Kate laughed. "I'll watch for him." Plopping onto the rocker, she propped her elbows on the window sill beside the cat, but rolled her silver-gray eyes toward her aunt. "Unless you want to."

"*Ich hab Arivet fe schaffe* (I have work to do)." Bustling to the stove, she drew a long breath. Her brother's oldest daughter was too smart for her own good. Jonas was seemingly getting more serious, so maybe she should start inviting him for meals without having Sara Kate present. She frowned. What exactly were the man's intentions? Grasping a spoon, she stirred the mixed vegetables.

"Here he comes." The girl sang the words.

Ignoring the implication, Rachel took the pot of potatoes to the sink, picked up the stomper she had placed there, and began to mash vigorously. Sara Kate jumped up and hurried into the living room as though she didn't wish to answer the door. Rachel didn't blame the girl. Jonas hadn't tried to cover his aversion to having her underfoot almost every time he came to call. Rachel had no intention of catering to the man's whims. When footsteps resounded on the porch, she went to open the door.

"Hello." Jonas stepped through the portal, his tall frame dwarfing the entrance. A smile brightened his features. "*Wie gehts?*"

Jonas shut the door, but before he could hang up his black hat, Prissy raced around him and streaked into the living room. Scowling at the spot where the feline had disappeared, Jonas removed his jacket, hung it on a peg, and moved farther into the kitchen. His black broadfalls contrasted sharply with his light-blue shirt. Closing his eyes, he inhaled deeply. Pot roast?"

"*Ja*." She hurried back to finish the potatoes.

"Mashed?"

"*Ja*."

He sniffed. "Apple pie with lots of cinnamon?"

"*Ja*, Jonas. Just the way you like it."

Nodding his approval, he vanished into the living room. When Rachel realized her lips were taut, she relaxed her features. The man appreciated a good meal. Most men did. But he seemed to be more interested in the food than in her. Was there something wrong with her? With her looks? Was Jonas weighing his gratitude to see if having a wife was worth the effort?

Sarah appeared beside her. "I hope you marry him soon, Aunt Rachel," she whispered.

Rachel's eyes widened. *"Fer wass?"*

"Because I'm tired of baby-sitting you two."

"I didn't think you minded." She handed the girl the bowl of potatoes.

Setting them on the table, Sara Kate turned. "He doesn't like my being here."

"Vell . . . I do." Smiling, Rachel patted the girl's slender arm. "I'll lift the pot roast. You can put the vegetables into a bowl."

When they were seated around the table and silent grace had been said, Jonas reached for the meat platter. Smiling, he took a large portion, then handed the platter to Rachel. Sara Kate passed the mashed potatoes and the vegetables. Eating slowly, she watched Jonas. When he became aware of her scrutiny, he seemed uneasy.

"Do you have a problem, Sara Kate?" he asked.

Not taking her eyes from him, she shook her head.

Noticing a movement from the corner of her eye, Rachel turned to see Prissy sitting in the back of the rocker nearest Jonas. He noticed the cat about the same time and the two stared eye-to-eye. Amused, Rachel watched. It was Jonas who blinked and turned away first. Prissy's tail twitched victoriously.

Jonas's fork clattered to his plate; his dark eyes sought Rachel's. "After supper, we will go for a walk. Just you and me." He nodded as though underscoring his decision, then returned his attention to his plate.

Rachel felt as though she had sipped vinegar. Shouldn't he have asked her, not told her? If he was that domineering before marriage, what would he be like afterwards?

Had he been pressed by exasperation or was this his usual behavior?

Reaching for the pitcher of gravy, he poured more over his beef and potatoes. "You're the best cook in this county, Rachel."

"*Gross Dank.*" How many times had the man told her that? She liked compliments, but she would prefer he told her he liked her eyes, or her smile—or her personality. Sipping her tea, she pondered. The man had once told her she was pretty, but mostly he enjoyed her meals and remarked favorably to the way she kept house. Hoping it wasn't prideful to desire compliments from one's intended, she took a bite of beef and chewed methodically. Why had he never mentioned the way she cared for *Kinder*?

Sara Kate tapped her fingers on the side of her water glass as she took a drink and continued to peer at Jonas. Was the girl trying to irritate the man—or pressure him into action?

The wind howled and hurled clouds of snow against the windows. Rachel was thankful to have a warm house. She thought about the walk with Jonas and shivered. Was it from envisioning the cold stroll—or from apprehension over what he might say?

When he had cleared second helpings from his plate and finished a huge piece of pie, he stood and pushed in his chair. "I'll get your cape."

Her stomach knotted. In an effort to stall, she picked up her plate. "I must do the dishes."

A frown shadowed his broad brow. "Sara Kate can do them."

"It would be improper not to help!"

"*Ach!*" A smile created dimples in Sara's round pink cheeks. "I'll do the clean-up. You and Mr. Yoder have a nice walk."

Rachel wanted to glare at the girl, but figured Jonas would see her corrective expression. Sara was being kind, but this time Rachel wasn't happy over her generosity. Donning a heavy sweater to keep out the December chill, she jerked on boots and put on a scarf. Tying her bonnet, she wrapped her cape around her shoulders. Jonas bundled into his jacket.

As they stepped from the porch, a brisk wind tore at their clothing. The icy air took Rachel's breath. What Jonas had to say must be very important. Again, her stomach cramped.

"*Kom ann.*" Grasping her hand, he led her across the barnyard to the carriage shed. Inside the building, he motioned for her to get into the carriage. Doing so made her feel silly. She sat staring at her hands. With no horse hitched to the conveyance, they couldn't be going far. Rachel smothered a laugh, then the possible seriousness of her situation seized her heart and squeezed her insides.

Jonas joined her on the seat. "*Vell,*" he said slowly. "I've been doing a lot of thinking."

Rachel's heart lurched. Although she had prayed much and considered every facet of their relationship, she hadn't been able to come to a conclusion. According to her sisters, a lady should be anxious and expectant when she thought a gentleman was about to propose marriage. The thought of spending life with Jonas should make her heart pound in joyous expectation. Hers felt gripped in a vise! Why?

Reaching, Jonas took her cold fingers in his. "You are a wonderful woman, Rachel." His smile created creases at the corners of his dark eyes. "I should have asked you this before now." He cleared his throat.

Rachel drew a quick little breath. Should she just sit here and listen to a question she wasn't ready to answer? *Should I jerk free and run for my life?*

CHAPTER EIGHT

"Ja, Jonas?" Figuring she might as well get this proposal over with, Rachel gazed up at the big man on the carriage seat beside her. The last time she had visited her dentist she hadn't felt this tense and frightened. *Is this the way a woman is supposed to feel?*

"*Vell*, Rachel, my dear . . ." Releasing his grip on her fingers, he rubbed a large hand across his face.

She supposed she should make it easier for him, but she had decided to let him ask her to marry in his own fashion. She burrowed her hands into the folds of her cape, partly to keep them warm, but more to hide their trembling.

"Martha Marie is *koming* next Tuesday."

What does his sister have to do with his taking a wife?

Clearing his throat, Jonas blurted, "I'd like you to clean my house and get it ready. Also, I'd like you to cook the meals while Martha Marie is here."

"Oh." The syllable issued forth in a whisper. For the first few seconds, Rachel felt relieved. Then the realization of what this man expected her to do dawned upon her. All this nervous energy used up just to be asked to be a housekeeper and cook! She laughed.

"*Wass* is funny?"

The genuine puzzlement on Jonas's face made her laugh harder. Then forcing a sober continence, she took a deep breath. "*Ich wehr froh gwest fe du was ich koent fe dich helf* (I'd be glad to do what I can to help you)."

"*Ach! Hertzlich Dank!*" The creases of concern seemed

to melt from his expression. "I knew I could count on you."

Was disappointment wriggling within her? It was wonderful to be counted on, but must it always be as a friend and helper? Would she never be a bride? Fighting tears of frustration and disillusionment, she stepped from the carriage. Why had the man brought her to the shed to ask such a question? "We'd better go in, now, Jonas."

"*Ja.*" Jumping to the shed floor, he rounded the buggy with a spring in his step and reached for her hand. "We should consider something more permanent before too long."

Was the man thinking of marriage after all? His warm smile drew her, and she placed her hand in his. Maybe love wasn't always as emotional as her sisters had said. She had hoped for more. Should she settle for what she considered less?

At the porch steps, Jonas paused. "When can I expect you and Sara Kate to clean?"

"Will Monday be all right?"

"*Ja.*" He gently squeezed her fingers. "I'd like you to fix roast chicken with baked sweet potatoes and peas for dinner on Tuesday. They're Martha's favorite."

She nodded. "Since you don't care for sweet potatoes, I'll bake some white ones, too."

"It's like you to think of everyone." Opening the door, he stepped aside for her to enter the kitchen.

Turning to peer curiously at them, Sara Kate plunked another plate into the dish water. Her warm-brown eyes were questioning and her grin obvious.

Hanging up her cape, Rachel sat on the bench to remove her boots. Prissy had been dozing in the rocker by the window. At the sound of Jonas's voice, she sat up and stared at him, her eyes shimmering green slits.

"You should keep that feline outside," he grumbled.

"Ach. She's part of the family," Sara Kate said.

As though to mock him, the cat tilted her head and flicked her tail. Rachel smothered a laugh over their obvious dislike for each other.

"*Vell* . . ." Jonas took off his hat, then shoved it back on his head. "I'll be going." Pausing with his hand on the knob, he looked back at Rachel. "I'll see you Sunday at meeting."

She nodded.

"*Gross Dank* for supper. *Es war wonderbar gut.*"

Smiling was easy, for even though Jonas's compliments didn't make her ecstatic, they made her feel warm and comfortable. After he left, she moved to the sink to help Sara with the dishes.

The girl rolled her eyes toward Rachel. "*Vell?*"

"*Vell wass?*"

"*Wass* did Jonas want?"

Rachel shrugged, hoping to look more nonchalant than she felt. "He wants me to clean his house and get it ready for Martha Marie's visit."

Sara's eyes widened. "That's all?"

"*Vell* . . . he asked me to do the cooking for his sister's family."

"*Ach!*" Sara flipped her hands, sending a shower of soap bubbles over Rachel. "I thought he was going to ask you to marry!" She laughed until she doubled over. "He took you out to be alone just to ask you to be his housekeeper?"

"*Vell*, Martha Marie looks for cobwebs in corners, and she expects good meals."

"Then Jonas should take a wife. Even Prissy knows that!"

Giving the girl a playful swat, Rachel laughed. "It's just as *vell* he didn't ask me."

"You like being an old maid, *gel?*"

Rachel's smile froze on her face. She never thought of herself as a spinster, but was that how others were categorizing her? Would being a wife in a friendly relationship beat living the rest of her life alone? If she waited for emotional love, would she wait in vain? *Maybe Jonas intended to propose tonight, but had lost his nerve. If he asks me to marry, maybe I should accept him.*

Rachel tested the rising loaves of bread on Jonas's counter, found them ready, and popped them into the oven. By the time they were baked, the chicken would be stuffed and waiting. Her dark-blue skirt swished as she turned to yank open a cabinet drawer to get the tablecloth with embroidered roses. She hadn't looked for spots and hoped it was in perfect condition. She wished Martha Marie weren't so fussy—especially since she didn't help much.

Jonas came in from doing the barn chores as Rachel removed the golden crusted loaves of bread from the oven. The aroma of baking bread permeated the kitchen. He sniffed and eyed the golden loaves as she bumped them from their pans and set them on racks to cool. After buttering the tops, she turned to look at Jonas. He looked sheepish. *Fer wass?*

Hanging up his jacket, he moved to the table and gripped the back of a chair. "Martha Marie has to go into the hospital for tests."

"*Ach!* Then she won't be *koming?*"

"On the contrary. She is leaving her five *Kinder* here for me to watch."

A vision of Martha's rambunctious brood blasted Rachel's senses and her lips parted. "You?" The syllable came out in an amazed whisper.

"*Vel* . . ." Ramming his fingers through his thick dark hair, he groaned. "Since her husband can't be here, I should accompany my sister to the hospital." His troubled brown eyes searched her face. "You can stay with her *Kinder, gel?*"

Had he known of this before he asked her to cook the

meal? Surely Martha had told him. "When is she going to the hospital?"

"In the morning. She and I will have to leave about eight."

Rachel had decided to refuse him, but reading his woebegone expression, she relented. "I'll *kom* about a quarter till."

His features relaxed and he let out the breath he had apparently been holding. "*Hertzlich Dank!*"

Feeling as though she were being taken advantage of, Rachel slid the roaster containing the stuffed chicken into the oven, then turned to the cupboard to count plates. Jonas went to the rocker in the corner, unfolded the latest copy of *The Budget* and read while Rachel set the table. Everything in the kitchen was under control, so she went into the living room to make sure all was ready. She and Sara Kate had dusted the furniture yesterday, but knowing Martha Marie usually noticed specks, she shined the small tables, again.

The howling wind made Rachel shiver, although the house was warm. Envisioning a steaming cup of tea and a few minutes to relax, she returned to the kitchen, filled the kettle with water, and set it on the stove to heat.

"*Ach!*" Jonas hurried to a front window as a vehicle stopped by the gate.

Whirling, Rachel stared open-mouthed. Martha Marie was an hour early! The image of the woman's children underfoot while she put the finishing touches to supper was enough to give her heart palpitations.

Jonas shoved his arms into his jacket. "I'll help with Martha's luggage." He hurried outside.

Rachel peered through the glass. Instead of handing him a suitcase, the woman practically flung her squirming infant into his unsuspecting arms, then turned to give orders to the driver of the van. Four *Kinder* poured from the vehicle like bees from a hive and swarmed toward the house. Three of them veered to splash through partially frozen muddy water. Thumping onto the porch, they squealed. The door swung inward and crashed against the wall as they spilled into the kitchen. Laughing, seven-year-old George raced around the table. The younger three chased him. Rachel stared in alarm as they left four sets of smeared tracks in their wake. Four-year-old Tim seized George, knocking him off balance and tipping over a chair. Five-year-old Linda laughed. Three-year-old Mary stared at the bedlam.

Rachel's hands flew to her face. "*Ach!*"

The driver banged Martha's boxes onto the porch as the woman followed Jonas into the house. Stopping with a jolt, she thumped her bag onto the bench and peered at her wild brood. Her hazel eyes swept over the muddy footprints on the formerly-spotless green-and-white kitchen vinyl, then rested on Rachel.

Feeling as though the woman was blaming her, Rachel tried to smile.

Baby Thomas began to howl. Jonas looked dismayed as he tried to untangle the tiny boy from the blankets that covered him. Finally getting him unwrapped, he awkwardly cradled him.

Martha went to the living room door and peered in. "I see you managed to borrow a crib this time, Jonas."

He sighed. Moving toward the woman, he tried to hand her the baby.

Ignoring him, she propped her hands on her ample hips. "George! Go to the bench and take your boots off." Her eyes spanned the room. "You other three get out of your jackets." She turned to her brother. "I imagine you made arrangements for me to use the first-floor bedroom."

Jonas looked flustered, betraying that he had expected to use his own bedroom, then he shrugged. "*Vell . . . ja.*"

Thankful her thoughts weren't audible, Rachel retrieved a mop.

Slumping to a chair, Martha groaned. "I'm not a well woman."

The statement was probably true, but well or not, she rarely offered any assistance. After cleaning up the myriad of tiny brown puddles that dappled the vinyl, Rachel picked up the four jackets that had been tossed in a heap in the corner of the kitchen and straightened the four small sets of boots strewn in front of the bench.

Martha sniffed. "I guess we're having roasted chicken and sweet potatoes?"

"*Ja*." Putting the mop away, Rachel went to the stove to stir the vegetables.

"You fix mushroom sauce for the peas?" Hauling herself out of the chair, Martha moved to the stove, peered into the pot, and nodded approval.

Plopping the now screaming baby Thomas into the crib, Jonas fled out the back door. Rachel would have laughed over his hasty retreat if the situation hadn't been so grim. Hurrying to get supper on the table, she hoped Martha would supervise the *Kinder* during the meal. George was the trouble-maker. At seven, he should be helping to manage the younger ones. Instead, he seemed to enjoy leading his siblings into near riot. If George were under control, peace could easily be maintained.

Martha began to gather her *Kinder* and tell them where to sit. Jonas returned. Standing at a distance, he watched, an expression of disbelief shadowing his features. Baby Thomas had finally quieted, but the rest of the woman's offspring seemed to be in constant motion, making continuous noise and creating confusion. This type of commotion was unusual for an Amish family. Rachel wondered if Martha's husband really couldn't get time off work to accompany her, or if the unruly offspring was the real reason he had remained behind. What did the man do at home, hide in the barn?

Looking as though he might yell, Jonas ran his fingers

through his hair. Grabbing George, he plopped him onto a chair at the table.

"Stay put." Swooping five-year-old Linda off her feet, he plunked her on the chair next to her brother. He glanced at Rachel. "Get Mary." He glared in the direction that four-year-old Tim had gone.

Finally they made an attempt at the silent grace. Rachel tried to concentrate on prayer, but she had to fight a grin over how the four *Kinder* wiggled, squirmed, and peeped at Jonas from under lowered lashes. Were they assessing what their uncle would permit them to get away with.

Hours later, stretched out on her bed, Rachel reveled in the beauty of peace and quiet. She hadn't had as much turmoil raising her eleven siblings as she'd had with Martha's five little ones this evening. After helping the woman get them ready for bed, Rachel had gladly raced for home.

The wind howled. The temperature was dropping, and it was snowing again. Tiny ice crystals tinkled against the window pane, encouraging her to snuggle deeper under her quilts. Since her younger sister had married, Rachel had been using one of the two upstairs bedrooms for her quilting frames and one as a guest room. Unless she was quilting or had visitors, she didn't heat the upper floor.

A few hours of helping with Martha's family had taken more out of her than a week's housework. She sighed. Tomorrow, she would have to take care of the *Kinder* alone. Did Jonas really have to accompany Martha—or was it his way of fleeing the house?

"How do I get myself into such messes?" she whispered into the night. She didn't need an answer. Her compassionate heart knew.

Sleep came quickly. So did morning. Dragging herself from the warmth of her blankets, Rachel cooked oatmeal for her breakfast and was glad that she wasn't expected at Jonas's until nearly eight o'clock.

A bowl of oatmeal and a cup of steaming tea boosted her outlook. She checked her outdoor thermometer. It read twenty-nine, but the snow had stopped and the sun was shining. Maybe the day would not be as bad as she had expected. Pulling on boots, she donned her barn clothes. She must milk Judy and feed Muddy Foot before leaving for Jonas's place. Prissy was waiting on the porch and accompanied Rachel to the barn. The feline sat watching Rachel milk, then mewed expectantly and pranced near her dish. Rachel poured her a liberal amount of warm milk, then returned to the house to get washed and change into her deep-rose dress.

The trek through the field to Jonas's was harder walking than on the lane, but it was closer. As she crossed the footbridge over the small stream that separated the properties, she smiled. Jonas had built the bridge years ago when he had courted her. During his marriage, it had fallen into decay. Last fall he had repaired the foundation and replaced worn and broken planks. This had informed Rachel of the man's intent to call on her, for she and Jonas were about the only ones who used the bridge.

She could hear the din before she reached the house. Pausing in the freezing wind with one gloved hand resting on the top of Jonas's gate, she considered fleeing. The door opened with a jerk and Jonas stepped onto the porch. His jacket was unfastened, one of his boots seemed loose, and his hat was crooked. When he noticed Rachel, he grinned.

"*Dank der gut* Man you're here!"

She opened the gate and moved down the path toward him. "Are you going to hide in the barn, again?"

He laughed. "I have to do the chores."

"*Ja*? Aren't you getting a later start than usual?"

He shrugged. "It's a wonder I'm getting a start at all." Laughter danced in his warm-brown eyes. "You have fun today."

Deciding to tease him, Rachel summoned her most serious expression. "I decided to go with Martha and leave you with the *Kinder*."

His eyes widened, and he instantly sobered. "You're joshing, *gel*?"

Unable to maintain a straight face, she laughed. "It's a temptation, but I promised to watch them."

His relief was audible in a sigh. "You're an angel." He grinned with one side of his mouth. "Martha made oatmeal for breakfast. It's a bit lumpy, but there's some left."

"*Gross Dank*, but I've eaten." Suffocating a sigh, Rachel went inside. Martha stood by the sink, a faraway expression capturing her features. Last night, in the glow of the gas lamp, she had appeared a bit pallid, but in the morning light, she looked ghostly. Her dark hair was thinning on top and scarcely showed in front of her prayer cap. Her thumb in her mouth, Mary clung to the woman's dark-blue skirt. Thomas kicked and cooed in the crib. The riot in the living room drew Rachel to the doorway. George and Tim had rolled Linda up in a brown carpet; she could barely wiggle. Her wails of protest hurt Rachel's ears. Moving quickly into the middle of the chaos, she pulled the boys away and released the captive. Sitting up, Linda sniffled and rubbed at her tears with a fist.

"Can you boys be quiet for awhile?"

"*Ja*." Tim laughed.

George rumpled his brother's tousled straight brown hair, gave him a shove that sent him reeling, and laughed. Taking him by the arm, Rachel guided him to a chair and gently pushed him into it. Grabbing Tim as he tried to streak by, she placed him on the couch on the opposite side of the room. Instead of the separation helping, the two began making faces at each other. Mary had begun to cry, so Rachel went back to the kitchen. The child, tiny for three, had a pretty heart-shaped face with a small nose and narrow chin. Her delicate features were contorted, portraying her dismay.

Sighing, Martha bent to pat the girl's head. "You be a good girl for Mama. Aunt Rachel is going to play with you today."

Rachel was no relation to these *Kinder*, although she would become their aunt should she marry Jonas. The oldest three tried her patience, and Thomas was more demanding than most babies she had cared for, but she had taken a special liking to little Mary. Moving forward, she picked the child up and cradled her.

"Can Aunt Rachel rock you while Mama gets ready?"

Tears were swimming in the little girl's big blue eyes as she peered quizzically into Rachel's face. "*Mem* gonna go away."

"Just for a little while, Mary."

Martha changed into a purple dress and came to the kitchen as a tan car stopped at the gate.

Jonas came into the house. "Our ride is here, Martha."

She nodded, donned her bonnet and cape, hugged all her *Kinder*, then left, not delivering her usual last-minute warnings and instructions. Rachel caught her lower lip between her teeth. What was this feeling of pending disaster that gripped her?

The morning continued, noisy, but without mishap. Sitting on a blanket on the floor, Thomas played with a chain made from tied-together jar rings. Linda sat at the table munching a cracker while the boys tussled in the living room. Little Mary stood on a chair by a window, her expression woebegone, and her thumb in her mouth as she stared down the lane in the direction her mother had gone.

If I ever have a child of my own, I'd like her to be just like Mary, Rachel thought as she went to comfort the little girl.

Thomas began to demand attention while Rachel was trying to fix dinner. Pancakes had been a mistake, although

George and Tim had requested them. Soup would have been easier and would not have taken so much individual attention. Finally, she got Thomas to sleep and put him in the crib. The boys were good for a change as they ate. Linda, more than a little chubby, ate four pancakes and asked for another. Mary sat quietly pushing bite-sized pieces around in the syrup on her plate. Rachel played a game with her to get her to eat and ended up holding the child on her lap for the remainder of the meal.

"You older *Kinder* can help with the clean-up," Rachel said, setting Mary on the rocker and handing her a doll.

George stared wide-eyed, his mouth agape; Tim raced into the room; Linda simply shoved a large piece of raisin muffin into her mouth and washed it down with a gulp of milk. Shaking her head, Rachel moved to the sink and began to prepare dish water. George vanished into the room.

"Linda, bring me the plates."

"*Fer wass?*"

"Because at five, you're old enough to learn how to do simple chores. When your mama comes home, she'll need your help."

Sliding from her seat, the girl gripped her plate and carried it to Rachel. Eventually, all the plates and tableware were cleared and in the dish pan. Rachel hugged Linda and told her she could go and play.

Before she had the dishes in the cupboard, a shouting match between George and Tim created a din. Mary began to cry. Swooping her up, Rachel went to settle the living room fight. Linda picked up the book that had caused the squabble. Now the wrestling bout was between Linda and Tim. Mary cried more loudly.

"Hush," Rachel pleaded. "You'll wake Thomas."

As though punctuating her statement, the baby began to wail.

"I can't stand this fracas!" George put his jacket on

and headed for the door. "I'm goin' skating."

"No you're not."

"*Ja*, I am."

"Hang your jacket on the peg and go into the room," Rachel commanded. Hurrying to the crib, she picked up Thomas. He had spit up on the sheet and he needed his diaper changed.

Jerking the door open, George went out. Alarmed, Rachel put Thomas back in the crib and chased after the eldest boy. George had crossed the porch and was running across the yard toward the barn. Grabbing Jonas's jacket, because it was the closest garment, Rachel donned it quickly and chased after the boy. She intended to grab him and make him come back inside. He headed for the pond in a run.

"George!" The pond had frozen over, but she didn't know how thick the ice was. The thought of what could happen chilled her marrow.

Stepping onto the ice, George slid his feet. Laughing, he skated along the shoreline, then angled toward the middle.

"*Kom* back!" Stopping at the edge of the pond, Rachel wrapped her arms around her slender body. Wind whipped under her skirt and reached icy fingers under the huge jacket that hung over her shoulders. The sleeves covered her hands, for which she was thankful.

George turned to look at her, his expression defiant. Moving backwards, he grinned. "If you want me, *kom* and get me."

Rachel stared at the ice. How thick was it? The boy was out at least fifteen feet. The ice seemed to be supporting his weight, but her added ninety-five pounds could be too much.

George whirled in a circle, leaped into the air, and landed with a thud. A cracking noise made his eyes widen.

"Lie down!" Rachel commanded, knowing it would help

to distribute his weight. Not used to obeying, George stood unmoving, fright branded on his face. Another crack made him run toward shore. His pounding feet proved too much and the ice broke through. Rachel screamed. How deep was the water? "Grab the edge of the ice!"

George managed to grasp the edge. It broke off and he grappled for another handhold.

"Do your feet touch bottom?"

"No!"

Rachel knew the boy's boots would be filling with water, making it more difficult for him to hang on. Her added weight would break the ice before she could reach him. If she tried and fell in, she could drown. If she didn't haul George out, he would die. She glanced around feverishly. There was no one in sight. If she took time to go for a rope it might be too late.

"It's . . . cold," George cried, his teeth chattering. He blinked. "I can't hold on much longer!"

Wind swept across the field, as though intent on ripping off the large jacket and tearing her skirt from her body. Gritting her teeth, she did the only thing she could do. She gently lay on her stomach and began to work her way toward the stranded child. The ice groaned. Visions of horror tumbled over themselves in her mind, then gyrated in a wild frenzy.

"Can't . . . hold . . ." The boy's eyelids drooped and his body lowered another few inches. His chin was already touching the water.

She wanted to continue to encourage the boy, but cold from the ice was penetrating her clothing, sapping her strength. Finally, she was almost close enough. "Reach toward me," she urged, praying she could grab his hand.

With a feeble gesture, George shook his head. "If . . . I let go, . . . I'll . . . sink."

She prayed for strength as she inched herself forward. Only a few more inches and she would be able to reach him. Thrusting her arm forward, she gripped the boy's glove. Only another couple of inches and she would be able to grasp his wrist. The ice groaned and creaked. George slipped farther into the water. Rachel tugged, then gasped in horror as the boy's glove came off in her hand.

CHAPTER NINE

Shards of horror ripped through Rachel. *If George vanishes under the water, the chance of finding him is slim.* In one last desperate thrust, she managed to grasp his wrist. The relief that waved over her was short-lived. If the groaning ice gave away, would she be able to keep her hold on George while struggling to keep from drowning?

She tried to yell for help, but her voice was gone. The wind seized her skirt with angry fingers, jerked the fabric one way, then yanked it another, exposing her stocking-clad legs to the frigid air. Her bare fingers were going numb; her arms weakened. *Dear Lord, don't let me lose my grip!*

George's eyes closed. Since he didn't respond to her pleas, she assumed he'd lost consciousness. Would he be a victim of hypothermia? Was it already too late to save him? If she lay prone on the ice much longer she would also pass out and both of them would die. Her mind was becoming fuzzy; she could hardly move. *If the Lord doesn't intervene soon, . . .*

Had someone shouted her name? Were pounding feet coming closer? Striving to remain alert, she shook her head.

"*Heeb oo* (Hold on)!" Wayne yelled.

Rachel's heart rejoiced.

He stopped at the edge of the pond. "We heard your scream."

She recalled screaming when George had broken

through the ice. *Hertzlich Dank, dear Jesus, for prearranging our rescue.*

"Grab the line," Wayne called.

The loop of a rope slapped the ice near her. *I can't move!* Breathing a rapid prayer, she strained to curl her nearly frozen fingers around the rope. The struggle seemed futile. Forcing what felt like a claw at the end of her arm, she strained to grip the rope tighter. She had to have help, but Wayne wouldn't dare add his weight to the ice.

Sensing power she knew came from her heavenly Father, Rachel dragged the loop closer. Fighting not to pass out, she worked the lifeline around George's limp body. The ice creaked and moaned as she wrestled to thread his arms through the loop.

Gross Dank, Jesus.

Wayne pulled the rope taut. "Work your way backward, Rachel. Rachel!"

Although she tried to obey the voice that sounded more and more distant, she drifted deeper into a gray abyss. Her head lowered until it rested on the cushioned hood of Jonas's jacket. A peaceful oblivion claimed her.

Something jerked her leg. "Rachel. Rachel!"

She fought to respond, but her head was too heavy. Strong hands tugged her toward a black void. She felt her body being yanked backwards.

"Rachel!" Wayne called.

A pair of hands held her firmly. "I got her." It was Henry's voice.

She blinked her leaden eyelids; through a misty haze, she saw her brother's relieved face. "George?" she mumbled as someone wrapped her in a blanket.

"We got him," Wayne said.

Thanking God for having given her courage and the strength to hang on, she relaxed and was vacuumed into a deep and silent tranquility.

Friendly but distant voices coaxed Rachel to consciousness. She was in an overstuffed chair in Jonas's parlor, cocooned in a thick comforter. A crackling blaze stretched warm fingers from the fireplace to caress her cold cheeks.

"Hi, *wie gehts*?" Rosy's cheerful round face loomed near.

Rachel strained to focus on Wayne's wife. "George?"

"Wayne and Henry are working with him. He'll be fine."

Sara Kate touched her arm. "Don't worry, Aunt Rachel. I'll watch the rest of Martha Marie's unruly chicks."

"*Gross Dank.*" Rachel cuddled deeper into her quilt, peered at the crackling logs, and absorbed the tranquility.

"Drink this." Rosy handed her a mug. "Hot cocoa will warm you up."

Rachel gratefully accepted it.

Rosy shook her head. "Maybe this is what it took to show George the importance of obedience."

As Rachel took grateful sips of the steaming cocoa, she hoped Rosy was right. When she had finished, Sara took the mug.

A gust of wind swept into the room; then the kitchen door closed with a bang. A moment later, Jonas knelt in front of her. Grasping her hands in his, he peered into her face. Admiration shimmered in his dark eyes. "*Gross Dank* from my sister and me for saving George's life." He smiled. "You're an angel."

Her cheeks warmed. "Oh, Jonas, I only did what anyone would have done under the circumstances."

He shook his head. "Anyone would race for help. Few would risk their lives—especially for someone else's *Kinder*."

"You would have—wouldn't you?"

"*Vell . . . ja.*" A frown flickered across his face. Getting up quickly, he turned to the fireplace, his changing expressions betraying the complexity of his thoughts. He stroked his beard as he stared at the blazing logs.

Was he worried about Martha Marie? An image of little Mary drifted into Rachel's mind. The child was so attached to Martha. She seemed more sensitive and shy than her siblings. If something happened to the woman . . . As though perceiving her thoughts, Mary came to her side and gazed into her face. Rachel smiled. The child quietly crawled into her lap and rested her head against her shoulder. Her heart extended arms of love and wrapped little Mary in a cocoon. Humming softly, Rachel prayed for a little girl of her own—just like Mary.

Warm and comforted, Rachel closed her eyes and drifted into slumber. Jonas clasped her hand, encouraging her to race through a flowered meadow. At the footbridge, he released her fingers, crossed to the other side, then turned to face her. She stared at his outstretched hand, but remained on her side of the stream.

"*Kom ann*," he said, his eyes beckoning.

Lured, she stepped onto the first plank.

"Aunt Rachel!"

She turned to see Mary struggling through the high grass, and went back to help her.

"Rachel!"

Glancing over her shoulder, she noticed Jonas's frown and became puzzled. "Wass?"

"I want you to be my wife."

She smiled. "First, I must help Mary."

"You've given enough of yourself and your time to other women's *Kinder*! It's your turn, now—and mine."

"Mary needs me."

"It's your choice."

Mary's cries drew her away from Jonas. Picking up the whimpering little one, she turned back. Jonas was gone!

Something startled Rachel awake. A door closed and muffled voices drifted from the kitchen. Still, her heart thudded against her ribs, and loneliness gripped her. She felt empty, then realized she was no longer cuddling little Mary. What had the dream about Jonas meant? Probably nothing—yet . . .

The voices came closer. Jonas had visitors! *After my ordeal on the ice, I could be a rumpled sight!*

It was her youngest sister who knelt beside the chair to hug her. "Rachel. Oh, Rachel. *Dank der gut* Man you're all right."

"Hi, *Wie gehts*?" Matthew Yoder, Susan's husband, bent his lanky frame to tug on a truant black curl that had escaped Rachel's cap. A teasing gleam sparkled in his deep-blue eyes. "Never caught you disheveled before." He chuckled, then grew serious. "You are all right, *gel*?"

"I don't know if I'll ever get warm, but I'm fine."

Susan kissed Rachel's cheek. "You are such a loving sister. I don't know what we'd do without you." Moisture pooled in her eyes. "Please take care of yourself. It's your turn, now."

The statement underscored the one Jonas had made in Rachel's dream. Was this the Lord's way of showing her she was free to choose a life? She believed it was so; then something strange wriggled within her.

Two-year-old Annie gripped the arms of Rachel's chair and peered into her face. "Hi."

Reaching out, Rachel gently touched the child's dimpled cheek. She had taken care of Annie when Susan's second baby was born. *Baby Susan is already three months old!*

"We stopped in at your house, but you weren't there," Susan said. "We noticed a commotion over here, so we decided to find out what was going on. Giggling, she bent to whisper in Rachel's ear. "I thought maybe you and Jonas had married and you hadn't invited me."

"*Ach*! I'll invite you." Studying her sister's grin, Rachel realized the girl had tricked her into admitting a relationship existed between herself and Jonas. Warmth, not from the fire, bathed her cheeks.

Susan laughed. "We came to ask you to take care of Annie and baby Susan for a few days. Matt and I have been invited to go ice-fishing and figure they'll be better off in your warm cottage."

The horror that Rachel had just experienced exploded in shards of anxiety. "Not on the ice, *gel*?"

"*Ja*. We're going to Lake Erie." Her smile brightened her oval face. "The ice is very thick, so there's nothing to worry about."

"*Vell*, I'll be overjoyed to watch them." When she looked at Annie, the child smiled, deepening her dimples.

"We're to leave next week. Will you be all right by then?"

"Oh, *ja*. Martha and her *Kinder* will be gone by then, so I'll have lots of time."

Laughing softly, Susan hugged her.

Wayne lugged the crib his youngest had just deserted to Rachel's cottage and set it up in her downstairs bedroom for baby Susan. When the preparations for taking care of her sister's little ones were completed, Rachel made steaming tea and set cups on the table for her brother and herself. Heaping a plate with chocolate chip cookies, she set it in front of him.

Tasting one, he smiled. "Jonas is right when he says you make the best cookies in the county."

She laughed and waved a hand toward him, but the compliment had pleased her. Too anxious to sit, she moved to a window and peered at the freshly falling snow. "I wish Susan and Matthew would wait for summer to go fishing."

"There's no ice in July."

"*Ja*. They could use a boat."

Wayne chuckled. "Now, mother hen, there's a time to let the chicks make decisions for themselves, *gel*?"

She sighed. Her brain acknowledged the fact, but her heart was unwilling to let go. Susan was her youngest sister. When she had married and left home, the adjustment had been difficult for Rachel. Even though she had still had two young brothers to care for, a vacant space had bubbled into her chest and remained. Then, the boys were gone, too. "My cottage echoes the vacancy in my heart and life."

"*Ach.* Jonas has begun to call on you."

She smiled at her brother. How could he know that Jonas didn't have a place in her heart, yet?

A burgundy van stopped by the gate. In a bustling hustle, Susan collected bags and boxes and pointed to them as she spoke to the driver; then she and Matthew hurried up the path, each carrying a bundled child. Within minutes the little girls were ensconced in their temporary abode. Baby Susan was snug in the crib and Annie sat in a child's wooden rocker with her doll. Susan and Matthew went laughing on their way. This would be the first trip for the young couple since their wedding visits three years ago.

Standing at the kitchen window, Rachel gazed down the lane in the direction the van had gone. A feeling of desertion yawned within her. Scolding herself, she turned away. Wayne was watching her. "Rosy will have your supper ready."

He nodded. "If you girls need anything, let me know."

"*Viel Dank.*" She watched him cross the field to his house, then straightened the pillow in the rocker she had moved near the fireplace and smiled at Annie. The child had moved to a braided rug by the hearth and was patiently trying to fit blocks together. Kneeling beside her, Rachel showed her which ones fit. Annie looked up and smiled. The child's gray eyes reflected the orange and yellow flames and seemed to dance with life. Rachel kissed the little girl's dimpled cheek.

Baby Susan began to whimper. Rachel retrieved a bottle from the gas refrigerator and plopped it into a pan of warm water, then went to the crib. Scooping the baby into her arms, she cooed to her. Susan blinked her long dark lashes and peered up at Rachel.

"You have your mama's eyes." The infant quieted as Rachel changed her diaper.

Cuddling the infant, Rachel took her and the bottle to the rocker. A knock drew her to the kitchen door. It was Jonas.

Slipping out of his jacket while he was still outside, he shook the snow from it, then entered the house quickly. "I hope this storm doesn't last long. The snow is half-melting and the roads could get slippery."

"*Ja.*" She thought about the accident on an icy highway that had killed Jonas's wife. Was he remembering, too? Picturing the hired van in a collision, she shivered. "I pray for Susan and Matthew's safety."

He looked at Annie, at baby Susan; then his gaze met Rachel's. "You're at it again."

"It's temporary."

"*Ja*, but . . ."

Sitting in the rocker with baby Susan, she rocked gently.

Jonas knelt on one knee near Annie. "Wass are you making?"

She smiled up at him. "Build house."

Choosing a few blocks, he built a foundation, then began to pile blocks to form walls.

"Door?"

"*Ja.* We'll make a door and two windows."

Watching them, Rachel smiled. Jonas was good with children—when there was only one good-natured one to contend with. It was a shame he and Linda had never had any. She bit her lip. *Had they had several, I would probably be the one to raise them.* That would have been all right, but she wanted little ones of her own, too. When Susan was asleep, Rachel took her to the crib, then returned to the living room.

Jonas stood and went to the couch. "Rachel, I want to talk to you."

Sitting on the other end of the couch, she faced him. Annie joined her. Picking her up, she rested her in her lap.

He looked at the child; then his troubled eyes met Rachel's. "How can you concentrate with interruptions?"

"*Wass* interruptions?"

He frowned. "*Vell* . . ." Shrugging, he sighed. "Since I never get to see you alone, I guess I'll have to make do." His fingers drummed on his knees. "I've been alone for two years."

Her heart lurched, then cried, *No!*

Clearing his throat, he said, "I think we should marry."

Rachel swallowed hard. She had decided to accept his proposal, although she didn't love Jonas, yet. But, sensing a restraining hand of the Lord, she remained silent.

Puzzlement blossomed on Jonas's face. "This couldn't be a surprise."

"*Vell*, no, but . . ." Lowering her gaze, she fussed with the hem of Annie's dress.

"But *wass?*"

"I . . . need time to pray, Jonas."

His eyebrows rose and remained high. "I thought we had an understanding."

"You never asked me before. A woman shouldn't take a gentleman for granted."

"*Ach*." He laughed. "You just don't want me to think you were waiting and hoping, *gel?*"

It was her turn to raise her brows. "Jonas!"

Apparently chagrined, he sobered. Slight color bathed his cheeks above his beard. "*Vell*, a man likes to think a woman dreams of marriage."

"I sometimes have." She sighed. "I've had many responsibilities."

"*Ja*, but now you don't have anyone but yourself. We could make a good life together."

"I want to make sure I am doing the will of *der gut Man*. Please give me a little time, Jonas."

He scratched his head. "It's been two years since your youngest brother left! How long does it take you?"

"Marriage is for a lifetime, Jonas. I want to pray about our relationship."

He scowled. "I think you're being obstinate."

"I don't wish to be difficult. I just ask for time."

Appearing uncomfortable, he glanced at his watch. "*Vell*, it's time I start the barn chores."

It was still early, but she understood his urgency to disappear. "I'll fix you a plate of chocolate chip cookies."

His dark eyes sparkled above his warm smile. "I can't think of a better peace offering."

That wasn't how she had meant it. Besides, if there was to be a peace offering, shouldn't he be the one giving it? Slightly irked, she arranged the treats. Shoving his arms into his jacket, he plopped his hat on his head. She proffered the plate; instead of accepting it, he reached beyond it to grasp her shoulders and pull her forward. His lips found hers in a lingering kiss, although the plate between them kept him from holding her close.

When he drew away, something unfamiliar to Rachel shimmered in his eyes. "I hope you decide to marry me quickly," he said, his voice husky.

"I will decide, soon." Being so small, Rachel had to lift her chin high to look up at him. His six-foot-two frame seemed to fill the doorway between the kitchen and living room. She felt intimidated in his shadow. She wondered about that, too. He said good night and left. She watched his broad-shouldered frame fade into the darkness. Rachel figured a girl should be ecstatic over a proposal of marriage, but she stood transfixed, wondering why she felt nothing. She had decided to accept Jonas; but when the time came, she knew the Lord was warning her to be hesitant.

Annie tripped over the carpet by the door and sprawled onto the floor. Dismissing her ponderings over Jonas, Rachel hurried to pick her up. She heated bath water for Annie and hauled the round wash tub into the kitchen. Pouring cold water in first, she added the hot, making four inches of perfect-temperature water. Dribbling in bubble bath, she whipped it with her hand, making bubbles that delighted Annie. When the child was squeaky clean, Rachel left her to play with a toy boat while she got Susan tucked in for the night. Then, toweling Annie dry, she slipped a soft flannel nightgown over her head and took her to the rocker for a story.

Finally, Rachel stretched out in her own bed. The day had been wonderful. She chewed her lower lip. How should she answer Jonas? "Show me Thy ways, O Lord," she whispered.

Still praying, she drifted into slumber. A dream invaded her sleep. She called to George, but he ran onto the ice-covered pond. She screamed as the ice cracked and the boy plunged into the murky dark water. This time, her attempts to rescue him failed. She slipped from ice she had been clinging to and sank. She searched the frigid depths, but grasped only rocks and sunken logs. Desperate for air, she tried to surface. To her horror, she could not find the opening. An ice roof kept her from getting her head above the water. Her lungs began to burn and lights exploded in her brain, still, she could not find George or the break in the ice.

Waking, she gulped air. Her heart thundered in her chest and her pulse throbbed in her temples. Too upset to sleep, she got up, checked the sleeping little girls and went to the kitchen to make herself a mug of hot cocoa. Her fingers still trembling, she spilled powdered cocoa mix on the counter. She lit the flame under the water kettle, then cleaned up the messy counter top.

Grabbing the kettle before it whistled, Rachel gripped her mug. Still distraught, she splashed hot water on her hand, but quickly plunged it into a basin of cold water to avoid a burn. She tried to tell herself her dream had been a trick of her mind; still, there seemed to be more to it. Sipping the steaming aromatic brew, she struggled to calm her frenzy.

The next day, the horror of her dream continued to haunt her. After the noon meal, she put both girls down for a nap and stretched out on her bed to relax.

Footsteps on the porch awakened her. She jumped up, straightened her skirt, checked her cap, and prayed she didn't look as though she had just gotten out of bed. What would Jonas think?

Wayne and Henry shook snow from their jackets and slipped inside. Closing the kitchen door, Wayne looked at her. "Let's go into the living room."

Her brother's expression caused her dread to mount. "Has something happened to one of your *Kinder*? To Rosy?" Her eyes traveled to Henry. His pale face portrayed trouble. "*Wass is letz?*"

Without answering, he gripped her arm and led her into the room. She sat in the center of the couch, a brother at each side, her pulse thundering in her temples.

Wayne held her tiny hand in his large calloused ones. "Rachel." His voice caught. He cleared his throat. "There's been an accident."

CHAPTER TEN

Huge tentacles of alarm coiled around Rachel as though intent on strangling her. Trapped in a vortex of whirling thoughts, she sat on her sofa between her two oldest brothers and stared into space.

"We wanted to be with you when you heard," Henry said, his voice choked.

"It's Susan and Matthew," Wayne said.

A vision of icy roads blasted her senses. "The van?"

He shook his head. "They arrived and made camp on the lake, then decided to continue to fish all night. The ice had been declared safe. As usual, several vehicles were on the lake, and a number of people were camped in tents. Apparently, the density of the ice had been miscalculated."

"No!" Rachel's hands flew to her face as her nightmare of struggling in a dark watery depth replayed through her reeling mind. "No! Oh, no!" She closed her eyes. A vision of her beloved sister drowning played on the back of her eyelids; blinking, she wrestled to erase the horror.

Henry cleared his throat. "Fourteen cars and trucks went into the water, along with tents and . . ."

"Susan?" Rachel's question hung like limp laundry between them.

Finally Wayne spoke. "She's...missing. So's Matthew."

Rachel didn't want to comprehend. Still, she had to know. "Was there no rescue attempt?"

"*Ja*, but Susan and Matthew aren't accounted for."

Shock and disbelief washed over her; then tears came. Rosy left her younger *Kinder* with Sara Kate and came to comfort Rachel, but there was no balm for her agony. "Poor little Annie and baby Susan," she said, sniffing.

Rosy patted her hand. "They are your little girls, now."

Realization washed over Rachel. When Annie was born, and again when Susan had given birth the second time, Rachel had promised the couple to care for their *Kinder*— should anything happen to them. "I meant my promise, but I never dreamed . . ."

Henry hugged her. *"Vell,* this time you won't have to raise a family alone. Jonas will help with these little ones."

That's my answer, she thought. *I'll marry Jonas.*

Lancaster County. Liz Ann bundled herself in her warmest sweater and flipped her winter cape over her shoulders. She wanted to be at Zooks in time to help Leah with Emma and Jacob's *Kinder* while Leah prepared dinner. Eli took the bricks she had warmed for her feet to his carriage. Joy bubbled within her as she climbed to the seat and snuggled in the thick quilts.

Icy fingers seemed intent on forcing their way under her wraps. When they were still a mile from Zooks', a vision of how warm it had been in Eli's car gripped her mind. Abashed over her thoughts and not wanting Eli to read her expression, she hid her face in the folds of the blanket. Then curious, she glanced at him. His sparkling blue eyes and dimpled grin told her he had read her thoughts. She must pray not to be tempted by worldliness.

As Eli halted Stomper by Zooks' gate, Liz Ann eyed Peter John's Trans Am and sighed. *We must do something to get Eli and Peter to join the church.* She struggled to relax the band that tightened around her heart. If she and Leah waited too long, all the other young men would be married. She and Leah could end up spinsters! *Like Rachel Kay.* Admiration for her cousin spread warmth through her. She would write and ask her to visit, soon.

Inside Emma's warm kitchen, Liz Ann hung her cape

on a hook by the door, then sat on the bench to take off her boots. Eli dropped to one knee to help. She returned his generous smile.

"Are you staying for dinner?" she asked.

"*Ja*, he is." Gripping five-year-old Elmer's hand, Peter came from the living room.

Carrying two-year-old Katy and leading four-year-old Anna May by the hand, Leah came from the lower bedroom. Her cap was askew and a smudge of flour streaked her pink skirt. "*Gross Dank* for *koming*, Liz Ann."

Noticing a pot boiling too heartily on the stove, Liz Ann moved to turn down the heat and stir the contents. "Umm, your famous stew. What can I do to help?"

"*Vell*, the *Kinder* are under control. Malinda and Amanda have been angels."

The twins appeared in the living room doorway, their welcoming smiles identical.

Grinning, Elmer clapped his hands. "Mama's gonna bring home two more babies!"

Sighing, Malinda rolled her eyes, but Amanda's smile broadened. Malinda went to the cupboard, took out bowls and began to set the table. Amanda counted silverware and napkins. The twins always worked in harmony without discussing who would do which chore. Liz Ann wondered if it came naturally or if Emma had trained them. Emma was a wonderful mother. Her *Kinder*, even the smallest ones, were mannerly and well behaved—most of the time.

"*Ach!*" Liz Ann reached into her pocket and withdrew a letter that had arrived that morning. "I didn't get time to read my mail."

Leah checked her stew. "Who's it from?"

"Rachel Kay Lapp."

A smile of understanding spread across Leah's face. "The lady who sacrificed marriage for her siblings."

"*Ja*, but she's free now." Opening the envelope, Liz

Ann withdrew a small folded paper and chuckled. "She's free, but apparently busy. She usually writes long letters."

As she read the note, she felt the color drain from her face. Her fingers trembled, and she slumped to a kitchen chair.

Leah moved quickly to her. "*Was is letz?*"

"Susan, Rachel's youngest sister, drowned in Lake Erie!" Tears filled her eyes and rolled down her cheeks. "Susan's husband was drowned, too. They were married three years ago and have two darling little girls."

"*Ach!* those poor little creatures."

Liz Ann read further and sighed. "Rachel's freedom is a thing of the past. She has accepted the responsibility of raising Susan's *Kinder*."

"How old are they?"

"Annie Kate is two, and baby Susan is three months."

Grasping a hot pad, Leah opened the oven and removed a pan of golden biscuits. "You said a neighbor was seeing her. If she marries him, he will help her with the little ones."

"*Ja.*" Liz Ann folded the letter and slipped it back into the envelope. "I hope she comes for a visit before she gets married."

Peter shrugged. "They could all *kom, gel?*"

"*Ja.*" Shoving the letter into her purse, she accepted the pitcher of milk from Amanda and filled the glasses. The shock of Susan's death washed over her; then an ache for Rachel's loss gripped her. Was there no end to the woman's suffering? Yet no matter what happened, Rachel's trust in the Lord remained steadfast. Liz Ann hoped that she would be as faithful as her cousin when adversity visited her.

Handing bowls of stew to Peter and Eli, Leah instructed them where to set each. "I got a letter from Samuel this morning. He's *koming* for a visit around Christmas."

"*Ja?*" Picturing Leah's tall azure-eyed brother, Liz Ann

smiled. "That will be nice."

A shadow crossed Eli's face. "Where's he staying?"

"With Elizabeth and Elam." She glanced at Liz Ann and winked. "He asked about you."

Eli's frown became full-blown. He turned to Peter, his expression serious. "You'd better keep him busy."

Peter laughed. "A little competition will do you good."

"*Vell,*" Leah sang. "Susanna said Amos is *koming* along."

It was Peter's turn to frown. Liz Ann thought about Susanna's brother and didn't try to harness her teasing nature. "You'd better be on guard, Peter John. Amos is sweet on Leah."

"Let's eat," Peter said, pulling out the chair Leah had designated.

Eli poked him. "Don't be so glum. A little competition will be good for you, too, *gel*?"

During silent grace, Liz Ann's mind wandered. She reprimanded herself, but the vision of Samuel remained before her. He was kind and had a great sense of humor. Last summer, he'd raced all over the country with a friend. He came home shortly before Elam and Elizabeth left for Bird-in-Hand. He moved into Elam's vacated house, joined the church, and assumed some of the responsibility for the family farm. She nodded. Seeing Samuel might prove rewarding. Something seemed to pinch her insides. She loved Eli. Could she learn to love someone else? She looked up and their gazes locked. Had he perceived her thoughts?

Ohio. Rachel Kay picked up a pile of laundered sheets and headed upstairs. Her bread was rising, the kitchen gleaming, and the girls were taking their afternoon nap. The past several days had been hectic. It was impossible to envision Susan being gone. More bodies had been recovered, but Susan and Matthew remained somewhere under the ice.

For the first few days, she had frequently glanced out the window, hoping to glimpse a vehicle bringing Susan home. She'd pictured the girl racing into the house out of breath and explaining how there had been a mistake. She would laugh and tell how she and Matthew had been safe in a cabin. They were sorry for causing such a commotion and they were overjoyed to be home. Days had passed. They hadn't come.

Tears spilled over and ran down Rachel's cheeks. Being alone with her sister's girls seemed to amplify her torment. Until today, some of the family had been with her. Now, she must face life head-on.

"Like *Mem* taught me to do," she whispered. The Lord had given her strength and courage to meet challenges in the past. He would again.

Entering the first bedroom, Rachel plopped the sheets onto a chair. This was the room she intended to fix over for Annie. But summer would be plenty soon enough for that. She would teach the little girl how to climb onto the porch roof—in case the cottage caught on fire. Envisioning it, a shudder raked her small frame.

Prissy strolled into the room, hesitated, then eyed the quilting frames.

Rachel pointed a finger at the temperamental cat. "Don't you dare!" If you put one snag in that quilt, you'll be banished to the barn forever."

Leaping to the bed, Prissy faced her. "Meow."

"*Ja? Vell*, as long as we understand each other."

Still feeling dazed by loss, Rachel went through the motions of making the beds. She knew it was wrong to wish her life away, but she longed for the next six months to be over. By that time, maybe she would have adjusted to Susan's death. Giving the last pillow a satisfying plumping, she went downstairs, Prissy at her heels. Jonas was coming for supper. Glancing at the clock, she sighed.

Rubbing sleep from her eyes, Annie staggered from the

first-floor bedroom; her curls were tousled and her thumb in her mouth. Grasping Rachel's skirt, she tugged. Swooping her up, Rachel hugged her.

With a chubby hand, Annie patted Rachel's face. "*Mem kom?*"

Choking back tears, Rachel kissed the dimpled cheek. How could she explain to the child that her mother would never come home? "My sweet little angel," she whispered, hugging her.

Annie's thumb went back into her mouth. She looked puzzled, then rested her head against Rachel's shoulder.

"We have to get supper for Jonas." She propped the little girl on one slender hip,. "*Wass* shall we fix?"

"Chicks and tatas."

"Okay." She had two chicken breasts that would be good oven barbecued. She had scrubbed potatoes to bake earlier. "Shall we have green beans?"

Annie shook her head. "Car-wotts."

"Shall we have them cooked in broth or candied?"

The little girl's eyes widened. "Candy?"

Rachel laughed. "Not exactly. They have brown sugar on them." Setting her on the counter, she retied her shoes. Annie was her little girl, now. So was baby Susan, and she would love them as though they were her very own. The moment she set Annie on the floor, Prissy dived from behind the rocker and swiped at the child's shoe laces. So that was why Annie's laces were untied so often! "Prissy, you naughty girl."

"Pris." Giggling, Annie stroked the cat's head, down her back and the full length of her long tail. Prissy turned for another soothing swipe.

By the time Jonas arrived, supper was ready. Rachel had baked an apple pie. Susan woke and Rachel fed her before she served supper. While they ate, the infant kicked and cooed in a basket on the table. Jonas seemed meditative.

"Your pie *war wonderbar gut*, Rachel." Without glancing her way, he took another bite.

"*Gross Dank.*" She hoped her tone wasn't as flat as it sounded to her.

"Your pastry isn't the only thing that's exceptional."

She smiled, but the seriousness in his expression sobered her. He had something on his mind. Was he thinking of marriage, again? He seemed cautious. Maybe he was afraid of being turned down. Could he tell she wasn't deeply in love with him?

"Moe candy." Annie pointed to the carrots.

Rachel put a spoonful on the little girl's plate. She had prayed about her relationship with Jonas and felt that the Lord was urging her to go slowly. She had decided they could wait until next fall to marry. If he really cared, he would wait.

About the time Rachel was ready to serve coffee in the living room, Baby Susan began to cry. Jonas looked perplexed.

Rachel lifted the infant. "Help yourself to coffee. After I take care of her, I'll join you."

Mumbling, Jonas filled his cup and retreated. When Rachel entered the living room, he was kneeling in front of the fire, stabbing at the half-burned logs, the poker in one hand, the steaming coffee in the other. Standing, he slumped onto a stuffed chair beneath a wall shelf of china plates and cups.

Rachel went to the rocker with the baby. Annie squeezed in beside her. The rocker was small for an adult, but since Rachel was tiny, as well as Annie, the arrangement worked well. The little girl watched her baby sister. Color picked up from Rachel's dress made her eyes shimmer like blue pearls, and lights from the fire danced in their depths.

Jonas's labored sigh drew Rachel's attention. He propped his elbow on the couch arm and scrutinized her.

Was her mother image giving him ideas? She smiled; he looked away. Puzzled, she decided to ease his discomfort by telling him she would marry him next year. She opened her mouth to speak, but noticed Prissy on the china shelf above Jonas. Apparently Sara Kate hadn't taken her home when she left. How had the cat gotten to the wall shelf?

Prissy stretched onto her stomach, dangerously close to the sewing basket Rachel had placed on the end of the shelf. One paw dangled over the edge as Prissy looked down at Jonas. Her eyes narrowed and her tail switched. Rachel wondered what the cat could be thinking. Standing, she intended to put her out.

"I've been . . . considering things," Jonas said.

Rachel hesitated. "You mean . . . about us?"

"*Ja.*"

Her knees weakened and she sank back to the rocker. It felt as though inebriated grasshoppers were holding a jumping contest in her stomach. Handing Susan's bottle to Annie to hold, she put the baby on her shoulder and took a deep calming breath. "Some time ago, you asked me to consider our relationship, *gel*?"

"*Vell . . . ja*, but . . ." He glanced at Annie, then at the infant in Rachel's arms. "That was before you accepted the responsibility of raising your sister's *Kinder*."

"Does that make a difference?"

"Can't Wayne and Rosy take Susan's offspring?"

"Rosy's weight and weak back make it difficult for her to chase after her own."

"*Wass* about Henry? He'll probably marry soon."

"I was the one who promised; besides, I want these little ones."

"I think you should consider letting one of your other sisters raise these two."

"*Fer wass?*"

Jonas began to fidget. "I wanted us to marry, Rachel. That meant just the two of us."

She stared at him. "You mean you've changed your mind because of my keeping Annie and Susan?"

"Your life will be taken up with their care."

Astounded, Rachel blinked. Before considering the intrusion of her question, she asked, "You and Linda never had *Kinder. Fer wass*?"

He jolted as though she had slapped him. She expected him to get angry, and she figured she deserved a strong retort. Instead of lashing out, Jonas took a long breath, then said, "We never had *Kinder*, because I didn't want any."

Her eyes widened. "But, how did you—" Heat crept up her neck and across her face.

He shrugged. "We had separate rooms-most of the time."

Struggling to comprehend the depth of his statement, she peered into the fireplace. A log shifted, sending orange-and-yellow sparks up the chimney. She shivered, although the room was warm. And to think that she had nearly agreed to marry this man. *Dank der gut* Man she had been spared a life of loneliness and heartache. How could she marry a man who would deny her children? "Vell," she said slowly, "I guess this means we will go our separate ways, *gel*?"

At that moment, the sewing basket crashed onto Jonas's head, tipped, and showered him with pins, needles, thimbles, yarn and patches. Spools of thread avalanched to his shoulders, into his lap, then bounced on the floor and rolled. Jonas sat up straight. He gritted his teeth and his face darkened. A green quilt patch draped over one of his ears; a red thread trailed over his head and across one eye. Rachel broke into laughter.

Jonas leaped to his feet. Whirling, he glared at Prissy, who sat primly on the shelf above him. With a deep growl, he dived for her.

CHAPTER ELEVEN

Prissy yowled. Wise to Jonas's probable intent, she sprang to the chair Jonas had vacated, leaped to the floor, and raced up the stairway.

Slowly Jonas turned to Rachel. "That cat doesn't like me."

"She knows you can't stand to be around her."

"I don't trust her!" He waved his hand at the mess. "Look at what she did!"

"My sewing box needed sorted; now I'll get at it."

"*Ja*." Jonas shook his head. Crossing the room, he sat on the couch and sighed. "You're a wonderful woman, Rachel. We can be friends. And we can continue to see each other, *gel*?"

An old suspicion that had been tiptoeing around the fringes of her thoughts began to stomp. "You like my cooking, *gel*?" She watched his expression, reading him completely for the first time. "You need someone to clean for you and keep you company on long winter evenings, *gel*?"

"*Vell*." He waved a large hand. "We enjoy each other's company. I don't see why that has to change."

She liked company, too, but didn't relish being taken advantage of. "I think I'm going to accept my cousin's invitation and go to Lancaster County after the first of the year."

He looked startled. "Who will take care of your place?"

"My brothers."

"But . . ."

The baby was asleep, and Annie was slumped against

her side. "Excuse me, Jonas. I must put my *Kinder* to bed."

Getting up slowly so as not to disturb Annie, she carried the baby to the crib. Jonas gently lifted sleeping Annie and followed her. He was a good man, for the most part, but his hidden selfishness was something she could not abide. She frowned. Had it been so hidden—or had her loneliness blinded her?

When baby Susan was settled in her crib and Annie in the other side of Rachel's bed, Rachel went to the kitchen and put the kettle on to heat. She would give Jonas a cup of tea before he left. While the water heated, she emptied her cookie jar of peanut butter cookies. She put them on a paper plate so he would not have to return it. This evening was finalizing another chapter in her life. What would the next one bring?

Jonas sat quietly at the table, slowly eating the piece of apple pie she had set before him. This was the end of a chapter for him, too. Already he seemed estranged. When he had finished, he strode to the door and put on his outside wraps, his dark-brown eyes pleading like the cocker spaniel she once had. What did the man expect her to do?

"*Vell* . . ." He cleared his throat. "*Viel Dank* for everything." His fingers tightened on the knob as though he were reluctant to go.

Her smile felt plastic. Tears that had been threatening were building up pressure. She wished he would just say good night and be on his way so she could cry. In spite of her struggle, a tear escaped captivity and rolled down her cheek.

Moving to her, Jonas took her in his arms. "It doesn't need to end like this." His warm lips pressed against her forehead.

"All I have to do is give Annie and Susan to one of my siblings to raise, *gel*?"

"That shouldn't be difficult. You've only had them for a

couple of weeks."

She sniffled and pulled away. "I can't. I won't. They are all I have left of my dear Susan."

His body stiffened. "I'd better be going." Turning he jerked the door open.

"Wait."

Whirling, he eyed her expectantly. "*Ja?*"

"You forgot your cookies."

"Oh." The single syllable hung in the cold air between them. He accepted the cookies and looked at the porch floor. "You'd better close the door, you're cooling the house for your precious *Kinder*."

"*Ja*. They are precious." Closing the portal softly, she leaned against it. Had Jonas's remark been as sarcastic as it had sounded? Had he really meant it? "Probably," she whispered, wondering if the man would ever soften or have a change of heart. The way he felt, it was better he not become the girls' papa.

Not wanting Jonas's pie plate and cup to be there in the morning as reminders, Rachel washed them. Sighing, she dressed for bed and slipped beneath the quilts. Annie was curled into a ball, her tiny fist tucked under her chin. Resisting the urge to hug the child, figuring it would wake her, she gently kissed the small chubby cheek. Wayne had said he would bring over a cot for Annie, soon.

Rachel's bed seemed strangely empty, even with the child beside her. Was it because she'd dreamed of sharing life with Jonas? She frowned. He'd said he'd slept in his own bedroom to avoid having *Kinder* to Linda. *That poor woman*, Rachel thought, knowing Linda loved little ones. Even though she knew the Lord had spared her future heartache, tears wet her pillow.

"I had thought I was so close to Eden," she said into the night, remembering the story Liz Ann had written to her about a young woman named Rebecca who had left home to search for her Eden. Instead of fulfillment, she experienced trouble.

"Eventually she found happiness," Rachel murmured into her covers. Closing her eyes, she willed sleep.

An hour later she was still tossing, gently though, not to disturb Annie. On her back, she stared at the darkened ceiling. "Lord help me," she said, closing her eyes. "Dear Lord, I have strived to do Your will." Her eyes flew open. That was the last prayer her father had uttered. Smiling weakly, he had gently squeezed her fingers. Rolling his head on his pillow, he had peered at her with love in his eyes. "I know you'll take care of the *Kinder*." Closing his eyes, he breathed his last.

"Oh, *Pap*, I could use a talk with you right now." Another tear, this time for the father she had lost sooner than she had expected to, slipped from the corner of her eye and lost itself in her hair.

Determination to do the Lord's will flooded Rachel. She would stop pondering what might have been between her and Jonas.

The Christmas season would soon be here and there would be a lot of family visiting. Rachel thought about how her Old Order Amish church district celebrated on the old date which was January 6th. There would not be much work, for instead of a feast, it was a day for fasting.

Rachel decided to write to the Christopher Lapps and ask if the end of January would be convenient for a visit. The trip would be difficult in mid-winter, but it would be a balm to talk to Liz Ann. The trip would be good for Annie, too. Rachel had been telling her about Aunt Naomi, Liz Ann, and other members of the Lapp family. The child had asked many questions and seemed to be looking forward to meeting their Lancaster relatives.

Her lips moving in silent prayers, Rachel drifted into the sweetness of sleep.

Lancaster County. Michael Zook stoked the morning

fire in the wood burner in the corner of his living room and turned to Charles Grayson, his *Englischer* guest. The six-foot-three man towered over Michael's lean five-foot-two frame. Charles had slept overnight on the navy couch and would probably leave before dinner. Michael didn't know whether he had enlightened the man about Amish ways or further confused him. He smiled. "Breakfast will be ready soon, Charles."

"Thank you." The man looked bleary-eyed, betraying that dawn was early rising for him. He combed his thick dark hair with his cigar-shaped fingers and followed Michael to the kitchen. Sighing, he settled his bulk in the rocker in the corner. A generous smile rounded his face. "Before I go, I'll help you cut a Christmas tree."

"*Vell* . . . we Amish don't trim Christmas trees." Michael usually waited for Lydia, his twelve-year-old daughter, to start cooking breakfast, but feeling a bit uncomfortable in this *Englischer's* presence, he sliced ham and arranged it in a skillet, then put the griddle on the propane stove and dumped flour into a bowl to make pancakes. No one made them as fluffy as his wife had, although his daughter's were coming close.

Charles rubbed his naked chin. "What if I help you nail up a few strings of colored lights?"

Michael measured the baking powder. "We don't decorate with lights." A glance at the man's surprised face made him laugh.

Slapping his shaven cheek, Charles shook his head. """That's right. You don't have electric." His forehead furrowed. What do you do?"

"We bring in greens and place them around. Sometimes we have candles."

"That's all?"

"We get together in groups to visit." Picturing some of the delicacies the ladies fixed, his mouth began to water. "And we eat—although some days are fast days. One such day is December twenty-sixth." He dumped the eggs, oil, and milk into the flour mixture and beat them into a smooth batter.

Charles watched. "What about Santa Claus? If you don't have a tree, where does old Saint Nicholas pile the presents?"

"We Amish don't believe in Santa Claus. We give a few gifts to friends. I purchase one gift for each of my four *Kinder*. When a family is large, members draw names, so each person provides one gift." Moving to the stove, he dropped spoonfuls of batter onto the hot griddle. They sizzled and a pleasant aroma curled through the room. He turned the heat on under the ham. "Would you like a cup of coffee?"

"Yes, please." The man straightened his bulk in the rocker to accept the steaming cup of liquid Michael proffered.

When holes formed on the top of the pancakes, Michael flipped them over. He was getting pretty good at fixing them light and fluffy, but he would never be able to master the art as his wife had. A twinge gripped his heart as it always did when he thought of her. The Bishop had said it was her time or the Lord would not have taken her home. He had accepted that—still the emptiness remained.

"Those smell terrific!" Charles held up his cup. "I say men are the best cooks."

Michael smiled, but not agreeing, he remained silent.

"*Pap.*"

He turned to see his five-year-old daughter. Her honey-colored ringlets bobbed around her face, and her hand-me-down nightgown dragged the floor. The stuffed brown-and-white cow she slept with hung precariously, facedown, from the crook of her arm. He grinned at her. "Your sister up?"

She nodded, bouncing her curls; then her deep-amber eyes warily studied their guest.

He smiled. "Good morning, Miriam."

She looked at her father for approval, read his slight nod, and faced the man. "Hi."

"Miriam was Moses's sister."

"*Ja.*" A slight smile curved her tiny mouth and she lowered her gaze to the blue-and-white vinyl floor. "Moses is my brother, too." As though remembering her cow, she adjusted her grip on the animal.

As Michael stacked the first six pancakes on a plate and spooned more batter onto the griddle, he thought about Moses and wondered why he was becoming more and more obstinate. Setting the bowl of batter on the counter, he opened the cupboard and counted out six plates and glasses. Glancing over his shoulder at Miriam, he smiled. "I bought a bottle of homemade maple syrup from Mister Yoder."

Her eyes twinkled. "*Gross Dank, Pap.*"

Lydia, Michael's twelve-year-old, gracefully descended the stairs and strolled into the kitchen. She was tall for her age and looked older than her years. Michael supposed the responsibility of becoming the lady of the house at a young age had matured her early. Her dark hair was neatly combed and under a prayer cap, and her apron was pinned straight over her light-blue dress. She was an obedient child, and he was depending more and more on her. She had been only eight when her mother had died. Emma Zook had taken over and continued the girl's training. He could count on Lydia's coming downstairs at dawn, ready to begin the day.

"Your pancakes smell *un wonderbar, Pap.*" Smiling, she reached for the pancake turner. "I'll finish."

Gladly surrendering the tool, he dragged a wooden chair closer to Charles and sat down, but looked at Lydia. "Are Andrew and Moses up?"

"*Ja, Pap.* Their *koming.*" She spread a white tablecloth on the table. Loading her arms with plates and glasses, she set the table, then counted napkins and silverware.

Thumping down the stairs in his stocking feet, eight-year-old Andrew rubbed sleep from his light-brown eyes. Flipping a strand of medium-brown hair away from his slender face, he yawned and slumped onto a chair at the table.

Moses clomped down the stairs in his heavy work boots. How many times had Michael and Lydia told him to take them off at the door and leave them under the bench? Unless sternly reminded, he invariably wore them to his bedroom. Often he left small clumps of mud or manure on the steps or in his room. Why did he so frequently fail to clean his boots before entering the house? Many things the boy did frustrated Lydia, but she was a patient girl who rarely scolded her siblings.

Michael thanked the Lord for an angel daughter like Lydia. He smiled as he pulled his little girl onto his lap. Miriam followed in her big sister's footsteps. He felt blessed, although he suffered from loneliness. His marriage had seemed flawless; thus after the agony of Bethany's premature death, he had decided not to remarry and risk another heart-wrenching loss.

Lydia brought the platter of pancakes to the table, then set a tray with fried glazed ham beside it. Retrieving a pitcher of milk from the refrigerator, she sliced bread and spooned applesauce into a bowl. Turning to her father, she smiled and nodded, the signal he knew meant to take a seat at the table.

He took Miriam to her place. Moses stood gazing out a window at the snow. Not wishing to correct the boy in front of company, he cleared his throat. Moses didn't move. Michael turned to Charles. "You may sit here beside Andrew."

Moving quietly to his younger son, he gripped his shoulder and turned him toward the table. Pink hue crept across the boy's rounded cheeks. The dimples that Bethany had loved were only slight impressions, for he rarely smiled anymore. He glanced sideways at his father. His expression wasn't hostile, but bordered on it. A cord tightened around Michael's heart. Was he losing the boy? Why?

Camouflaging his concern with a smile, he took his place at the table beside Moses. All heads bowed for silent grace. Michael quickly blessed the food, then concentrated the rest of his prayer on Moses. If he were to save the slipping relationship, the Lord would have to show him what to do.

"Amen." Michael helped himself to a slice of ham and passed the platter to their guest. Forking a pancake, he intended to put it on his son's plate. The boy's hand hovered in the way, forcing Michael to drop the pancake on his own plate.

"I can serve myself," Moses said, barely moving his lips.

"*Pap* only wants to help," Lydia said softly, touching his arm.

Moses jerked away. His glance told her to mind her own business. Michael prayed Charles would not perceive the tense thread that wound its way through his family this morning. He must figure out what was creating the emotional disturbance in his younger son.

Andrew finished, stood, and pushed in his chair. "I'll go to the barn and feed the horses, *Pap*."

"*Viel Dank*, Andrew." He glanced at Charles, saw that the man was preparing to go with them, and moved to the bench. He sat beside his older son to yank on his barn shoes. Donning his heavy jacket, he eyed Moses. "You *koming*?"

"*Ja*." Instead of leaving the table, he poured an inch of milk into his glass and drank slowly.

Puzzlement and confusion gripped Michael. The other three *Kinder* were kind and cooperative. Even Miriam smiled sweetly as she stood on a chair to help Lydia wash the dishes.

"We'll meet you in the barn, Moses." Michael opened the door for Daniel and Charles. He would have a serious talk with Moses when they were alone.

Holmes County. Rachel Kay sat at her kitchen window, her fingers flying as she crocheted a lace tablecloth. Prissy had come to visit earlier that evening. Now, the cat curled up, contentedly licking her paws at Rachel's feet. It was nearly dark, so Rachel would soon have to light a lamp. She had promised to have the tablecloth finished by the end of the week. If she were to be on time, she would have to work late into the night for the next four days. The little girls were asleep. With the *Kinder*, she had been unable to spend needed time upstairs at her quilting frames. Selling fancywork had been her source of income, and now, she had two more mouths to feed.

A moving shadow in the distance caught her attention, and she turned to peer into the twilight. Jonas tramped through the snow from his barn to his house. She sighed. It had been two weeks since he had come to call—and then he had dropped in at supper time. For the second time in her life, she wished for a row of trees to screen his home from her cottage. He didn't want to marry her, and she didn't enjoy watching him. She sighed. In the spring when he began plowing, he would be working even closer to her house. Would the feeling of rejection amplify?

"I'll get caught up, then go to visit Liz Ann." She returned to crocheting. She'd thought no one used crocheted tablecloths anymore and had been surprised when she'd been asked to make one. Although the hours it took were too numerous to count, it would bring a good profit. The woman had explained that she wanted the covering for display purposes. Rachel shook her head. Why would someone want something that wasn't serviceable?

Clouds gradually curtained the remaining light. Rachel

lit the oil lamp on her living room stand and relaxed in her armchair. Still, her fingers were busy. She thought about the unfinished quilt on the frames upstairs. A quilting bee would be nice, and the ladies of her district would probably enjoy an outing.

A noise made her straighten. She listened intently, thankful to be sitting out of the line of view from the windows. Footsteps on the porch made her heartbeat quicken. Was Jonas coming for a cup of tea? Her lips tightened. Why did she always think of him? She had vowed to stop remembering their good times. When no one knocked, she frowned.

Another thump on the porch made her swallow. Living alone had never bothered her, but now she had the girls to protect. Should she put out her light? She didn't have a fire in the fireplace, and didn't wish to be in darkness. Turning the lamp low, she set her crocheting aside and stood. There was someone on the porch. Why didn't they knock?

Prissy began to prowl. Apparently the cat was aware of someone's presence, too. Cautiously, Rachel slipped to the side of the window to peep out. Her breath caught. A stranger stood on her porch, looking toward her brother's farm. The man's shoulders were broad, made even more so by his fur jacket. His gloved hand rested on the porch post. He was too huge to be Jonas or one of her brothers. Her heart pounded and her mouth went dry. The bell was in the yard, and there was no way for her to signal for help. Maybe the man just needed directions.

Prissy jumped to the sill to look outside. At that moment, the man turned and looked at the cat; then his cold dark eyes lifted to meet Rachel's. Gasping, she jumped back and pinned herself against the wall. He could no longer see her, but he knew she was home! How could she get to the girls in the back bedroom?

Footsteps thudded to the window and a huge gloved

finger tapped against the glass. Rachel's hands flew to her throat and she stifled a scream. What good would her anguished cry do when there was no one to hear—except him?

"Dear Lord, please send someone to help me," she prayed.

The footsteps moved away from the window, and Rachel gulped for air. She hadn't realized she had been holding her breath. Was the man leaving?

A fist pounded on her door. She jumped, then felt faint. She could have slipped out the side door and raced for help, but the little girls were in the bedroom. To get to them, she would have to cross the kitchen in full view of the man on the porch.

The fist thundered again, rattling the door panels, and his curse split the air, vibrating her soul.

"Hey, in there!"

Leaping from the sill, Prissy fled behind the couch.

Rachel clutched her cheeks with icy fingers, her heart spasmodically leaping against her rib cage.

CHAPTER TWELVE

Cold rivulets of fear trickled down Rachel's spine; hot tears burned her eyes. She glanced feverishly around for a weapon. It was her Amish belief not to strike back, but she had to protect her *Kinder*.

"I know you're in there!" the bear-like man yelled. "If you don't open this door, I'm going to smash it."

She had no doubt that he could! Her heart drumming, she hurried across the room, seized the fireplace poker, and went to the kitchen. Straightening to her full four-foot-ten, she stopped in front of the kitchen door, looked through the window, and met the man's bloodshot eyes. Did she look as terrified as she felt? "What do you want?" Her voice squeaked.

"My truck slid into your ditch. I need your horses to haul me out."

"I don't have horses."

"That's a lie! I heard one in your barn."

"She's a carriage horse. She can't pull your truck."

His lip curled back over his teeth, reminding her of the mad dog that had challenged her mother so long ago. "You people should keep up your roads."

Rachel stretched and imagined she had added two inches to her stature. "You made a wrong turn. This is a private lane, Sir."

"Don't git lippy, little lady. Git yer man out here to help." He struck the glass hard.

Expecting it to shatter, Rachel jumped back. The man thought she had a husband. What would he do if he discovered she was alone? "We have no plow horses, Sir." She pointed toward her brother's place. "They can help you."

He turned his shaggy head to peer across the field, then glared at her. "I'm half frozen. Let me in to get warm."

Rachel tried to swallow, but her mouth felt filled with powder. Her fingers tightened on the poker. Would she actually use it? The man peered at her weapon, then laughed. As huge as he was, why would he be frightened of her?

Seizing the doorknob, he twisted it one way then the other. "I don't want to break your door, but your forcin' me to." Turning sideways, he braced his shoulder against the door. Rachel caught her breath; her heart drummed.

"Hey!" Jonas raced up the path and hurried onto the porch. "What are you doing?"

The man straightened. "This little lady won't help me."

"What's your problem?"

"My truck is in the ditch."

"*Kom* with me. We'll get my team." Glancing through the kitchen window at the poker in Rachel's hand, Jonas grinned. Feeling foolish, she lowered it. *Dank der gut* Man for sending Jonas to rescue me, again. Relief swept over her when the stranger accompanied Jonas through her gate and strode across the field. Prissy crept from her hiding place and rubbed against Rachel's legs.

"Coward." Rachel bent to stroke the cat; then she put the poker away. Turning the flame in the kerosene lamp higher, she picked up her crocheting and began to work. Her trembling fingers refused to cooperate. She dropped a stitch and had to unravel several to catch it. Not wanting to risk making a flaw that would greatly decrease the covering's value, she quit for the night.

"*Kom ann,* Prissy." Turning out her lamp, she went to open the kitchen door. "It's time for you to go home. Sara Kate will wonder where you are." The cat slipped out the door and streaked across the meadow toward Wayne's house. Going to her bedroom, Rachel dressed for bed and slid between the sheets.

Annie whimpered. "*Mem?*"

Reaching out, Rachel cradled her and hummed until the little one was again asleep. Her heart ached for Susan, too. How long would it take Annie to adjust to losing her mother? Baby Susan already seemed content. Rachel felt confident that Annie would accept her new situation, soon.

The next day, Wayne and Henry cut pine boughs and brought an armload to Rachel to place on her mantel and window sills.

"Should I bring you a sprig of mistletoe?" Wayne asked with a chuckle.

"No." The humor that danced in his brown eyes hurt. "Why would I want mistletoe?"

He shrugged. "*Englischers* put it above a door, then they can kiss their sweetheart if they catch her in the doorway."

"That's frivolous." She softened her words, not wanting to sound too prudish. Hoping to camouflage her loneliness, she added, "Besides, mistletoe is a parasite and I abhor parasites."

Henry's light-brown brows rose sharply above his blue eyes. "It's just a silly plant! Who said it was a parasite?"

"Jonas said it grows on mesquite trees in Texas. It gets its nourishment by sapping it from the tree."

Apparently Wayne decided to change the subject. "You coming over for supper Friday night, Rachel?"

"*Ja.* It will be good for the girls to get a change."

"And for you, too." Henry smiled. "Rosy is making candy this afternoon."

"Annie will enjoy tasting every kind."

His grin broadened. "Who was that ape on your porch last night?"

"Henry! You shouldn't use such terms." Her motherly expression sobered him. "He was a gentleman who needed help." She narrowed her eyes. "If you saw him, why didn't you *kom* over?"

"I thought you might have a new boyfriend."

"Henry!"

He laughed. "We were concerned. Wayne and I had dressed to come over, then we noticed Jonas taking him to his place. We went over there and helped him pull the guy's truck out of the snow." He shook his head. "That fellow used curse words I'd never heard!"

"*Vell*, we will pray for him." Moving to the stove, she put the kettle on. "Tea?"

"*Gross Dank.*" Shuffling to the table, he took a seat. "Any cookies?"

"Chocolate chip."

He rubbed his belly. "A half dozen will do—to begin with."

"Rosy baked cookies this morning!"

"Orange. If they aren't chocolate, they aren't cookies."

Wayne poked him. "Then why'd you already eat half of them?"

Rachel laughed. Henry would eat anything called a cookie, but he'd had a craving for chocolate since he was two. Serving her two oldest brothers, she thanked the Lord for her close loving family. She figured it was as good a time as any to let her brothers know of her plans. "I'm going to Lancaster County to visit Liz Ann Lapp the middle of January—providing there isn't a bad storm."

Wayne's cup stopped part way to his mouth and he lowered it to his saucer. "*Fer wass?*"

She shrugged with one shoulder. "It's time."

Henry pursed his lips. "What's going on between you and Jonas?"

She took a deep breath. It had been a month since the man's rejection. "He doesn't wish to marry a woman with

Kinder."

Henry's eyes widened, and Wayne choked on a gulp of hot tea. Both brothers stared at her.

Finally, Wayne found his voice. "*Wass* is wrong with him?"

"I suppose he has a right to live the way he wants."

Henry took a big bite of chocolate chip cookie, munched it, then washed it down with tea. "You're better off without someone like that, Sister." He grinned. "Don't despair. We'll find you someone else."

"Never mind." She laughed. "I've seen a few that you've suggested."

The good natured bantering continued until the teapot was empty and only crumbs remained on the cookie plate.

"We'd better go." Wayne stood and stretched. "The water in the chicken coop is frozen, and I want to thaw it before supper." He gripped his brother's shoulder. "Let's go, Henry."

Annie, still groggy from her nap, staggered from the bedroom. "Hi." Stopping beside Wayne, she looked up at him.

He swung her into his arms. "How's our Annie?"

Giggling, the little girl hugged him.

"Give Uncle Henry a hug, too, then we'll have to go."

When the men were gone, Annie peered at the empty plate, then looked at Rachel. "Cookie?"

Opening the cupboard door, Rachel brought out the treat she had kept out of Henry's sight.

Annie smiled as she accepted the cookie, then noticing the pile of greens, her mouth formed a circle and her gray eyes widened. "Uncle Hen-wee bring twees in?"

"Not quite. But don't the branches smell good?"

"*Ja.*" She skipped across the room to examine the boughs. "Per-tee." She petted a branch as though it were a kitten.

Rachel laughed softly.

Lancaster County. Michael had wanted time alone with Moses; now the two stared at one another from across the room. Michael's tongue felt thick and his brain stodgy. This was the chance he'd been waiting for, but words evaded him. It seemed as though Moses had locked something inside that was festering. Michael knew it would get worse if not confronted.

"Has something . . . been bothering you, Moses?"

The boy made a small gesture with one hand, but his light-brown eyes remained steady. The gold flecks made them sparkle and tiny black slashes made them appear mysterious. This boy was a small replica of himself, which created a bond between them. The thought that their closeness was being shattered tore at Michael's heart.

"If there's something wrong, Moses, I'd like you to tell me."

The boy sat there, perfectly still, saying nothing.

"You don't seem happy."

Moses lowered his gaze to his feet. "I love you, *Pap*."

Michael swallowed hard. Getting up, he joined his son on the couch. "How about your brother and sisters?"

"*Ja*."

"*Fer wass* do you neglect your chores?"

He shrugged. "I do them."

What could Michael say? Moses had eventually done his share, but it was his "no care" attitude that worried him. "When we're troubled, we should pray. Have you asked *der gut* Man to help you?"

"*Ja*." Again Moses flipped a hand. "He doesn't answer."

"He always answers."

The boy sighed. "Then He says, '*Neh*', and that's just as bad."

"*Vell* . . . that depends. Shall we talk about it?"

"*Neh*."

A knock resounded on the side door. Michael sighed.

"I'll be back, Son." He went to the kitchen and opened the door. Liz Ann Lapp and Eli Beiler stood on the porch.

"*Kom ann* in." He swung the door wide to let them enter.

Smiling, Liz Ann handed him a pie. "It's Dutch apple with loads of brown sugar and cinnamon and a hint of ground cloves."

Accepting the gift, Michael smiled. "*Viel Dank.*" Motioning them inside, he closed the door.

Liz Ann loosened her scarf, but didn't remove her cape. "Emma's twins baked the pie. Malinda said you liked it sweet and spicy."

He chuckled. "*Ja.*" Waving his free hand toward the table, he said, "You'll sample it with a cup of tea, *gel?*"

"*Viel Dank*, but we can't stay," Eli said. "I'm taking Liz Ann home, then I have to get to my place to help with the chores."

Michael would have to start his barn work soon, too. "Is Emma home?"

"Not yet. Leah's there. Three of your *Kinder* are visiting."

"*Ja.*" Michael glanced out a window at Eli's carriage. Snow swirled around Stomper's head and he shook his mane. "I have water hot and I can make cocoa in a jiffy."

"*Gross Dank*, but we really do have to go." Liz Ann's green eyes sparkled when she looked at Eli.

After they left, Michael went into the parlor. Moses was gone. The boy had slung his jacket over a chair instead of hanging it up. It, too, was gone. This was a prime example of Moses' actions. Michael hadn't told him to stay put, but the boy knew he had been expected to. The thought of searching for him, then giving a lecture on behavior wasn't appealing. *Am I shirking my duty as a father?* He must pray earnestly concerning this matter and ask the Lord to give him insight. Slumping into his armchair, he picked up the latest copy of *Die Botchoff*. He stared unseeingly at the words and pondered his family—his thoughts settling on Moses, again.

Leah Miller straightened the pillows on the couch and chairs in Emma's living room. It was the tenth time today she or Liz Ann had repeated the chore. She wondered if she should leave them tossed around the room. What if company came? Her lips tightened. "I'll hide them."

"Hide *wass*?"

She whirled. "Peter John, stop sneaking up on me!"

"*Ach*!" He laughed. "Amid this clamor, a dozen horses could gallop up to you and you wouldn't know it."

Surveying the room, she frowned. "How does Emma keep them quiet?"

"You're too lenient!" His eyes sparkled. "When you have *Kinder* of your own, you'll keep them more under control."

"Vell . . ." The thought of her own *Kinder* brought visions of marriage to Peter. Warm color bathed her cheeks. She flipped her hand in a vain effort to appear casual. "We have Emma's seven and three of Michael Zook's." She glanced toward the kitchen. "Was that a rap on the door?"

Peter pressed his hand against his forehead. "Hard to tell."

Going to the door, Leah opened it to find Moses Zook on the threshold. "*Kom ann* in."

He hadn't worn a cap and snowflakes twinkled in his sandy hair. Shirking out of his jacket, he headed toward the chaos in the parlor.

Leah grasped his arm. "You're going to take off your barn shoes, *gel*?"

He grinned sheepishly as he complied.

Towering in the doorway, Peter whistled. Silence fell. "We're going to play quietly, *gel*?"

Looking disappointed, Moses made his way to the corner where Dan and Andy were playing with his brother.

Kneeling, he picked up one of the small plow horses. Within seconds, the four boys were planning where to plant which crops. The twins and Lydia sat conversing in another corner; occasionally they giggled. The younger girls had dolls. The din had lowered to happy murmuring with frequent laughing or a joyful squeal. Turning to Leah, he grinned. "It looks like you'll have to marry me to keep your *Kinder* under control."

She hoped the heat that bathed her cheeks didn't mean they were turning from pink to scarlet. "I have no *Kinder*."

He touched her cheek with an index finger, which informed her he'd noticed their hue. "We don't—yet."

"You're not ready to take a wife, Peter John, *gel*?"

He took her hand and pulled her to a corner of the kitchen where they were screened from the children by the hutch. Taking her face in his hands, he kissed her. Her heart soared to new and lofty heights, and she melted into his ardent embrace.

Pulling away slightly, Peter gazed at her with longing. "I love you, Leah. Will you marry me?"

CHAPTER THIRTEEN

Marry Peter? *Ja, ja, ja!* Leah's heart rejoiced; but visions of his green Trans Am flashed before her, sealing her lips.

Peter watched her changing expressions. *"Vell?"*

"I . . ." She drew in a long breath and squared her slender shoulders. "When you sell your car and join the Church, I'll marry you."

Grasping her hands, he grinned.

"Until then—I'm going to look around." She wasn't completely serious, but he instantly sobered.

"You mean with Amos Yoder when he comes next week with Samuel Miller, *gel?*"

No man could take Peter John's place, but this wasn't the time to inform him of that. She lowered her lashes. "Amos has asked to call on me."

The color drained from Peter John's face, and he dropped her hands. "You wouldn't, *gel?*"

"Not if you sell your car."

"And if I don't?"

Leah didn't like to use pressure, but maybe this was the time to apply just a little. "A girl must think of her future *Kinder.*" The truth of her statement blasted her senses. She tried to picture having *Kinder* with someone other than Peter John, and a strange numbness washed over her.

"Can you *kom* in for awhile?" Liz Ann asked as Eli halted Trooper at her gate.

"I'd better be getting on home."

She grinned at him. "I baked a cake this morning and Ella promised to frost it."

"*Wass* kind is it?"

"Heart attack chocolate."

"Ah!" He laughed. "I can't resist that or you." Taking her in his arms, he kissed her.

At first Liz Ann had been in a playful mood, but Eli's warm lips took the frost from the air and cocooned them in an atmosphere of delight. Whirling in a colorful land of emotional wonder, she returned his kiss.

He pulled slightly away, his smile a little crooked. "I want us to marry, Liz Ann."

His words shocked her back to reality. "You're selling your car, *gel*?"

His brow creased and he looked away. "I will—eventually."

She sighed. Her heart still pounded a staccato rhythm against her ribs, but she forced her mind to think clearly. "I'll consider marriage after you join the Church."

His frown deepened. "But Samuel will be visiting soon."

"*Ja*." Liz Ann laughed softly. "And he asked Leah if he could call on me."

"You're not serious, *gel*?"

"Samuel joined the church this fall, Eli."

"But we had an understanding!"

"We did?"

"*Vell*, I want you to be promised to me before Samuel comes."

She loved Eli, but what if he never settled down? What if he left the community and turned *Englischer*? Her stomach tightened. She must not make any promises to him, yet. She poked him playfully. "Your piece of cake is waiting."

He climbed from the buggy, helped her down, and they headed up the walk together. He was silent, and it seemed strange. Naomi met Liz Ann at the kitchen door. "You have a letter from Rachel Kay."

"Maybe she accepted our invitation for a winter vacation with us, *Mem*." She took off her outer wraps, hung them on hooks and shoved her boots under the bench. Her mother must have been expecting Eli. The new blue-and-white checked cloth covered the table. The cake sat in the center. Noticing Ella in the parlor doorway, Liz Ann smiled. "You did a great job of frosting the cake."

"*Gross Dank*." The eleven-year-old's hazel eyes sparkled. "It probably tastes better than it looks."

Eli licked his lips and rolled his eyes at her. "It looks too good to eat—but we'll eat it anyway."

Ella giggled. "Mama had a hard time keeping my brothers from devouring it."

"Call them. We'll all have heart attacks together, *gel*?"

She laughed, creating deep dimples in her rounded cheeks. "Philip and Timothy are in the barn."

Anna Ruth came in from outside. A piece of straw stuck to the medium-blue skirt that showed beneath her navy cape. Setting her basket of eggs on the counter, she moved to Liz Ann. Light from the window made gold highlights in her light-brown hair. Her green eyes, much like Liz Ann's, twinkled. She had been taught that it was impolite to whisper, but cupping her mouth near Liz Ann, she motioned toward Eli. "He looks like someone struck him in the stomach with a poker. Did you turn him down?"

Liz Ann laughed, but it sounded forced. Her younger sister had too much insight for fourteen. "Get a knife to cut the cake, Anna Ruth. The boys will be *koming* soon."

Running footsteps thumped on the porch; the door burst open. Seventeen-year-old Philip bounded into the kitchen, his hat askew and his dark hair flying; his brown-green eyes were wide and his face white. "Timothy stabbed himself with a pitchfork!"

"*Ach!*" Naomi seized her cape.

Eli whirled, grabbed his jacket and raced for the door.

"He's in the barn." Philip ran back the way he'd come, Eli at his heels.

Ella and Anna Ruth stood as though turned to stone; Naomi raced after the boys. Liz Ann threw her cape around her shoulders, but hesitating, she told her sisters, "You stay here. I'll see how badly he's hurt."

As Liz Ann approached the barn, she heard her youngest brother's frantic cries. She wished her father hadn't gone to auction. Banging the door on her way through, Liz Ann hurried to Timothy. He sat on the straw-covered floor, his arms across his chest. Blood stained the front of his jacket and dripped onto his broadfalls.

"*Ach!*" Naomi cried, her ashen face twisted in horror as she knelt beside her wounded, twelve-year-old son. "Your chest?"

He shook his head, his tousled wavy brown hair swinging. "My arm!"

Liz Ann was thankful that her brother's lungs or another vital organ hadn't been punctured, but he was losing too much blood. Had he severed an artery?

Eli peered at her. "See. If I had my car I could rush him to the hospital. As it is—"

"Oh hush, Eli!" At times, she had a problem controlling her temper. How could Eli bring up the argument about owning a car when her brother was bleeding so profusely?

Eli knelt on Timothy's other side and stripped off his bloody jacket to examine the injury. Liz Ann gasped; Naomi cried out; Philip reeled back in shock. A prong of the pitchfork had entered the inside of Timothy's arm slightly above the elbow and ripped a six-inch jagged wound. Timothy stared at his arm; his pale face turned whiter, and he slumped to the straw.

"He may be going into shock," Eli said. He glanced at Philip. "Get some old blankets." He frowned at Liz Ann.

"He could have punctured an artery. We need a tourniquet. Get me a stick of wood and a strip of old sheet. Also, bring some cloth for a pressure bandage."

Liz Ann ran to the house with Philip. Inside, she seized a stick that had been used to prop open a window and rushed to the closet for a worn sheet kept clean for making bandages.

"*Wass* happened?" Anna Ruth followed her. "How's Tim?"

"It's his arm." Whirling, Liz Ann hurried to the barn. Before she reached Timothy, she heard his groans. Naomi tucked the blankets around him, then folded a section of sheet to press against the wound.

As Eli applied a tourniquet he gave Liz Ann and Naomi instructions.

"We know how to take care of him, Eli," Liz Ann snapped.

Eli shrugged. "He shouldn't be jostled in a buggy. I'll call an ambulance." He was gone in a flash.

As Liz Ann loosened the tourniquet and held the bandage tightly against Timothy's gaping flesh, her irritation continued to simmer. Who did Eli think he was to give her and her mother first-aid instructions? *Where does he think I've been all my life? And how does he think Mem raised eight Kinder without knowing what to do in an emergency?*

Blood oozed through the sheet bandage. Compassion and concern filled the cavity anger had left in its wake. Liz Ann had prayed to gain control over her temper. She'd been learning, but her reaction to Eli during this near calamity had proven that she needed to pray harder.

It seemed like forever before the ambulance sped up the lane and stopped at the barn. The attendants rushed in and put Timothy on a stretcher.

"I'm going with him," Naomi said.

Nodding, Liz Ann tried to swallow a lump in her throat.

Naomi looked at Philip. "You finish the barn chores." Tears made her hazel eyes glisten. "Be careful."

"*Ja, Mem.*"

Liz Ann went to the barnyard and stood mute as she watched the ambulance vanish down the lane. Eli was at her side, his arm around her. Philip stood statuesque, staring at the space the conveyance had recently occupied. Liz Ann turned to him. "You boys have had training with pitchforks since you were five years old. *Wass* happened?"

Philip sidestepped nervously. *"Vell . . ."*

Reading his reluctance and expression of guilt, she felt her right brow raise. "Were you boys fooling around?"

"Not-exactly." His two words went together in a mumble.

"Exactly *wass* were you doing—instead of the chores?"

Looking away, he scuffed the toe of his boot in a pile of dirty snow.

"Philip. *Pap* is going to ask, so you might as well tell me."

He turned a sheepish face toward her. "We were playing a game." His voice was barely audible, betraying his shame.

"With a pitchfork?" She had been tempted to yell at him, but she forced her voice into submission.

His nod was hardly discernable. "We took turns flinging it into a pile of hay, then we scrambled to see who could get it first."

"*Ach!*" Liz Ann's mouth parted. Philip was in for a lecture to top them all when Papa heard of his foolishness. Assuming his punishment would be severe, she clamped her lips shut. Her brother was aware of his Tomfoolery, and needed compassion, not her pointed finger. Stepping forward, she hugged him. When he went to speak, his voice cracked, portraying how close he was to tears. At seventeen, he had pictured himself a man. Now, that image was shattered. When she released him, he hurried back into the barn."

Liz Ann sighed. "You still want a piece of cake, *gel?*"

Eli's smile seemed forced. "It doesn't seem right with Timothy injured and the family dismayed."

"Timothy is being taken care of, Philip will suffer remorse for a time, but after Papa's reprimand, he will get over his chagrin and concentrate on becoming a responsible young man. Let's go into the house. We need to tell the girls that Timothy will be fine." She grinned. "Besides, we can't let that cake go to waste, *gel?*"

As though he already tasted the dessert, his grin became genuine.

Reaching up, she pressed a gloved finger into one of his dimples. How she would miss them, should . . . She refused to continue that line of thought.

Holmes County. Rachel Kay sat in Wayne's living room, surrounded by siblings, nieces, and nephews. Annie sat in the chair beside her; Sara Kate had baby Susan. Prissy perched on a hassock as though she were the queen of the house. Twitching her whiskers, she looked from one family member to another. Her tail, usually in motion, lay curled against her body. Occasionally, she squinted as though deep in thought.

"It's time for us to draw names for Christmas," Wayne said.

"*Ach!*" Henry feigned surprise. "I thought we got together to sample the tons of cookies Rosy and Rachel baked."

Chuckling, Rosy gave him a swat. "Sit, Boy. You've already sampled each kind several times."

Since Amish could get a small gift for a friend, Rachel planned to crochet a doily for Liz Ann. She thought about her twenty-two-year-old brother's recent announcement of his planned marriage. When couples were seriously dating, the young man might purchase his lady friend a set of china or table flatware. James had given china. David, another brother who had just begun to court had ordered a tablecloth for his friend's hope chest.

Rachel thought about Jonas and fought despair. The past two years he'd given her small gifts. There would be no gift from him this Christmas. This would also be the first Christmas without Susan. None of her siblings had said anything, but she figured they were all quietly grieving.

Wayne gave everyone a small slip of paper. Rachel wrote her own name on one, Annie's on one, and baby Susan's on another. Folding them, she dropped them in the hat that Henry passed around the room. She planned to make Annie new dresses, for the little girl was growing out of the ones she had. There was enough new material for three.

Henry passed the hat again. Reaching in, Rachel took three slips. "I'll look at Annie's first, then Susan's. Mine will be last."

Strolling across the room in the pretense of soothing baby Susan, Sara rounded Rachel's chair. Knowing the girl intended to look over her shoulder at the names, Rachel smiled. Taking her pencil, she numbered the folded slips.

Sara Kate grinned. "Aren't you going to look at them?"

"I'll wait. I like surprises. Now I'll have something to look forward to when I'm home alone."

Apparently realizing she had been outguessed, Sara grinned. Taking a slip from Wayne's hat, she quickly unfolded it, read the name, and smiled at Rachel. "You want to know whose name I got, *gel*?"

Playing along, Rachel reached for the slip.

"*Ach!*" Holding it high, Sara looked triumphant. "It's my secret."

The merriment continued until it was past Annie's bedtime. Full of cookies, punch and good cheer, Rachel bundled the girls and herself for their trek across the meadow. It was dark, but she had no fear; still, Henry walked her home. She wondered how much longer he would live with Wayne's family. At twenty-six, Henry should be married. She smiled. He had been slipping over to help Isaac Kauffman with his farm work. Rachel figured Rosemary, their oldest daughter, was the main reason he was so anxious to lend a hand. Henry was good-natured and big-hearted, but there was probably more to his frequent visits than that.

A week later, Wayne was notified that more bodies had been retrieved from Lake Erie. He and Henry traveled to New York to see if Susan and Matthew had been recovered. Rachel didn't know how to pray. If they found Susan's remains, she could be buried in the family plot; however, as long as she was missing, Rachel could hang on to a slim thread of hope that her sister was still alive.

Wayne and Henry returned devastated. Identification had been difficult, but convincing. Two days later they had the funeral services; now fresh mounds of earth covered Susan and Matthew's graves. Rachel wept.

December 25th came and went. Since Amish districts in Holmes County celebrate Christmas on the old date of January 6th, Rachel waited until the 8th to gather the green boughs from her cottage. Piling them on the porch for one of her brothers to burn, she went inside.

"You wait here at the window, Annie. You can watch me as I go for the mail."

The little girl grasped Rachel's skirt. "*Mem* take Annie."

Picking her up, Rachel wrapped her cape around the child. "We'll get the mail together, *gel?*"

"*Ja.*" Annie patted Rachel's cheek, then hugged her. "Susan wait."

"*Ja.* She'll sleep." Holding the cape shut, Rachel went down the path, through the gate, and headed for the mail box at the corner of her property. Her cape was too big, because it had belonged to one of her sisters who was two sizes larger.

"Annie git it, *Mem*." She stretched to reach the handle. Rachel leaned forward to make the chore easier.

Yanking the door open, Annie peeped inside. "We got some, *Mem*!"

Every time the little girl called her Mama, Rachel's heart swelled. The girls were becoming more and more her own. She collected the mail and went back inside. Playfully dumping Annie on the couch, she laughed.

The little girl giggled. "Annie bag of tatas."

"*Ja*, you are." Setting aside her copy of *The Budget*, the Amish newspaper published in Sugarcreek, Ohio, she flipped through the mail advertisements. An envelope fluttered to the floor. Scooping it up, she read the return address. "It's from Aunt Naomi Lapp."

Annie bounced. "Read, *Mem*. Read."

Rachel was anxious, too, but hung up her cape before she came to sit beside Annie. Tearing open the envelope, she unfolded the sheet of notebook paper. "Dear Rachel, Annie, and Susan, I hope you are keeping warm this winter. We have had a lot of snow storms, but I'm beginning to study seed catalogs for my garden. I'll need to plant more cucumbers this year. The family ate all the pickles I did up last fall."

"I like pickles," Annie said.

"*Ja*, you do." Noticing that Naomi had written about Susan's death, Rachel scanned the rest of the letter.

"Read me, *Mem*."

"Aunt Naomi says Timothy had an accident with a pitchfork, but he's doing fine, now. He gets out of forking hay and lifting anything very heavy."

"*Fer wass?*"

"He hurt his arm. It will be all better, soon."

Annie blinked. "Then we kin visit, *gel?*"

"*Ja.* Pretty soon."

Annie bounced on the couch until she had loosened

her prayer cap. It dangled for a time, then toppled to a cushion. She slid to the floor and rolled across the braided rug.

"Aunt Naomi asks if we can come to visit right away."

"Oh, *ja!*" Jumping to her feet, she ran to the couch, seized her prayer cap and put it on sideways. One string dangled down her back, the other hung across her sweet, heart-shaped face.

Rachel laughed. "She didn't mean today."

Sara Kate came in. "I'm here to watch the girls. Is it too early for you to milk Judy?"

"We can visit first, if you like."

"*Vell* . . ." Her slight frown betrayed her anxiousness to be elsewhere.

Rachel stood. "I guess Judy won't mind being milked a bit early."

In the barn, Rachel found her cow a bit jittery. Usually the bovine was affable and cooperative. Her large brown eyes rolled as though searching the barn for something. For a time, she held back her milk. Rachel stroked the animal's neck and patted her shoulder. "*Was is letz*, Judy?"

When the cow calmed, Rachel milked her and set her full pail aside. Wayne wanted to take the animal to his place so that Rachel wouldn't have to milk twice a day, but Rachel felt that Judy was almost a member of her family. Besides, Sara Kate didn't mind watching the girls. *I have to feed and care for my horse anyway*, she thought. A carriage horse was expected to be in service about twenty years, and Muddy Foot was already nineteen and slowing down. She intended to remain faithful to the animal. Picking up her pail of milk, she headed across the cow shed toward the side door. A throaty growl made the hair on the back of her neck prickle.

Without moving, her eyes scanned the barn for the source of the warning. A huge dog with a shabby gray coat stepped from the corner to her left and stood between her and the door. An instant replay of the strange mad dog and the horror of her mother's injury blasted her senses, only this animal was four times the size of the one that had bitten Muddy Foot. She glanced around feverishly for a weapon. This, too, seemed to be a replay.

"*Geh heem* (Go home)!" Instead of sounding threatening, her voice squeaked.

Snarling, the canine rolled his lip back and bared his teeth. Rachel stepped backward. The dog advanced several steps. Rachel stepped back another step. Again the dog advanced two. This wasn't going to do! If she screamed, would the animal attack? If she didn't, would he go for her throat anyway? Cold sweat broke out on her forehead, and her mouth went dry. "Dear heavenly Lord, please help me," she whispered.

As though her voice had been a threat, the dog barked. She backed until the wall stopped her. A scream caught in her constricted throat. Growling, the dog slowly moved toward her.

CHAPTER FOURTEEN

"Jack!" a man yelled. "Git yer tail over here!"

The huge dog stopped inches from Rachel; his growls silenced. Glancing into the shadow in a corner of the shed that had hidden him, he woofed. It sounded friendly, not at all like the noises he had made at her.

A shabbily dressed man stepped from behind a pile of hay. "I'm sorry, Ma'am." Raking long slender fingers through his straggly orange-red hair, he cleared his throat. "Jack's ma watch dog."

She swallowed and found her voice. "I don't like him watching *me!*"

The man looked pained. His tattered jacket and hole-frayed jeans didn't look warm enough. "Jack's a mite feisty, but he's all I got." His Adam's apple bobbed as he spoke and he squinted as though he had a difficult time seeing. Dirt smudged one cheek and reddish stubble covered the bottom half of his face. "Besides, now that Jack knows yer okay, he'll be protectin' ya, too."

Because of the dim lighting and the man's shoddy appearance, it was difficult to tell his age. Rachel didn't know which to fear the most, the nasty dog or the unkempt man. She warily eyed the canine. He met her gaze, took one step forward, and wagged his bushy tail. Cautiously, she reached a hand toward him. Stretching his neck, he licked her fingers. She petted him; he blinked and wagged his tail more vigorously. Prissy's dish sat nearby. Moving cautiously, Rachel poured some milk into it. The dog lapped greedily.

"He'll love you forever, now, Ma'am." The man coughed, hawked up a mouthful, and spit.

Rachel's stomach convulsed. "Who are you?"

"Forest Grant, Ma'am. I'd be grateful if ya had a bite to eat. I don't want nothin' for nothin'. I'll work."

Sensing the Lord's urging, she said, "The small section of the shed needs forked out and new straw put down for Judy."

The man's head jerked as a pheasant's bobs when it's going through tall grass. "Judy?"

"My cow."

He nodded. "Where do I find a pitchfork?"

He scratched his head, from habit or because of crawlies, she didn't know. A twinge of conscience pinched her insides. This man looked cold, sounded sick, and was probably hungry. "I'll get you something to eat before you start the work."

"Mighty 'bliged, lady."

Gripping the handle of the milk pail, she headed for the house, Forest in tow. Jack bounded beside her as though she were his new mistress. She thought about the burly stranger who had threatened to smash her door. Having a dog like Jack around might prove advantageous. She frowned. That would mean housing Forest. *How, Lord; and Where?* She thought about the two-room cabin on Wayne's property. Her brother rented it to vacationers during the summer, but now it was unoccupied. She bit her lip. What about Jack? Would the huge dog be a threat to the *Kinder*?

She felt guilty inviting Forest to wait on the porch, but too wary to invite him in, she closed the door leaving him out in the cold. Jack appeared at the window, his eyes bright. Sara Kate shrieked, but Annie toddled to the window.

"Big doggie!" Giggling, she pressed her palms against the glass. Jack wagged his tail and licked the pane as though he could touch the little girl's fingers.

"He likes me, *Mem.*" Annie's gray eyes shimmered like blue pearls. "Can I play with doggie?"

"Not right now, sweet." Rachel longed to say, "Never," but didn't want to upset the happy child.

"He's a monster," Sara whispered, suspiciously eyeing the dog.

Prissy stalked to the window. Jumping to the arm of the rocker, she narrowed her eyes and glared at the dog. He looked at her, gave a friendly woof, and wagged his tail. Arching her back, Prissy hissed.

"So much for friendship," Sara Kate said. "Where'd he come from?"

Rachel sighed. If Forest were to stay at Wayne's, this girl would have to get used to the dog. "He belongs to an unfortunate gentleman who is hungry and will be dunging out the stable."

Frowning, Sara moved closer to the window to peer out, then jerked away and joined Rachel at the counter. "You can feed that mutt—as well as his mangy companion—if you like, but I'll be glad when they're both gone!"

Rachel retrieved the left-over meat loaf from the refrigerator and sliced slabs of fresh bread for sandwiches. "I thought your father would offer him a place in the summer house."

Sara gasped. "You don't mean that, *gel?*"

"Indeed I do. It's the eleventh commandment."

Sara laughed. "There are only ten!"

Rachel shook her head. "Moses was given ten. Jesus said, 'This new commandment I give unto you that you love one another. Even as I have loved you, you also love one another.' The way we do things for Jesus is to do things for people who are less fortunate than we are."

"*Ja*, but . . ." Frowning, she looked at the window.

"Get a mug from the cupboard, Sara. Forest will need a hot drink."

Retrieving the largest cup on the shelf, she thrust it at her aunt. "What are you going to put in it? The coffeepot is empty."

"The water kettle is hot. Get a pint jar and make him some hot chocolate." Going to the bear cookie jar, Rachel picked out an assortment of treats.

Sara Kate dug in the cabinet for the container of instant cocoa mix that Rachel kept for quick occasions. "I think you're making a mistake, Aunt Rachel." Sara glanced sideways at her as she stirred the cocoa. "You always take in wounded birds and stray animals."

Baby Susan began to cry.

Sara rolled her eyes. "Not to mention everyone else's *Kinder*."

Rachel's mouth dropped open and her eyes widened.

Sara giggled. "I thought that would shock you." Her smile remained and her dark eyes twinkled. "You let too many people take advantage of your compassion, but we all love you, Aunt Rachel."

"*Vell, Dank der gut* Man for that."

The sweet aroma of chocolate emanated through the kitchen as Sara poured the hot liquid into the jar. Rachel dug in a drawer for a lid. It tinged as she dropped it on the counter. Seizing it, Sara twisted it onto the jar. Rachel thunked a small cardboard container onto the table, packed the lunch in it, and carried it to the door.

Sara opened the portal, but stood out of sight behind the panels. Prissy vanished behind the stuffed chair, mimicking her mistress's apprehension.

Wind howled and swept into the kitchen in feverish gusts as Rachel handed Forest the box. "I put some ham trimmings and a crust of bread in for Jack."

"He'll thank ya, Ma'am." Graciously accepting the offering, Forest headed for the barn, Jack in tow.

The cat stepped boldly from her hiding place, leaped to the window sill and switched her tail as she watched the dog retreat.

"That's probably the last we'll see of him," Sara said as though she hoped it was true. "You'll have to dung out your own cow stall—or Papa will."

Annie looked distressed. "Doggie go bye-bye?"

"For now." Patting the top of the little girl's head, Rachel headed for the bedroom. Baby Susan was beginning to kick up more of a fuss. The peaceful feeling she had in her heart told her she had done the right thing concerning Forest. Scooping up the baby, she returned to the kitchen. "Sara Kate, can you stay with the girls for an hour longer?"

The younger girl's eyes narrowed. "So you can talk Papa into harboring that creepy stranger, *gel*?"

Rachel rarely pointed a finger, but this was one of the times. "Young lady, you had better ask Jesus to help you with your attitude toward the less fortunate."

"Maybe that man's situation is his own fault."

"*Ja*. But maybe he's an angel in disguise. If so, *wass* would Jesus think of your attitude?"

Sara turned away, but her sigh was evident. "I didn't mean to be nasty," she mumbled. "Don't tell Mama."

Rachel hid her smile in Susan's blond ringlets. The point had been made, and there would be no need to bring it up, again.

After changing the baby, she retrieved the warming bottle of milk and sat in the rocker. While feeding the infant, she pondered. Forest seemed harmless, but she would not trust any stranger with the children. She didn't even want to leave the little girls with Sara while she went to speak with Wayne. It was too cold to take the little ones, and she didn't want Sara to go home by herself—not with big Jack on the loose. Sara was terrified of large dogs. *Lord, I know you want me to help this man, but I don't know how. Show me the way. Should I speak with Wayne? Should I contact Jonas?*

"That would be feasible," she mumbled. Jonas was a

man without a family to protect.

Still, the image of Wayne and Henry played before her.

Hands on hips, Sara looked at the floor. "I hate your black-and-gray vinyl, Aunt Rachel. Every footprint and crumb shows like a stop sign."

"I don't like the color either, but why a stop sign?"

Retrieving a mop, the girl cleaned up a couple of spots. "These marks say, 'stop! Look! Rachel is a poor housekeeper."

Rachel laughed. "I mop it every day."

"*Ja*, but others don't know that." She put the mop back, allowing the handle to clack against the wall of the closet. She flipped a hand toward the cupboards. "That white counter top is a pain, too!"

"It takes a lot of work, Sara. I didn't choose the colors."

"Whoever did was dumb."

"Your Papa and Henry chose the floor covering, cupboards and counter top when they refurbished the cottage."

"Oh." She shrugged. "What do men know, *gel*?" She studied Rachel and chewed her lower lip. "Why did they choose the colors for *your* kitchen?"

"I was in Bird-in-Hand visiting Aunt Naomi Lapp. My brothers wanted to surprise me."

Sara laughed. "I bet they did that all right!" A knock on the kitchen door made Sara freeze, her hand hovering in the air, her eyes wide. "That could be that man!" she whispered. "Did you lock the door?"

"*Ja*." Getting up, Rachel handed Susan to Sarah. She had not locked the door during the day until she had received custody of the little girls. Now, she rarely left it open. Peeping out the side window, she grinned. "It's your Papa." She flipped the lock, knowing that this was an answer to her prayers.

"Rosy sent over a cream pie for your supper." Wayne

slid the still-warm dessert onto the counter and turned to Rachel. "I noticed a huge gray dog over here in your barnyard and thought I'd check it out."

"*Gross Dank.*" She made a pot of tea and poured him a cup. While he sipped the aromatic brew, she told him about Forest. Wayne was open to whatever he thought the Lord wanted him to do. To Rachel's relief, he agreed that the summer cabin would be the proper place for the man to stay.

He cleared his throat. "It's settled, then." He eyed her. "Providing the dog is friendly and the *Kinder* will not be in any danger."

"We'll make sure."

Forest gratefully accepted the arrangement, but insisted on taking care of Rachel's livestock during her visit to Bird-in-Hand. The next few days, Rachel packed for herself and the girls. She finished last minute details. They had a family supper to say temporary farewells.

Forest, bathed and in clean clothing, joined them. Rosy had invited him to eat his evening meals with them. His brown eyes gradually took on a luster; his shaven face was lean, but had lost its haggard appearance. Rosy cut his hair. When Rachel saw it she fought a laugh. The style was neat, but it made the man look Amish! He told her he liked it because it made him feel closer to the family. He refused to discuss his past or future, which made them suspicious, but he was doing his work well, keeping Jack completely under control, and settling in as though he figured he might stay.

Jack quickly became a part of the family. He loved the children, especially the tiny ones. They pulled his ears, clung to his bushy tail, and yanked on his whiskers, but he only looked distressed, then seemed to smile crookedly. The youngest children used him like a toy horse, riding him around the yard. Annie called him her doggie. Rachel knew when Forest left and took the mutt, Sara Kate and Prissy would be ecstatic, but her little girl would be devastated.

To Lancaster County. The first Monday of February, the van Rachel had hired to take them to Bird-in-Hand stopped by her gate. Her siblings who lived nearby came to wish her well.

Mark, her youngest brother, took her bags to the van. "Don't worry about anything, Rachel. I'll come over every night and light your lamps, so no one will know your cottage is unoccupied."

"*Gross Dank.*"

Rachel and the girls were soon headed eastward. Rachel's heart pounded. This was her first major trip in five years. Would all be the same as it had been? Hardly. Would she remember the members of the Lapp family? What about their friends? Her mind whirled with faces. Some had names. Some didn't.

"When we be there, *Mem*?" Annie asked.

"We have a long ride ahead." Rachel had brought sandwiches, cookies, and milk, but wanted to keep them until Annie grew restless. Susan seemed to like her rented baby car seat.

"Dun't like this box!" Frowning, Annie yanked on the straps that secured her.

Rachel patted the little girl's tiny hand. "*Kinder* must use one in a car."

Annie's eyes studied her face. "We kin take the cawage."

Rachel laughed. "It's too far. Muddy Foot would get too tired." Digging a Bible story book out of her bag, she opened it, pointed to the pictures, then began to read.

When Annie fell asleep, Rachel rested her head against the back of her seat to relax. Apprehension gnawed at her, for she sensed that after this trip her life would be forever changed. What awaited in Lancaster County?

"We're almost there, Mrs. Lapp," Brentwood Austin said as he steered his van onto a secondary road.

Rachel peered at the back of his bald head and opened her mouth to correct him, then decided explaining her marital status might complicate matters—especially since Annie called her *Mem*.

"We made good time." He pointed. "There's Christopher and Naomi's place."

The house was a rectangular wood frame dwelling painted white. It was newer than some in the area, but very similar to other Amish houses. A porch stretched across the front of the house. An addition to the lower left was the summer kitchen. Liz Ann had said bathrooms were permitted as long as they were on the lower floor and didn't need a pump to get the water to the fixtures. Maybe she would stay longer than one month.

The van stopped by the hitching post. Rachel's pulse quickened as her anxiety grew. Andrew, the oldest Lapp son, came out of the house. The wind whipped his medium-brown hair and a broad grin stretched his handsome face. He and Peter John had brought Liz Ann and Martha, the two oldest Lapp daughters, to visit last summer. Rachel recalled that Martha had light-brown hair and green eyes and hoped she would recognize her.

Andrew opened the van door, and his velvety-brown eyes met hers. "Hi. *Wie Gehts*?"

Returning his smile, she handed him her traveling bag.

He slung the handles over his arm, then reached for Annie. "I'll help the little lady to the porch."

Annie blinked. "Su-san's the 'ittle one."

"*Ach*, so she is." He reached to unbuckle Annie's seat. "*Wass* if I take this big girl to see Aunt Naomi?"

"*Ja*." She reached her arms to him.

Picking her up, Andrew headed for the house. With baby Susan in her arms, Rachel followed him down the brick path to the house. Brentwood opened the back of the van and carted the luggage to the porch. Liz Ann had said there would be a crib available, as well as other infant paraphernalia, so Rachel had packed light.

A German Shepherd pup peeped through a hole in a cardboard box that sat in a corner. Then wiggling through the opening, he waddled toward them. When Annie squealed with delight, Andrew stood her on the porch. Bending, she gripped the dog's fur. The puppy yipped excitedly and made a puddle.

"*Ach.*" Andrew swept the little girl into his arms and stepped through the door that Naomi had swung wide.

Rachel followed him into the large cheery kitchen. Not wanting to track across the spotless vinyl, she sat on the padded bench inside the door to remove her boots. A crisp two-tone blue checked cloth covered the large rectangular table that took up a great deal of space in the middle of the room. A wooden butter bowl filled with oranges, apples, bananas, and grapes graced the center of the table. Winter sun spilled through the windows above the sink and made shiny splashes of light on the floor.

Naomi smiled at Annie and her fingers moved as though she itched to hug her, but apparently not wishing to overwhelm the little girl, she held back.

Annie wiggled to get down and ran to her. "You Aunt No-me?"

"*Ja.*" Kneeling she wrapped her arms around the child. "And I've been looking forward to your visit."

"*Mem kom.* And baby, too."

Over Annie's head, Naomi's warm-brown eyes met Rachel's gaze. "She is adjusting *vell.*"

Rachel nodded. She noticed a few more silver strands glimmering in the medium-brown hair that showed at the front of Naomi's prayer cap. Martha, Anna Ruth, and Ella had been patiently waiting across the room, but as Rachel unwrapped baby Susan, they were instantly at her side. She scanned all three faces, knowing each hoped to get the baby first. Standing, she again met each pair of eyes. "*Ach*, this is a dilemma!"

A warm smile spread across Martha's oval face. "I want her, and I'm the oldest, but I'll give my turn to Ella."

Surrendering the infant to the youngest Lapp daughter, Rachel hugged Martha. Her impression of the girl's kindness hadn't been exaggerated. One-by-one she was hugged by everyone at least twice.

Martha swooped up Annie and showed her the potted gardenia above the sink. The little girl gently touched a white blossom and grinned, flashing deep dimples at Anna Ruth—who now cradled Susan.

Supper's in the oven," Naomi said. "As soon as Christopher and Peter John get home we can eat."

Susan began to fuss. "Hush, hush." Anna Ruth gently rocked the infant.

Martha glanced at her mother. "Is Michael *koming* to look at the horse *Pap* wants to sell?"

"*Ja*." Naomi took a huge loaf of bread from the bread box and sliced it with great swishes.

"Will his *Kinder* be with him?"

"He'll have Moses with him." She piled the slices on a flowered plate. "I hope they'll stay for supper."

A pensive expression captured Martha's features. "I think he's having a discipline problem with Moses."

Naomi turned toward her. "*Wass*? He's only seven years old!"

"*Ja*, but . . ." She pursed her lips in thought. "Moses is a good boy, and his actions only border on disobedience. That's what makes it hard to correct him."

Ella was also peering curiously at her older sister. "Who told you?"

"Lydia."

A sigh escaped from deep within Naomi. "I don't know what Michael would do without that dear girl."

Rachel assumed they were talking about Jacob John

Zook's younger brother. Liz Ann had mentioned the man in a couple of her letters. If so, he'd been widowed for five years and was raising his four *Kinder*.

Timothy came in from the barn and took off his jacket. Rachel noticed his bandaged arm. "*Wass* happened?"

"*Vell* . . ." the twelve-year-old's freckled cheeks turned bright-pink, then he chuckled. "I just got a little wild with a pitchfork."

"*Ach!* I forgot."

Philip came in. When he saw Rachel, he stood tall and squared his seventeen-year-old shoulders. Her eyes met his brown-green ones and she smiled.

Naomi turned to Andrew as he strode from the living room. "Will Liz Ann be home for supper?"

"*Neh*. She's helping Leah with Emma's *Kinder*."

Disappointment showered Rachel. "Will she be home tonight?"

"Oh, *ja*. Peter will fetch her this evening." Opening the cupboard, Naomi counted out a pile of plates and handed them to Ella. "We'll get Andrew to fetch the old high-chair for Annie." She turned to Rachel. "I keep it ready for visiting little ones."

As Rachel counted out silverware, she pondered Emma's expected new twins and the possible danger of losing them. "Have the new babies arrived?"

"*Ja!*" A smile brightened Martha's pretty oval face and added more sparkle to her green eyes. "Last week."

"They're doing fine, *gel*?"

"Oh, *ja!*" Martha grabbed a handful of tableware and began to place settings around the plates. "Yesterday, Liz let me go with her to help. Both Rose Anna and David are perfect and beautiful!"

Nine Kinder, Rachel thought. She remembered how overwhelmed she had felt at seventeen when she'd taken on the responsibility of raising her eleven siblings. The gracious Lord had sustained her; he'd given courage at every point. *Even when I lost Jonas so many years ago,* she thought, then relived losing him again when she had accepted Susan and Annie. She wasn't suffering from anything but feelings of rejection. *And hurt pride,* she thought, shuddering at the horror of having pride. She was thankful that part was over. Deep in thought, and with her back to the kitchen door, she paid no heed when it opened—nor did she register the conversation in the room. Then a strange voice penetrated her revery.

"You have a new friend, Ella? *gel?*" the strange voice asked.

"Oh. *Vell . . . ja!*"

Rachel turned. Her eyes slowly swept the room; then her gaze halted on the stranger's surprised face.

CHAPTER FIFTEEN

Rachel wondered if the gentleman was surprised or embarrassed. To put him at ease, she smiled, unknowingly flashing dimples at him. When she realized that their gazes had locked, warmth crept across her cheeks.

Martha laughed softly. "Rachel, I'd like you to meet Michael Zook." She drew Rachel toward the man.

"Your . . . back was to me. I thought you were a child." Michael's light-brown eyes appeared golden in the evening sunlight.

Rachel extended her hand. "Hello, Mr. Zook. *Wie gehts?*"

"*Vell* . . . a bit abashed."

His rich baritone voice spread over her like warm honey. "It's nice to meet you," she said quietly.

Timothy giggled; Martha elbowed his ribs, and Anna Ruth threatened him with a glance.

Michael drew a small boy forward. "This is Moses, my youngest son. He's seven."

The boy appeared shy, but slicked his sandy-colored hair down with his hands as though he intended to make a good impression. His hair and features, as well as his amber eyes, duplicated his father's. Stepping forward, he smiled and proffered his hand.

"*Vell*, introductions have been made." Peter John chuckled. "Let's eat."

"You sit here at the end beside the high-chair, Rachel dear," Naomi said. She glanced at Michael. "You can sit here." She designated a chair across from Rachel. "Moses

187

can sit beside you." She took her place; the family took theirs, and all heads bowed for silent grace.

"Amen," Christopher said.

As though on cue, baby Susan began to cry.

Martha rested a hand on Rachel's shoulder. "I'll get the baby." Smiling, she skipped to the living room.

Michael met Rachel's gaze. "How many *Kinder* do you have?"

"Two girls."

Ella bounced on the edge of her chair. "After Rachel's mother died, Rachel raised her eleven brothers and sisters."

Michael looked impressed. "Alone?"

"Oh, no. We had Papa." Her voice lowered. "Until my youngest sibling was four." In an attempt to appear normal, she forked a bite of roast and put it into her mouth.

Naomi set her cup on her saucer. "Joseph Wayne, Rachel's father, took it very hard. We feel it hastened his premature death."

Moses had become attentive. His fork rested on his plate, his slice of bread motionless in his left hand. His amber eyes searched Rachel's face. "You didn't have a *Mem*?"

"I did until I was nineteen."

The little boy nodded. "Then you took care of your family—just like Lydia?"

"*Vell . . . ja.*"

He grinned and the few freckles on his cheeks bounced.

Michael cleared his throat. "Eat your supper, Moses."

Spearing a slice of carrot, Rachel trailed the circle through the rich brown gravy on her plate. Most men towered over her, making her feel insignificant. She was about four inches shorter than this man.

Martha carried Susan to the table and took her chair. Susan seemed contented in the girl's arms. Rachel glanced up, and her gaze locked with Michael's; warmth bathed her cheeks as his eyes probed hers.

He smiled. "Your husband unable to make it this trip, *gel*?"

"I have no husband."

He looked sympathetic. "You're a widow?"

"I never married."

"Oh . . . But . . ." He looked at Annie, then at baby Susan. "These *Kinder* aren't yours, then?"

"Oh, *ja*. They're mine."

Michael looked puzzled; then his right brow rose a few degrees.

Peter John laughed. "She grew them in her garden, Mike."

Ella giggled, but Anna Ruth gave him a gentle poke.

"Annie and Susan were Rachel's sister's little girls," Naomi said quietly. "There was an accident, and Rachel undertook to rear them."

Anna Ruth looked at Michael. "Isn't that *wonderbar*?"

"*Ja*." He shrugged. "*Wass* else could she have done?"

During the meal, their eyes frequently met, although Rachel struggled to keep her attention elsewhere. He made her nervous. *Fer wass?*

After supper, the men went to the barn to discuss the horse sale, but Moses lingered behind. He seemed intrigued with Annie and played with her while Rachel helped with the dishes. When Susan began to fuss, Rachel took her to the rocker in the living room. Moses followed, but hung back. Finally, he ventured to the stool beside Rachel. He seemed pensive. Then he faced her.

"You're not really Annie's *Mem*, *gel*?"

"*Vell*, I'm her *Mem*, now."

The boy nodded. "Her first *Mem* died, *gel*?"

"*Ja*. She was my sister."

He studied baby Susan. "Their *Pap* die, too?"

"*Ja*." Rachel was going to explain what had happened, but a vision of dark icy water gripped her mind, squeezed her heart, and constricted her throat.

For a time, Moses silently stared at the multi-colored braided rug at his feet. Then he sighed. "My Mama got sick when I was little. Lydia tells me about her, but I don't remember." Again he sighed. "Everyone else has a Mama, but it seems like I never had one."

The look on the little boy's face made tears burn the back of Rachel's eyes. This little guy was hurting. A desire to comfort him began to grow within her. She was taken completely by surprise when he stood up quickly and whirled to face her.

"Will you be my *Mem*, too?"

Rachel's lips parted. What could she say that would help him to understand? How, without hurting him, could she tell him his request was impossible? Excess moisture collected in his light-brown eyes, making the gold flecks sparkle; minute black slashes that she hadn't noticed before gave them depth. He swallowed, betraying how close to tears he was. Propping Susan in one arm, Rachel reached to hug the boy. His arms encircled her neck. It was *her* cheeks that suddenly became streaked with trails of salty droplets.

"The woman your Papa marries will be your Mama, but I'd love to be your Aunt Rachel."

"*Pap* says he's never gonna marry, again. I have lots of aunts. I want a *Mem*."

Her embrace tightened. Adjusting baby Susan to one side, she pulled the little boy into her lap. "Do you know what I do when I want something with all my heart?"

"*Wass*?"

"I pray. I tell Jesus what I want." She kissed the boy's forehead and noticed how gold highlights played on the crests of his wavy sandy hair. "After we ask Jesus for what we want, we must let it up to Him. He knows what is best for us."

Sitting straight, he eyed her. "How could it be best for

me not to have a *Mem*?"

She smiled. "You must wait for Jesus to answer your prayer. Sometimes it takes awhile. We must be patient. You have a good *Pap*. *Dank der gut* Man for him."

A man cleared his throat. Rachel looked up to meet the puzzled amber eyes of Michael Zook. Peter John stood in the doorway, his six-foot-frame towering over the man. Moses turned, saw his father, and slid from Rachel's lap.

"You ready to go home, Son?" Michael asked.

Shrugging, Moses went to the kitchen for his jacket and boots. Michael followed the boy from the house. Rachel strolled to a window, but tried to remain out of Michael's line of vision as she watched them climb into their gray carriage. She chewed her lip. What was the strange feeling that wriggled within her?

Excited over her cousin's visit, Liz Ann breezed into the kitchen, yanked off her boots and hung her cape on a hook. She whirled to see Rachel in the living room doorway, a smile dimpling the woman's rosy cheeks. Time had been kind to her. Liz Ann had expected her to look her thirty-three years, but Rachel was still youthful. Hurrying forward, Liz Ann hugged her. "It's so good to have you here! *Wie gehts?*"

Rachel laughed softly. "I'm overwhelmed with everyone's love. Did I hear a car?"

"*Ja.*" Liz Ann felt her anger rise, but stomped it into submission. "Eli Beiler has one. He used to keep owning it a secret—but not anymore."

"*Ach*! And he's the one you . . ."

"*Ja*, he is."

Rachel patted her shoulder. "He belongs to a good family. You must be patient. He'll settle down."

"How can I be sure?"

"Wayne and Henry had cars. It worried me, but they eventually got rid of them and joined the Church. My two youngest brothers also tried motor vehicles." She laughed softly. "So did one of my sisters!"

Ella skipped down the stairs. "Liz Ann is afraid of waiting too long and ending up a spinster."

The girl had meant no harm, but Liz Ann could tell the word "spinster" had gouged a deep furrow in Rachel's heart. In a letter, she had told Liz Ann that after losing Jonas for the second time, she had accepted her role and was trying to adjust to it. Rachel was so pretty, as well as sweet and kind. Liz Ann figured a man who was free and wasn't interested in her cousin would have to be mentally and emotionally deficient.

Rachel studied Liz Ann's face. "*Wass* are you thinking?"

Laughing, Liz Ann linked her arm in her cousin's. "Let's go up and see how my sisters have arranged our room."

Ella bounded up the stairs ahead of them. "We put a small cot near your bed for Annie, and there's room for the crib along the inside wall. Peter and Andrew will bring it up when we're ready to go to bed."

The room looked a bit crowded, but comfortable. A patchwork quilt, mostly in tones of blue and lavender, covered Rachel's bed. A small multi-colored design brightened Annie's cot. The little girl had accompanied them upstairs.

"Here's your bed, Annie," Liz Ann told her.

Smiling, the little girl moved to the cot and set her stuffed dog by her pillow. Liz Ann noticed that Annie's eyes were the same unusual gray as Rachel's. Her hair was dark, too, and the child's heart-shaped face and delicate features resembled her aunt's. Annie would easily be taken as Rachel's child.

"I have a big doggie at home," she told Liz Ann.

"What's his name?"

"Jack."

Liz Ann noticed Rachel's frown. "*Was is letz?*"

"Jack belongs to a drifter who is temporarily residing in Wayne's summer house. Annie has become so attached to the dog, I'm afraid she'll be devastated when Forest moves on."

"*Vell*," Liz Ann said. "You could get her a dog like Jack."

"*Ach*! That mutt weighs more than I do and eats heartier than Muddy Foot!"

Liz Ann laughed. "Maybe you could hitch him to a buggy."

"Girls," Naomi called up the stairway. "I have water hot for tea and the blueberry muffins are out of the oven."

"Let's go downstairs," Liz Ann said. "I always give the family a report on Emma's new twins."

On the third day of her visit, Rachel left her little girls sleeping and joined the ladies in the kitchen to help prepare breakfast.

Liz Ann smiled at her. "Eli is stopping by for me later this morning. Would you like to go with me to see the new Zook twins?"

"I'd love to, but Annie has been sniffling. I wouldn't want her to carry a virus to Emma's *Kinder*." A frown played around her mouth, but she struggled to cover her disappointment.

"Maybe next time."

Naomi looked pensive. "I was going to invite you to accompany the girls and me when we go into Millersburg for dress material." She looked concerned. "Since it's raining, you probably don't want to take Annie out."

"It would probably be wise to keep her in today."

Ella crossed the kitchen, a bouquet of silverware clutched in one hand. "You'll be here alone. Tim is going to the neighbor's to watch their young son. The other boys are going to auction with *Pap*."

Rachel smiled to put them at ease. "I'll start supper."

"*Un Wonderbar!*" Ella chirped, holding the silverware

up as though they formed a torch. "We have our own special maid."

"Ella, you naughty girl," Liz Ann said around a laugh.

The family gathered for morning Bible reading and prayer. Christopher read Scripture, then read prayers from the *Christenpflicht* (the prayer book). Afterward, the family left.

Naomi had told Rachel to relax and enjoy herself. Annie crawled into a dark-green armchair and opened the book Martha had given her. Baby Susan kicked and cooed on the blanket Rachel had spread on the floor. Sitting on the green couch, Rachel straightened the skirt of her gray dress and sighed. "The rest of the morning and most of the afternoon to do nothing!" She chuckled. How many times had she wondered what it would be like to have no chores to do? Propping her feet on a stool, she watched dust motes dance in a ray of sunlight.

Five minutes ticked by. Unused to idleness, Rachel began to fidget. Andrew had asked for chocolate chip cookies, but Naomi and the girls hadn't had time to mix up a batch. Leaving Susan blowing bubbles and making happy noises, Rachel went to the cupboards. She felt like a snoop and wondered if she was violating a trust; but when she quickly located the ingredients, her guilt leaped into oblivion.

She had to stop in the middle of her baking to change and feed Susan. When the baby fell asleep, Rachel put her on the couch with a chair propped against the cushions to form a crib.

Annie followed her to the kitchen. "Cookie, *Mem, gel?*"

"*Ja.*" Boosting her to the counter, she let the little girl choose her own treat.

"Me help."

"You can help Mama put the cookies into the crock when they cool." She usually gave the child a simple task while she was baking, but knowing she would have to wipe scattered flour from the counter and floor, and it would soon be dinnertime, she set her at the table with a paper and crayons.

By eleven-thirty, the cookies were put away and the counter clean. Naomi had left a pot of vegetable soup for Rachel to warm for the noon meal. Rachel peeped into the pot. There was too much for her and Annie.

A horse and carriage stopped at the gate. "*Ach!* Visitors." Rachel brushed a smudge of flour from her skirt and made sure her hair was neatly under her cap. Remembering that she sometimes ended up with a splotch of flour on her face, she wiped it quickly with the back of her apron.

Michael Zook climbed from the driver's seat and headed up the walk. Her heart lurched. Her palms moist, she gripped the doorknob. Why was she suddenly nervous? It wasn't her nature. Taking a deep breath, she opened the door. "Hello, Mr. Zook. *Kom ann* in."

Stepping inside, he glanced around and sniffed. The sound was barely audible, but Rachel was used to the way men honed in on baked treats. She hid her grin by turning to pick up Annie.

"Is Christopher about?" Michael sidestepped apprehensively.

"He and the older boys went to auction. Naomi and the girls are shopping."

"*Vell* . . ."

"I expect Naomi back shortly. If you'd like to wait, I'll fix you a cup of coffee and some chocolate chip cookies."

"*Vell* . . ."

Rachel had to strangle a laugh. The choice between leaving quickly to prevent possible gossip or giving in and accepting the treat was giving him an inner battle. She could make it easier by offering to put some cookies into a bag for him to take home, but something prodded her to leave the decision to him.

"They smell tempting." He unfastened his jacket, signaling that his stomach had won the debate.

"I've heated soup and there's plenty."

"*Vell* . . ." He rested his hands on the back of a chair.

Ladling steaming soup into bowls, Rachel set them on the table and poured coffee into two mugs. Figuring Michael's appetite matched her brothers, she piled a dozen cookies on a plate and set them near his cup. He took a seat at the table. Rachel waited for him to say the amen after silent grace.

After eating, he sipped his steaming brew and eyed the cookies, but he kept his fingers wrapped around his cup. Smiling, Rachel passed the plate.

He helped himself. "*Gross Dank.*"

She offered one to Annie.

The little girl's eyes sparkled. "*Denke ou, Mem.*"

Michael slowly ate one as though savoring the taste. Swallowing the last bite, he faced her. "*Es war wonderbar gut.*"

Something strange and different fluttered within her. She felt light and young. What did this area and its people have that was lacking in her district back home?

An uncomfortable silence stretched between them. Rachel's thoughts scrambled through her brain in search of something to say. She had never been tongue-tied before. What was the peculiar nervous sensation that crept into her bones? Embarrassment opened her lips. "Moses said he had an older sister named Lydia. How old is she?"

Michael smiled. "Twelve, but she seems much older." His smile faded and a winsome expression took its place. "My wife died when Lydia was seven. I guess the responsibility of being the oldest of my four *Kinder* matured her early.."

"Most Amish widowers would have remarried by now."

He laid his half-eaten cookie near his cup and sighed. "I'll never remarry."

"Never is a long time."

His eyes snapped to her face, and his features became a kaleidoscope of expressions.

Heat seared her cheeks. *What should I say or do now?*

CHAPTER SIXTEEN

Rachel bit her tongue. If only she could retract her statement. Michael looked disturbed; then dismay settled on his face. His changing expressions seemed humorous, and without warning, a laugh bubbled into her throat.

Michael shrugged. "I guess everyone has a right to voice their opinion."

"*Ja*, but not another one who says she'll never marry."

He finished off his cookie in two bites and stood quickly. "I'll *kom* by to see Christopher tomorrow." Grabbing his jacket, he jerked the door open and went out before he had his arms in the garment.

Remaining at the table, Rachel stared at his half-empty coffee cup. She shook her head. Was just the thought of marriage so terrifying to him? *Fer wass?*

Annie slipped from her chair and went to the window. "Where Mike go, *Mem*?"

"He . . . had work to do." A thought seized her mind and made her gasp. "Does Michael think I'm hunting for a husband?"

"*Wass?*" Turning, Annie peered curiously at her.

Realizing she had spoken aloud, she laughed. It sounded more like a giggle. *Am I getting senile?*

The little girl turned back to the window. "Horsey go fast!"

"*Ja*. He did." *So did Michael. Fer wass?*

"Mike have doggie, *Mem*?"

"I don't know." Still feeling the sting of his hasty departure, Rachel collected the soiled dishes and wiped the

199

crumbs from the tablecloth. Not wishing to answer Naomi's questions or suffer Ella's teasing, she washed the items and put them away. Grabbing a mop, she scrubbed every spot from the vinyl as though to eradicate Michael's having been there. *Why can't I erase his presence from my mind?*

Several times that afternoon, she relived Michael's visit and wondered how she could have better handled their conversation. The next time, she would steer away from mentioning his wife or future relationships. *The next time*, ricochetted through her brain. Would there be another time? Why did it seem to matter?

She was still pondering when Naomi and the girls came home.

Ella entered the house ahead of the others, her green eyes twinkling with mischief. "You had a visitor, *gel*?"

Rachel blinked. How had the news of Michael's visit traveled so far so fast?

The girl grinned. "Your hesitation makes me suspicious." She sang her words teasingly.

"*Vell*," she said, testing to see how much the girl knew. "*Wass* makes you think I had a visitor?"

A laugh bubbled from Ella. "Buggy wheel tracks in the fresh snow and many, many hoofprints near the gate." Her grin remained. "Besides, there was horse manure out front."

Rachel swallowed a gasp. Michael had been in such a hurry, he hadn't even checked to see if his horse had dropped something before he raced away! What had spurred the man to negligence?

"You had a gentleman caller, *gel*?"

Rachel tried to act nonchalant. "Mr. Zook was here to see your father about the horse he's buying from him."

"Ha! So it really was Michael!" Ella tossed her head as though she were pleased with her detective work. "As many hoofprints as there were out there, it must have taken him a long time to discover *Pap* wasn't here."

"*Vell*, I . . ." Rachel felt foolish. Why had she gotten herself into a position to allow this ten-year-old to corner her?

Packages in their arms, Martha and Anna Ruth came thumping and bumping into the house. Naomi followed. Rachel opened her mouth to mention the cookies to keep Ella from misleading the family, but the girl beat her.

"Guess *wass*?" Ella said loudly around a hearty chuckle. "Rachel had a gentleman caller."

Martha smiled. "Who?"

Heat burned spots on Rachel's cheeks. She opened her mouth to explain, but her throat had gone dry. Reading their expectant expressions, she shook her head. "Christopher had a caller. I thought you would be home any minute, so I invited him to wait."

"Mr. Zook visited with her all afternoon," Ella spouted.

"No!" Rachel swallowed. "He only ate a bite, then he had to hurry home."

Annie had been listening wide-eyed to the conversation. "Mike's horsey wun home fass!"

Laughter eased the building tension and the ladies turned to hang up their coats and take off their boots.

"Martha, get potatoes from the cellar," Naomi said. Ella, set the table. Anna Ruth, you can scrape and slice carrots." Digging into a bag of groceries, she withdrew a package of ground meat. "I'm going to mix a meat loaf."

Thankful the attention had shifted to preparations for supper, Rachel moved to the cabinet drawer to count silverware.

Peter John brought Liz Ann home. Her expression told Rachel that she had something to talk to her about. If the topic weren't personal, Liz Ann would have spoken in the presence of the others. The fact that she hadn't created trepidation within Rachel.

Supper seemed to take forever and clean-up even

longer. Finally, Rachel put the little girls to bed and faced Liz Ann. "You want to talk, *gel*?"

Going to the bedroom door, Liz Ann peeped out, then returned to sit on Rachel's bed. "Lydia Zook came to see Leah and me today. She said her father had been acting peculiarly."

Rachel felt peculiar, too, but wasn't going to admit it—at least until she figured out what was going on with her thoughts. Liz Ann seemed to be waiting for her to say something, so she obliged. "Did the girl say what was bothering her father?"

Liz Ann removed her prayer cap and her long black hair tumbled down her back. "She said he went to see my father and returned acting funny." Her green eyes probed Rachel's face. "I know Papa wasn't here, and that Mama went shopping with my sisters. Did Michael show up?"

Rachel flipped her hand, acting more nonchalant than she felt. "He stopped in. I said no one was here but me. I invited him in for coffee because I'd just baked cookies. He gobbled a couple, then hurried away." Her explanation sounded funny, even to her, but it was as close to the truth as it could be.

Liz Ann grinned. "Yesterday, he told Leah that he'd met you and that he thought you were a fine lady. Moses sure likes you!"

"He's a dear little boy."

"*Ja*, but troublesome."

Rachel stared at her. "*Wass* do you mean? He was a perfect little gentleman."

"Hum." Liz Ann looked pensive. "The way he talks about you upsets Lydia."

"*Fer wass*?"

"I don't know. The girl has been so sweet and works so hard for her family. Michael depends heavily on her."

"What happened to his wife?"

"Cancer, I think. He doesn't talk much about her illness." She sighed. "He's enshrined the memory of her and hasn't shown interest in any other woman. Lydia says he'll never marry, because no one can ever take her mother's place in his heart."

"*Ach*." What was the canyon that yawned within her? Rachel had never felt loneliness so acutely before. She frowned. Was she homesick for Jonas? That part of her life was over. By the time Annie and Susan were raised, Jonas would be married to someone else, again! Feeling fingers on her arm, she looked up to find Liz Ann studying her. She smiled to camouflage the emotional upheaval that was gyrating her insides.

"We can talk about anything that bothers you." Liz Ann's tone overflowed with compassion. "Aren't we close friends?"

Rachel hugged her. "We are." She felt like Liz Ann's older sister. That was good, she supposed. One thing she knew for sure, she must not permit her thoughts to dwell on Michael Zook. He was handsome, gentle, and kind. She could like him—maybe a lot—and he had made it clear that he wasn't available.

Liz Ann yawned as she reached for her hairbrush. Rachel undressed and slipped a plain white nightgown over her head. She felt ravaged by the day and could not understand why.

"Annie seems to be over her sniffles. Maybe you can go with me to Emma's on Friday." Yawning, again, Liz Ann slipped under her quilt. "I'll see you at breakfast."

Usually, right after saying her prayers, Rachel would drift into peaceful sleep. Tonight, she lay awake, staring at the ceiling. A strong February wind whistled through the pine outside the window. Was it the prelude to another snowstorm? Spring would be here, soon. The tobacco plants that Naomi had placed in planters in the house were growing like weeds. The Lapp family would plant them outside when the weather permitted. Rachel frowned.

Did she believe in growing tobacco? Amish in Ohio didn't grow it. Her family had never discussed the crop. *I don't even like the smell of it.* She could hate the plant if she liked, but she didn't feel she should judge the families in Lancaster County who used it as a cash crop.

Why am I thinking about tobacco? Her thoughts spiraled back to Michael. Was she trying to fill her mind with other things to keep from thinking about him? Why would she have to?

Vowing she was going to sleep, she turned to face the wall. Michael's smile lingered as warmth remains in the bricks after the sun has gone down. Concentrating on forgetting him only made the remembrance more vivid. *I'm losing my mind,* she thought, but the feeling in her heart warned her that danger of an emotional conflict lurked around the corner. Eventually, she slept, but Michael haunted her dreams. In the morning, she was more tired than when she had gone to bed. *If this is what it is like to be attracted to a man, loving one must be horrid!*

Dragging herself out of bed, she donned her deep-rose dress. Thank goodness her little girls were still asleep. She needed a cup of strong black coffee. Naomi and the girls were bustling around the kitchen. Breakfast was soon served and eaten; before the dishes were washed, a buggy stopped at the side of the house.

"It's Michael," Andrew called, going out to meet the man.

Rachel's heart had quickened at the sound of the man's name. She touched her face. Her fingers felt cold against her heated cheeks. *This is ridiculous!* The door closed. Assuming Andrew was outside with the man, she turned. Michael had stepped inside. Their gazes locked.

"Good morning, Mister Zook," Rachel said, amazed at how controlled her voice sounded.

"Good morning," he echoed. "*Un wie Machts?*"

"Fine, *Gross Dank.*" The formality between them was

staggering! What had happened to the easy friendship they had seemed to be cultivating yesterday, before he took off like a scared puppy?

Christopher came from the parlor. Apparently not noticing the strange tension between her and Michael, he grabbed his jacket. "You decide to take the two piglets with you today?"

"*Ja.*" Michael chuckled. "My Andrew said he wants to take the responsibility of raising them."

"Moses seemed to be interested."

Michael's smile waned. "Moses . . . isn't . . ." Apparently choosing not to finish his statement, he shrugged. "I'll take the pigs today and come for the horse tomorrow."

Nodding, Christopher yanked on his barn shoes and went out. Michael followed, but turned at the door to glance at Rachel. He moved his lips slightly as though he wanted to say something; instead, he gave a slight nod of his sandy head. She returned his nod. It was as though they had communicated without words. She knew he wanted to talk and figured he would be in later to do so. That had never happened with Jonas. *Fer wass?*

"I need to go to Abe Zimmerman's this morning, Rachel," Naomi said. "His wife is ailing and there are three little ones to watch."

"I'll go with you to help."

"*Ach,* there isn't that much to do, dear. Besides, Annie and Susan are still asleep." Naomi looked pensive. "It would be a bigger help if you stayed here and started dinner. I probably won't be back before noon." She made a list of what she intended to fix and where to find the ingredients.

Rachel watched her walk down the lane, the breeze whipping her long skirt; then she turned back to the quiet house. Liz Ann had left for Emma Zook's, the older boys were in the barn, and the rest of the Lapp *Kinder* were in school. Rachel wondered what she would do all morning.

When she heard a buggy leaving, she assumed Michael was gone. When the door opened, she turned.

"Hello," Michael said. He had his straw hat in his hand and his jacket unfastened. "I'd like to talk to you about Moses."

She smiled. "He's a sweet little boy."

"*Ja*, but..."

"We can talk better over coffee."

"*Viel Dank*." Moving forward, he sat on a kitchen chair. "Moses is a good boy, but I have a problem with him."

She retrieved the coffee cups. "What sort of problem?" Filling his cup, she placed it before him.

Michael sighed. "He won't cooperate, yet he doesn't disobey. He neglects his work in school, but I know he's smart. He draws away from the rest of the family and just sits quietly, staring at nothing in particular. I don't know if he sometimes doesn't hear when we speak to him—or if he doesn't want to answer."

Wondering why he was explaining private family matters to her, Rachel took her chair. "Is there something I can do?"

"*Vell*..." He took a few sips of coffee, then faced her. "Moses says he wants you to teach him his numbers."

An unexpected thrill raced through her veins, and she nearly splashed coffee into her saucer. "I'd be happy to try."

"I can bring him over each morning for about an hour or so before I drive him to school." He withdrew into silence and traced a block in the tablecloth with his finger. "I'll have to bring Miriam. She isn't in school, yet."

Rachel smiled. "Naomi is helping neighbors and her girls are in school, so if my girls wake, you'll have to watch them while I work with Moses."

Chuckling, he agreed. Their eyes met and a friendly trust began to bud. "Your eyes pick up the blue color from my shirt, and shimmer like bluish-silver pearls."

"Oh," she whispered. Warmth began inside her, then spread like tentacles until it filled her. She knew her cheeks were pink. He smiled, and joy showered her.

Days seemed to fly by. Moses studied each lesson and blossomed with Rachel's teaching and nurturing. After each session, Michael would leave sweet little Miriam with Rachel when he drove Moses to school. He would stop on his way back through for the little girl. Usually he stayed for coffee and a baked treat. Rachel's fondness for the man swiftly matured into adoration. Each day before he arrived, her heart beat faster and her pulse throbbed in her temples. A new excitement bubbled within her; enchanting dreams invaded her sleep, and happiness washed over her with the morning sun. Was this friendship—or the beginning of something more complex? *What will I do when I have to go back to Ohio?* The thought made her heart cramp.

February tumbled into March. Rachel had extended her stay, but felt she would have to leave before too long. The middle of the month was breezy, but sun streamed through the window and bathed her in warmth. Michael had been there, but had taken Moses to school.

Miriam came from the parlor. "I think Annie's awake." She placed a small foot on the bottom step. "May I go up and help her dress? I'll make sure she doesn't fall down the stairs."

"Annie would like that." Rachel smiled as she watched the five-year-old vanish up the stairs. Buggy wheels rumbled up the lane, and her heart raced. Taking a deep calming breath, she strolled to the porch.

Michael returned her smile. On his way up the path, he studied the sky. "Good plowing day. If it doesn't rain, I'll be able to finish the corner field." Entering the kitchen, he paused, sniffed, and glanced around until he saw the cherry coffee cake on the counter. His eyes met hers, and he chuckled. "Do I get a slice with my coffee?"

"*Ja.*"

When they were seated, he reached for her hand. As his fingers clasped hers, heat radiated up her arm and lodged in her chest.

He smiled, and a luster crept into his eyes. "If I *kom* by this evening, will you go for a drive with me?"

Her heart was screaming, "*Ja.* Oh, *ja.*" But, not wanting to seem overanxious, she spoke slowly. "That would be nice, if one of Naomi's girls can watch my *Kinder.*"

The rest of the day seemed to drag, although Rachel felt as though she were floating. As the time for Michael's arrival approached, her nerves tingled. In all her thirty-three years, she had never experienced this elation. When she was finally on the carriage seat beside him, she could almost hear her heart beating. Could he hear it, too?

Michael turned Luke, his carriage horse, down a secluded lane. Leaning back, he reached for her hand. "Things have happened fast for me, Rachel. I care deeply for you."

Her blood raced, but her brain warned her to be careful. "But, you said . . ." *This man had vowed he wouldn't remarry, and I don't want to appear presumptuous.* "You told me there'd never be another woman."

"*Vell* . . ." He cleared his throat. "That was before I got to know you." He turned to her and gently took her into his arms. "I've wanted to—" His gaze lowered to her mouth and lingered there.

Rachel's breath caught. Was he thinking about kissing her? She wanted him to, but didn't know how to show him without seeming bold. As though her body had a will of its own, she leaned slightly toward him. It was the only invitation he needed. The next thing she knew, she was in his arms, his warm lips caressing hers. The Earth seemed to whirl faster. Her heart leaped to the top of the highest mountain, carrying her with it. She wanted to be in Michael's arms forever. *So! This is what my sisters meant!*

When he pulled back slightly, the flecks in his light-brown eyes sparkled like shards of gold, and his gaze was misty. "I love you, Rachel."

"I love you, too," she whispered.

"Does my having four *Kinder* bother you?"

"Oh no. Wass about my two?"

His smile engulfed them. "Six *Kinder* make a perfect family, *gel*?"

"*Vell* . . . Maybe . . . to begin with." When she realized the implication of her statement, she covered her blazing cheeks with her fingers.

Catching her hands in his, he laughed, and the space between them seemed to be electrified with the joy that encompassed them. "Something tells me that we're going to have a big family."

"But, you haven't asked . . ."

"*Ach*! So I haven't. Will you?"

A woman doesn't get a proposal for marriage every day, and she wanted to hear him say the words. Feeling as giddy as a school girl, she touched his cheek with a finger and blinked up at him. "Will I *wass*?"

He hugged her. "Rachel Kay Lapp, will you be my wife?"

"Oh, *ja*. Forever and ever."

Liz Ann sat rigid on the passenger seat of Eli's Buick, her fingers curled into tight fists in her lap. Weeks ago, he had promised to sell his vehicle. When he stopped for her that morning, she reluctantly got in for the ride to Emma's. It was to be the very last time. She hoped she had made that clear.

Taking several deep breaths, she tried to relax. She didn't want Emma's family to witness her wrath—or to become aware of her aching heart.

"When do you want me to *kom* for you?" Eli asked.

She faced him, knowing green sparks danced in her eyes, but did nothing to stop them. "Eli Beiler, you've had it."

He turned on his innocent expression. "What time?"

"Your time is up." Getting out, she slammed the car door. The immature act made her feel rotten, but she was through talking, pleading, and waiting.

She was still breathing hard when she entered Emma's kitchen. Partially from anger, partially from fighting tears. Five *Kinder* peered at her, then silently hurried into the parlor. Did her emotions show that much? She closed her eyes and asked the Lord to help calm her.

Emma came out of the first-floor bedroom where she had been resting. "*Ach! Was is letz?*"

Tears pooled in Liz Ann's eyes. "I . . ." Against her will, droplets escaped and trailed down her cheeks. "I told Eli we were finished because of his car."

"*Ach.*" Moving to the stove, Emma put on a kettle of water. "We're going to drink a lot of tea this morning." Getting three cups out of the cupboard, she clattered them to the counter.

Leah came from the living room, her eyes red and swollen.

Liz Ann moved quickly to her. "*Was is letz?*"

CHAPTER SEVENTEEN

Leah bit her trembling lower lip and sniffed. Liz Ann turned to Emma for an explanation.

Emma sighed. "Last night, Leah told Peter John he wasn't to call anymore."

"So that was what was ailing him when he got home!" Liz Ann sighed. "He went to bed early and, according to Andrew and Philip, he tossed all night. This morning, he got up and left without eating breakfast."

Retrieving the sugar bowl, Emma clunked it onto the table. "Leah's going home."

Liz Ann glanced at Leah. "To Mercer County?"

Leah nodded.

Emma counted out three tea bags and put one in each cup, their strings dangling over the sides like tails. "The babies are five weeks old." She eyed her sister. "I wish you'd stay one more week. By then, with the help of Amamda and Malinda, I'll be able to manage."

Leah agreed.

"Your leg seems to have healed well," Liz Ann said.

"*Ja!*" Chuckling, Emma kicked. "I felt so free after getting rid of that cast. Now, exercise has limbered and strengthened my leg. I feel great." One of the babies began to cry, then the other twin screamed. Emma rolled her hazel eyes and her dimples deepened. "It's a good thing I feel good, *gel?*"

The babies quieted, signaling that Amanda and Malinda had answered their wails.

Leah turned to Liz Ann. "If you're smart, you'll go to

Mercer County with me."

An image of Samuel Miller crowded into Liz Ann's thoughts. If she went home with Leah, would Samuel think she had come to spend time with him? Would she inadvertently hurt him? She massaged her temples. Might she fall for Samuel on the rebound? Even so, leaving for a time might be a good idea. "Rachel Kay will be returning to Ohio in a week or two."

"Then you're free to go with me. Eli has to realize how serious you are."

Liz Ann didn't want to hurt Eli, and she hated to see Peter John hurting the way he was, but Leah was right. Before she changed her mind, she said, "I'll go."

"Good." Leah sniffed, then reached for a tissue to blow her nose. "I wrote to Amos Yoder and said I'd be glad to welcome his calling when I get home." A tear escaped and made a shiny wet ribbon down her face.

Liz Ann choked hers back.

Emma looked concerned. "I hope you ladies don't act too hastily. Eli and Peter John are just taking longer to settle down than most."

"I can't stand it any more, Emma!" Leah said.

Liz Ann would follow suit, although her heart refused to cooperate.

Emma poured boiling water into each cup. "It looks like Rachel Kay is making out in the love department."

Leah's eyes widened. "*Wass?*"

"*Vell*, Christopher told Jacob that Michael has been making trips over to Lapps, nearly every day." A smile dimpled her rounded cheeks. "He says Michael looks happy for the first time in years."

"*Un wonderbar!*" Sitting at the table, Leah sipped her tea.

Liz Ann was happy for her cousin, too. "Michael brings Moses over each morning. He has been having trouble in school."

"*Ach!*" Emma waved her hand. "He's a smart little boy."

"*Ja*, but he seems troubled."

Leah straightened. "*Fer wass?*"

"I don't know. Neither does Michael. Moses has taken a liking to Rachel. She has been tutoring him and he is doing very well." Liz Ann laughed. "Naomi goes over to Zimmerman's each morning to help the old lady. Ella, Anna Ruth, and Martha are in school, so Michael stays to take care of Annie and Susan while Rachel is occupied with Moses."

Emma chuckled. "I told you Moses was a smart little guy."

Leah shook her head. "Michael is against remarriage. He said no woman can take his late wife's place."

"*Ach!* Just give it time."

"*Vell*," Liz Ann hated gossip, but she enjoyed being the bearer of glad tidings. "Michael has changed his mind since he met Rachel. My cousin told me that he asked her to marry."

"*Un wonderbar!*" Leah said, sniffing again and reaching for another tissue. She eyed Liz Ann. "It's time we find gentleman who are settled down, too."

There were light footsteps on the porch, then a fist pounded on the door. Emma got up to open it.

"Oh, Aunt Emma," Lydia wailed, rushing in and flinging herself into the woman's arms. Her eyes were red and her face blotched, betraying many tears.

Leah moved closer. "*Was is letz?*"

Liz Ann was on her feet, too, wondering if something had happened to Michael or one of his children. Lydia was usually composed and quiet. Liz Ann had never known of her to become hysterical, and the girl should be in school.

"Oh, Aunt Emma!" Lydia cried. "*Wass* am I going to do?"

"*Kom* now, dear girl, nothing could be this bad." Emma

tried to calm Lydia's frenzy.

"It's worse!" Sobs racked the twelve-year-old's slight frame. "Our life is ruined!"

Patting Lydia's shoulder, Emma guided her to a chair. "Has there been an accident?"

Lydia shook her head.

"Is anyone hurt?"

"We all will be!"

Emma retrieved another cup. "Some nice hot tea will settle you, then we'll talk about this terrible trouble."

"I can't just drink tea! I have to do something to stop him!"

Emma stared at the girl. "Stop whom, dear?"

"*Pap.*" Another flood of tears streamed down her face.

Malinda came from the living room with one of the new babies. Amanda followed with the other. Several of Emma's younger children quietly peered around furniture and doorways at the weeping girl.

Setting the unwanted cup of tea in front of Lydia, Emma sat beside her. "What's your Papa doing that distresses you?"

"He wants to marry her!"

Emma patted Lydia's hand. "And you're against it?"

"Oh, *ja*! She would move in and take over."

"*Vell*," Emma said softly. "Wouldn't it be wonderful to share the responsibilities with someone older?"

Lydia shook her head. "I don't need some woman taking over and telling me to do things her way."

Liz Ann pulled out a chair and sat on the other side of the stricken girl. "Rachel is one of the kindest persons I know, Lydia. I'm sure she wouldn't want to shove you aside to do things her way."

"It won't be the same."

"Sometimes changes are good. Everyone loves Rachel."

"Vell I don't!" Lydia struck the table with her fist. "This is all Moses' fault!" A new kind of determination shone in her expression. "I'm not going to let *Pap* make a big mistake."

Liz Ann sighed. All was not going to be utopia for her cousin, either. She searched her mind for something that would convince Lydia of Rachel's genuineness. "Your *Pap* loves Rachel."

Lydia drew her lips taut. "It's her sweet, face and those cute dimples that attracted *Pap!*" Her fingers curled into fists. "He says her gray eyes are like pearls and shimmer so clearly that he can see himself in them." She pushed the tea farther away. "I wish she was six feet tall, instead of so tiny and delicate! *Pap* says she makes him feel like a man."

Emma rested a hand on the girl's clenched fist. "You should be happy your Papa has found someone to love."

Bits of blue fire seemed to spark in Lydia's eyes. "I hope something awful happens to her pretty face!"

Emma's eyes widened. "*Ach!*"

Liz Ann cringed. What would Rachel do about Lydia's hostility? Would she marry Michael and hope for the best—or would she go back to Ohio and stay, hoping the girl would soften? Would Lydia mature and her faith deepen—or would she create a wedge between Rachel and Michael that would ruin their relationship? Liz Ann prayed Rachel would not be hurt, again.

Liz Ann shoved her new deep-purple dress into her suitcase and snapped the lock. Rachel had left for Ohio the last week in March. She wanted to put things in order before she came back to marry Michael. He hadn't told her how extensive Lydia's resentment was. He felt that in time the girl would accept Rachel and learn to love her. Moses was elated. He had confessed to his father that not having a mother had been what had been eating away at him. Practically overnight, he had changed into a loving, happy little boy—except for being troubled over Lydia's hostility toward Rachel.

Sighing, Liz Ann took her bags downstairs. Her parents were concerned about her trip to New Willmington, but had said nothing to discourage her or to convince her to remain. She hugged them and her siblings, all but Peter John. He wasn't there. Eli hadn't come, either. Did they think her and Leah's leaving had been an idle threat?

With a heavy heart, she made her way to the waiting hired van. Matthew Zimmerman had already picked up Leah. Too close to tears to speak, she nodded and took the back seat beside her. Leah's eyes were swollen and red. Liz Ann knew hers were, too. She almost jumped from the vehicle and ran back to the house. What was she going to do without Eli?

Every mile carried them farther from the men they loved; every minute added to Liz Ann's misery. Elizabeth Miller had packed them a lunch, and Naomi had put in a box of fruit and cupcakes, but neither Liz Ann nor Leah could eat.

The trip was long and exhausting. When the car finally stopped at Jonah Miller's, Liz Ann was tempted to stay put and ride back to Lancaster County, but Mattie opened the door and hurried down the path.

"Welcome home, Leah, dear," she said. "Your old room is ready." She smiled at Liz Ann. "It's good that you could come with my sister-in-law. We're so glad to have you."

Liz Ann accepted the woman's proffered hand. "Hello. *Wie gehts?*"

"*Kom ann* in. I have soup on." Her smile broadened. "You should see how little Jonathan has grown. He sure is his *Pap's* joy." She laughed. "And mine."

"How's *Mem* and *Pap*?" Leah asked.

"Doing fine, but asking every few minutes when you'll be here."

Liz Ann remembered how the inability to conceive had made Mattie bitter. When the woman finally became pregnant, she had prayed and had begun to change. Now, she was a pleasant, compassionate woman.

After greeting elderly Rachel and Jonah, Leah's parents, Liz Ann was presented with one-month-old Jonathan. His little fists were tucked under his double chin as he slept. When he woke, he opened his blue eyes and looked around. Liz Ann touched the blond fuzz on the top of his nearly bald head.

"I hear Emma's twins have lots of hair," Mattie said.

"*Ja*." Leah filled the family in on the new little Zooks.

Jonathan came in, the joy of fatherhood illuminating his face. "Mattie and I will have to hurry if we're going to catch up with my sister."

Mattie threw up her hands. "I love one baby. I'd like several, but Emma has nine!"

Jonathan patted the top of her head. "Nine too many?"

She grinned at him, her cheeks glowing pink. "*Vell, neh*."

An hour later, Liz Ann followed Leah to her bedroom. She opened her suitcase to arrange her clothing on the hooks. Leah had explained the dress code of her district, so Liz Ann had made a purple dress and a dark-blue one and left her pastels at home.

Leah looked out her window. "I see Samuel's light is on."

Joining her, Liz Ann saw a glimmer across the field. "Was that Elam's house?"

"*Ja*."

"Did Elizabeth watch it from here, before she and Elam married?"

Leah chuckled. "She probably would have, but the corn was high when she was here and cut off most of the view."

While she watched, the light went out. "It isn't nine o'clock, yet. Does Samuel go to bed so early?"

"*Ach*, no." Leah patted Liz Ann's shoulder. "He knows

you were coming. He would have given you a chance to get settled, but he's probably on his way over."

Mixed feelings muddled Liz Ann's brain. If she was going to get over Eli, seeing Samuel would be a good way to start. She watched as his buggy came up the lane and stopped in front of the house. Moonlight turned his carriage to a dark-orange-gold. Another buggy came up the lane from the opposite direction, pulled in, and stopped beside Samuel's. Amos Yoder climbed from the driver's seat. Liz Ann laughed softly. "You have company, too."

Leah sighed. "I'd rather not entertain, but I promised I'd see him."

The girls stood at the top of the stairs, listening as Mattie invited the young men inside. The older folks had gone to the *Dawdy Haus* and to bed.

"Leah!" Mattie called. "You girls have company."

Liz Ann entered the living room ahead of Leah. Samuel sat on the couch, Amos on a wooden rocker opposite him. Both men stood. Samuel's blond hair gleamed in the light from the oil lamp. His azure eyes twinkled expectantly as he met Liz Ann's gaze. Amos's hair was a shade lighter than Samuel's; his green eyes were on Leah.

Liz Ann glanced around the room. "Where are Jonathan and Mattie?"

"*Vell* . . ." Samuel waved a hand. "They decided to sit in the *Dawdy Haus.*"

His innocent expression didn't fool Liz Ann. She was too used to Eli's. *Be on guard*, she warned.

Amos moved to Leah. "Why don't we go for a ride."

Leah smiled. "Let's all go for a walk."

"That sounds all right to me." Samuel guided Liz Ann toward the outside door.

Leah and Amos followed. Samuel walked faster than Amos, signaling to Liz Ann that he wanted to be alone with her. She figured there was no harm in socializing, for the country road wasn't a private lane. His hand found hers.

Gently she pulled her fingers away. "Samuel, I don't want you to get the idea that I am free."

"Are you promised?"

"Not exactly, but . . ."

He chuckled. It was a warm rich sound that invited companionship. "Any fish that isn't caught is fair game."

Liz Ann sighed. "Don't say I didn't warn you."

Grinning, he shrugged. "Ever since Elam's wedding, I've wanted to get to know you better."

"*Vell* . . . we can be friends."

She and Samuel rounded a curve which cut off Leah and Amos's view. Grasping her hand, Samuel pulled Liz Ann into the shadow of a large apple tree.

"Wait!" Liz Ann pulled free. Smiling, she endeavored to act casual. "There isn't a hook through my gills, but there's one stuck in my heart. If I get over Eli, it will take time."

He gently touched her cheek. "I'll wait."

The other couple caught up, and Leah said that it was time to turn back. After a few minutes of silent strolling, she glanced at Amos. "How's Elsie?"

He shrugged. "She's doing all right, I guess."

"Elsie likes Amos," Samuel said.

Amos looked at Liz Ann. "You remind me of her. She has a sweet heart-shaped face, black wavy hair, and green eyes. You could pass for cousins."

She turned to Samuel. "Why don't you call on her?"

He chuckled. "She's another fish with a hook stuck in her heart." He poked Amos. "All you'd have to do was reel her in."

"It's not funny." Amos grew quiet.

Liz Ann watched him from the corner of her eye. Did the man have deeper feelings for Elsie than he was admitting?

Holmes County. Mark Lapp, Rachel's youngest brother,

retrieved the can of kerosene he'd left on her hearth for convenience. Carting the fuel to the first-story bedroom, he filled the lamp on Rachel's dresser. He'd come over each evening to light a couple of lamps, then returned before going to bed to put them out. That way, no one knew his sister's house was unoccupied.

Rosy finished mopping Rachel's kitchen vinyl. "Make sure you fill all the lamps, Mark."

"*Ja.*" He sighed. He didn't need Rosy to tell him what to do. She was the one who had wasted energy cleaning a gleaming floor!

Sara Kate carried a still-steaming pie to the counter. "All is ready for Rachel's home-coming, *Mem.*" She rolled her eyes heavenward. "Even Jonas seems glad that she's returning."

Mark took the can of kerosene to the living room and filled the lamp by the window and the one on the small table by the couch.

"*Kom ann*, Mark!" Rosy fidgeted by the kitchen door. "We want to be gone when Rachel arrives, so she'll have time to settle without feeling she must entertain."

He needed to fill the upstairs lamps. He supposed he could do that after supper when he came over to welcome Rachel home. Gripping the handle of the kerosene can, he wondered if he should leave it or take it with him.

"Are you *koming*?" Rosy sounded impatient.

The can looked ugly. Mark knew his sister would not appreciate his letting it where it was in plain view. Feeling rushed, he lifted the fabric-covered box near the fireplace and set the can under it. I'll put it away later—after I fill the remaining lamps. He followed Rosy and Sara Kate from the cottage. Prissy scampered ahead. With a wave, he climbed into his black buggy and turned his horse toward home. Visions of his lovely wife, his infant son, and the scrumptious supper that awaited captured his mind. His heart rejoicing, he whistled a few bars of *How Great*

Thou Art, a song an Englischer friend had taught him.

Rachel Kay had fought dismay the entire way home, but her joy mounted as she thought about returning to Lancaster County and becoming Michael's wife. The Lord had graciously intervened to keep her from marrying Jonas and was blessing her with a wonderful future.

The car stopped by her gate. Home looked good, too. She had missed her siblings and their families. "We're home, Annie." She grasped the little girl's hand for the trek to the porch, then jostled baby Susan as she turned the key in the lock and entered her kitchen. Rosy and Sara Kate must have been there. The room sparkled from scrubbing; a fresh apple pie sat on the counter, and a delicious aroma issued from the oven. Annie stood beside her, and she cradled Susan in her arms. Still, the cottage seemed empty.

I miss Michael. She longed to rush back to him, but she must explain things to her family and get her house in order. When all was ready, she would move back to Lancaster County to marry the man she loved. With the Lord's help, they could overcome Lydia's negative reaction.

"Where's Jack, *Mem*?" Annie peered under the table; then racing into the living room, she peeped behind the chairs.

Forest Grant had probably moved on long ago. How was she going to tell Annie that the dog was gone? Would the promise of moving to Miriam's house be enough to solace her?

Susan was still asleep, so Rachel put her in the crib. When she came back into the kitchen, she noticed a piece of paper on the counter. Rosy must have left last minute instructions. Smiling, she unfolded the paper, then a frown slowly captured her expression. It was from Jonas. "Dear Rachel," she read aloud. "I've missed you. I hope you don't mind that I fixed our supper. I'll watch for you to come home, then give you an hour to get settled before I come over. I've done a lot of thinking, and I feel we should reconsider our future. Love, Jonas. P.S. Rosy baked the pie."

"*Ach!*" What was she going to tell the man? She thought about how she would have married Jonas, had he not rejected her keeping the girls. "*Der gut* Man knew what was best for me." She delighted in the image of Michael that nestled in her thoughts.

Annie's squeal shocked Rachel back to reality. She hurried into the living room. The little girl stood at the window, her hands against the glass. Jack stood panting on the other side, his eyes bright, his bushy tail wagging, and his tongue lolling out the side of his mouth. He had been groomed. His gray coat was smooth and shimmered like platinum.

"*Mem*, Annie play with Jack, *gel?*"

"Maybe after supper, we'll walk over to see Wayne and Rosy. Jack can go with us." She didn't know if she was relieved or disturbed that the monstrous dog was still on the property.

Pondering the possible awkwardness of the coming meal, she set the table. Rosy must have unlocked the door for Jonas. How else could the man have gotten in? She couldn't blame Rosy. She hadn't told her family about Michael, figuring it would be easier to explain in person. Now, she wished she had at least hinted.

Jonas came five minutes early. Prissy had been keeping watch on the porch, but as soon as the door opened, she streaked inside. Jonas scowled at the animal as she vanished into the living room. He had no sooner closed the door than he reached for Rachel. She stepped quickly away.

"We have to talk, Jonas."

"*Ja.* We'll talk after supper."

There he was, making the schedule according to Jonas. Michael always took her desires into account. Had Jonas ever asked her what she thought, or had he always assumed that he knew best? She avoided his hands a second time. Apparently he got the message for he didn't try again.

When they were seated at the table, Prissy made her entrance. Jonas glared at her; she glared back. Jumping to the chair that Sara usually occupied when she ate with Rachel, the cat squinted at Jonas.

He gritted his teeth. "When it isn't Sara, it's her beastly feline."

Rachel could not help notice how the cat seemed to delight in making the man uncomfortable. Jonas picked up the newspaper as though he were going to strike the animal. Prissy peered at him through green slits as though to say, "You wouldn't dare." Knowing the paper was an idle threat, Rachel laughed softly. Apparently deciding to ignore the cat, Jonas turned in his chair.

During the meal, Rachel chattered on about the Lapps and her vacation. Excitement gyrated through her as she described Emma's twin babies. Was she mistaken—or was he really uninterested? Since he didn't verbally complain, she continued. A thrill seemed to bubble in her veins as she told him how she had been able to help Moses. She explained that Michael had watched the *Kinder* during the lessons and how sweet Miriam was.

Scowling, Jonas clattered his fork to his plate. "So! Who is this Michael fellow?"

Her eyes wide, she stared at him. Had she said that much about Michael? Had she not been as tactful as she had planned to be? "*Vell*, Michael is Jacob John Zook's brother. And . . . he's a very nice gentleman who has four *Kinder*."

"And a wife?"

"She died five years ago."

A snort made him sound jealous. "I suppose he's looking for some unsuspecting creature to marry him to cook and look after his brood."

"Jonas . . . I . . ." Her voice faltered; she cleared her throat. "Would you like a piece of pie?"

"I'm not hungry."

She laughed, then interpreting his anger, she sobered. "But, you're always hungry."

"You're involved with this Michael, *gel*?"

"*Vell . . . Ja.*"

His chair squeaked on the vinyl as he shoved it back and stood. Seizing his black hat, he rammed it onto his head. His dark eyes bored into hers. "We've had an unspoken understanding for years, and the first time you visit out of state for more than a couple of weeks, you come back a tainted woman!"

Her eyes widened. Stalking to the door, he jerked the portal open, went out, and slammed it shut. As though his hasty departure were her doing, Prissy jumped from the chair and went to the window to watch him retreat. Rachel remained seated. She stared at the closed door, her soft lips parted.

"Jonas mad, *Mem*?"

The bewilderment on the little girl's face told Rachel she wasn't the only one flabbergasted over Jonas's raillery. A loud rap made her jump. She stared at the door. Picturing the burly stranger who had threatened her last winter, she shivered. Had Jonas locked the door on his mad dash for home?

CHAPTER EIGHTEEN

Another rap resounded.

Conquering her fear, Rachel went to the door, but saw no one through the small window. "Who's there?" she called.

"Forest and Jack, Ma'am."

She opened the door. He stood, straw hat in hand. His red hair was still bright enough to make one blink, but it was neatly trimmed, and his face shaven. Then she noticed his broadfalls and Wayne's shirt. "You want to become Amish?"

He shook his head. "I don't reckon I'll ever be good enough fer that, Miss Rachel. Rosy is mighty kind 'n she gave me new clothes." He nervously fingered the brim of his hat. "I was waitin' fer ya ta come so I could tell ya how grateful I am that ya trusted me. I did my best with yer animals while ya were gone. Now, I must be movin' on."

She opened the screen slightly. Jack pushed his nose into the crack. She petted him. Annie had followed her to the door. She reached to stroke the dog's nose.

"I wanted ya ta know that my daughter has asked me ta come ta live with her." He swallowed, making his Adam's apple bob. "I'd like ta ask ya fer one more favor."

Rachel met his brown eyes. "*Ja?*"

"Ma sister can't have no dogs at her place. I was wonderin', such as Annie loves Jack so much, if ya could take him in."

The thought of owning such a horse of a dog rendered her mute.

225

"*Ja Mem*. We keep Jack."

Before Rachel could recover, Annie shoved the screen open and dove for the huge dog. Wrapping her arms around his neck, she buried her face in his thick fur. "I love you, Jack. You be Annie's doggie, now."

Tears smarted Rachel's eyes. What could she do with such a monster dog? If she agreed to keep him, she would have to take him with her when she went back to Lancaster County. What would Michael say? Would he trust Jack around his *Kinder*? "Mister Grant, your dog is very nice, but I'm to be married and I don't know whether my future husband would want Jack."

Forest's eyes bugged. "Ya don't mean yer gonna marry up with Jonas?"

"No. There's someone else."

"Oh." Wrinkles formed across the bridge of his nose. "Jack hain't no bother, Ma'am. If ya jist feed him 'n give him a pet now 'n then, he'll be happy." He looked at Annie. She still clung to the dog's neck. "If ya don't take him, yer gonna have a heap of explainin' ta do."

"I promise I'll think about it—and pray for a sign from *der gut* Man. Will you give me a couple of days?"

"Sure. I hain't gonna leave 'til Sunday."

"Thank you." She pried Annie's arms loose from Jack and tried not to look at the little girl's face. The disappointment she knew would be there would grip her heart and maybe encourage her to make a wrong decision. "It's time to get ready for bed, Annie."

Reaching out, the little girl stroked the dog's snout. "*Gute naught*, Jack."

Rachel said good night to Forest and went inside. What else could happen to her tonight?

The house had been shut up and seemed a bit damp from the spring rains, so she built a fire in the fireplace. She glanced at the fabric-covered box on the hearth. It was close, but she decided it was far enough away from the blaze. Making sure the safety-screen was in place, she got the children ready for bed and tucked them in.

She had finished the lace tablecloth. The woman had picked it up and promised to send the money. Rachel hoped it hadn't been a mistake to trust her. All but one of the nine quilts Rachel had planned to make last winter had been finished. One with a patchwork pattern still remained on the frame. Her trip to visit Lapps had put her a bit behind. She wanted to complete the last quilt so she could take them with her to Michael's. After checking the slumbering little girls, she went upstairs, threaded a needle, and began to quilt.

Two hours later, Rachel straightened and massaged her back. When she quilted, she usually took a break every hour or so to stretch her legs. Getting up, she moved to the window and looked out across the moon-lit landscape. Nothing moved. The rain they'd had that day had left the trees refreshed. Their wet leaves glimmered in the dim light. She thought about Michael and his love for her, and her heart sang a song of devotion; peace surrounded her. She sighed.

After stretching once more and doing some bends, she went back to her seat at the quilt and picked up her needle. She took several stitches; then straightening, she sniffed. Something smelled hot. Had she put the screen back in front of the fireplace? She nodded to herself. She had a rule of never leaving the room without securing the safety screen in front of the blaze. Something wasn't right. Intending to go down to check the fire, she jabbed her needle into the quilt.

An explosion thundered through the house, shaking the foundation. Rachel leaped to her feet, stumbled, and grabbed the quilt frame for support. It crashed to the floor, sending pin cushions and thimbles flying. She tumbled on top of it.

My babies! blasted her senses. Scrambling to her feet,

she raced to the door and jerked it open. Smoke rolled up the stairs and into the room. She covered her nose with her hand and ran into the hall. Flames danced on the stair carpet. She couldn't descend and cross the living room and kitchen to the lower bedroom where the girls were sleeping.

"*Mem! Mem!*"

"*I'm koming,* Annie! Go back into your bedroom and shut your door!" Diving back into the room she had deserted, Rachel slammed the door. Racing across the room, she flung the window wide and crawled onto the porch roof. It was too far down to jump. If she broke a leg, she would not be able to get to the girls. Climbing back into the room, she seized the pile of eight finished quilts and stripped off the bed blankets and pillows. Returning to the roof, she chose a spot, and heaved her burden over the edge. Praying she would land on the cloud of blankets, she sat on the edge, dangling her legs over, then shoved.

She lit with a whoosh that knocked the wind from her, rolled, then clambered to her feet. Running around the house to the side door, she seized the knob. It was locked. She should have remembered that.

Racing around the corner of the dwelling, she paused under the lower bedroom window and thanked the Lord that she had instructed Annie to close the door. Maybe that would give the girls a bit more time and protection. She wondered what had happened, but didn't have time to ponder.

The window was too high! She could reach only the bottom part of the frame. She shoved upward. It refused to budge. Her heart thudded as she pushed harder. "It must be painted shut!"

There wasn't time to summon aid from Jonas or her brothers. She screamed, praying someone would hear her. Taking a rock, she smashed the glass in the window.

Smoke poured out into the night. The opening was too high for her to climb in. *The chair on the porch*!

Realizing the fresh air would give the fire oxygen to burn more profusely, she ran around the house and seized the chair.

Jack streaked from the barn.

Back at the window, Rachel looked at the dog and pointed. "The girls!" Rachel thumped the chair legs on the ground. Leaping to the seat, Jack bounded through the opening. Rachel retrieved one of the blankets and climbed onto the chair. As she flipped the fabric over the window sill, a splinter rammed under her fingernail. She cringed, but quickly forgot her pain. Jack appeared in the opening. He had grabbed a mouthful of Susan's nightgown and carried the baby to her as though the infant were in a sling.

"Bless you, Jack. Good boy. Get Annie!"

Again, the animal vanished into the smoke filled interior. Rachel hurried to the pile of quilts. Lugging them a safe distance from the burning cottage, she put Susan on them and raced back to the window. Terror writhed within her. Where was Annie? Jack wasn't back. Rachel rapidly climbed into the bedroom. "Annie!" She choked on smoke. Unable to breathe, she dropped to her knees. Disregarding the slivers of glass that slashed her knees, she crawled to the little girl's bed. Her hand swept the mattress. The cot was empty! Flinging herself across her own bed, she pawed the blankets. No Annie. Picturing the little girl cowering under the bed, Rachel thumped to the floor and rolled beneath the springs. There was nothing but storage boxes.

Scrambling free, she turned to the door into the kitchen. Her heart banged against her ribs; her pulse drummed in her temples. Annie had opened the door and had apparently been too terrified to close it! She must have tried to get out by going into the burning house! Flames roared through the living room. the sound amplifying Rachel's horror.

"Dear Lord. Oh, dear Lord. Please help me!"

Strangling on smoke, she crawled on raw and bleeding knees into the kitchen. The curtain hissed and flames licked the wallpaper beside her. She covered her nose with her apron.

Crackling, snapping sounds told her the ceiling was burning. intense heat informed her that the fire was spreading rapidly. By pressing her stomach to the floor and fighting for tiny breaths, she crept forward.

The dense smoke created a blackness inside the cottage that confused her; her brain became fuzzy and she lost her sense of direction. A dark shadow loomed before her. She tried to call Jack, but no sound came. The dog took her sleeve in his mouth and pulled. Praying, she followed him.

Stopping in front of the cupboard, he scratched its door.

Rachel was crazy from inhaling smoke, but not stupid enough to know that the bottom of the cupboard wasn't a way out. Grasping a handful of fur, she tugged.

Yanking free, Jack scratched the door more adamantly.

Realizing there must be a reason for the dog's insistence, she pushed the catch and yanked the door open. *Annie!*

The little girl lay in a crumpled heap. She tried to lift her, but her strength was waning. Jack seized the back of the girl's nightgown and pulled her free. Rachel hoped the door had been tight enough to keep out most of the smoke.

Annie was unconscious; Rachel crawled forward, keeping the little girl on the floor where the only air could be found. Jack continued to pull on Rachel's sleeve. Praying the dog knew where he was going, she inched her way after him.

She felt the panels of the side door. *Bless you Jack.* Rachel strained to reach the knob, but slumped back to the floor. Jack bumped her arm. Praying for strength, she forced herself upward, shoved the lock, grasped the knob and twisted.

The portal opened, but she slumped to the floor. Darkness washed over her in waves; she battled to remain conscious. Jack yanked her sleeve. She strained to reach the screen door hook, but failed. *Annie. Jack, save Annie!*

The dog scratched at the screen, then flung his bulk against it until it ripped.

The fresh air somewhat revived Rachel. She tried to get to her knees, but her arms buckled.

Something snapped and debris rained in the living room. The ceiling cracked and something clattered to the floor beside her. Scorching heat seared her. She screamed, but no sound issued from her parched throat.

Somewhere in the yard, Jack barked. Tortuous pain seared her left leg, then her arm. Again, she tried to scream. *Annie! Where's Annie?* Agonizing pain ripped at her flesh, then unconsciousness sucked her into a whirling dark void.

CHAPTER NINETEEN

Rachel became aware of excruciating pain. The fire! She must get herself and Annie out! Trying to move was futile. She felt strapped down. A moan escaped from her parched throat.

"Rachel."

She heard the summons and struggled to reply, but only a weak moan vibrated her throat.

"Wayne," Rosy said, "she's coming around."

Annie! Rachel's thoughts screamed. *Get Annie!*

A hand touched her right shoulder. "You're in the hospital," Wayne said. "You're going to be all right."

"Should we notify a nurse that she's conscious?" Henry asked.

"*Ja,*" Rosy said. "You go."

"How is she, *Mem?*" Sara Kate asked.

"Her burns are deep, dear, but she'll be all right in time."

"Her face!" Sara whispered. "*Wass* about her face?"

"Hush!" Rosy commanded.

Rachel fought to clear her foggy brain. Her face was on fire! So was her left leg and arm! Why didn't they get her out of the flames?

Finally, Rachel mustered enough strength to open her eyes. Rosy's round face loomed above her. "Annie?" Rachel choked.

"Thanks to Jack, she's going to be all right."

"Jack saved Susan, too," Rachel said, her voice a parched whisper. "Did you find her?"

"*Ja.* Both girls are fine. We arrived as Jack was lugging Annie out through the screen that he'd busted through. He barked and looked into the house, notifying Wayne that you were still inside. Henry smashed his fist through the screen near the hook and opened the door. Wayne grabbed you and pulled you out. Your skirt was on fire. Henry rolled you in a blanket to smother the flames."

Tears pooled in Rachel's eyes. She wanted to hug the huge dog. "Is Jack all right?"

"*Ja.*"

"He singed his pretty coat." Sara Kate made a face. "He looks half black and stinks awful."

Rachel thought about Jack's loyalty and figured he was now her dog. *That's fine with me.* She took a deep breath. "I hurt."

"I know, dear." Rosy stroked Rachel's right arm.

"My brain's addled," Rachel complained.

"That's from inhaling smoke—as well as the medication the doctor gave you to ease your pain."

"The drug isn't doing a very good job."

"*Vell,* burns cause some of the worst kind of pain." She held a glass of water to Rachel's lips.

Rachel gratefully took a sip. "I feel like I'm still on fire." The left side of her face felt as though she had rested it on a hot griddle. Where are my worst burns?"

"Your left leg and left arm have third degree burns and will take awhile to heal," Henry said.

She tried to focus on him. "My face?"

"*Vell* . . ." He frowned and looked at Wayne.

Wayne looked at Rosy. Rosy looked away. Horror smote Rachel. If her face looked like it felt . . . She reached to investigate.

Henry grabbed her wrist. "Don't touch your burns. They could get infected."

"Then, please tell me what my face looks like."

"It's . . . bad, but it will heal," Rosy said.

Rachel searched the woman's expression. "Without a scar?"

"*Vell* . . ." She looked flustered. "I'm not a doctor. I'm sure she will explain the degrees of your injuries and what you can expect."

Sadness mingled with Rachel's physical agony. She had been pretty when Michael had fallen in love with her. If her face was ruined, she could not expect him to marry her. What about her leg? What about her arm? Was she going to be crippled?

Oh, Michael! her aching heart cried.

Rachel's days and nights stretched into endless sessions of anguish and misery, blotted out only by periods of black holes created by medication. Consciousness brought back the reality of her burns, the scalding pain, and the emotional devastation of scarring.

A number of times she thought she had heard Michael's voice. He told her over and over how much he loved her, but when she woke, he was gone. If he did come to visit her, she didn't want him staring at her ugly burns when she wasn't awake to hide her face. She told Rosy she didn't want any company except her family and made them promise to make the nurses keep her door shut and everyone else out of her room.

Her drugged sleep sent her hurling into nightmares where she had no face and Michael turned away. She didn't know which was worse, the pain or the nightmares. She longed to be with him, yet she didn't want him to see her this way. Would this torture ever end?

Mercer County, Pennsylvania. Liz Ann sat on the porch swing at Millers' farm near New Wilmington. The chain squeaked as she moved back and forth. The aroma of new green growth drifted to her in wisps of a fresh April breeze; the scent of freshly tilled earth hung in the air, a sign that planting was near. Samuel, plowing the cornfield nearest the house, waved each time he drove the horses down a new furrow. His warm smile was a welcome, his dimpled cheeks a lure. She frowned. Was it because they reminded her of Eli? She opened the book Leah had loaned her. If she pretended to be engrossed, she wouldn't have to return Samuel's frequent greetings.

Leah came out and sat on the other end of the swing. "A lot has happened the past year." She smiled. "Elizabeth came last summer; now, she and Elam are married and expecting their first baby together."

"Sara Beiler and Joseph King are settled and expecting, too." Liz Ann closed her book. "Are Rebecca and Aaron?"

"Not yet. Rebecca is finishing her first year of nurse's training. She said when they expected their first little one, she would quit school, although she feels *der gut* Man wants her to be a nurse."

"Aaron's looking for another helper." Liz Ann pursed her lips. "I thought maybe Michael Zook would be interested."

"He is, but he's so worried about Rachel."

Liz Ann nodded. "My heart grieves for her. I pray several times a day that *der gut* Man will ease her pain and help her grow strong."

"*Ja.* So do I." She sighed. "She was so pretty."

Tears burned the backs of Liz Ann's eyes. "Wayne writes. The family is concerned, for Rachel could have scars. He asked us to pray that *der gut* Man will be merciful and heal her burns without many scars."

Mattie came up the lane from the mailbox. Waving letters, she scurried in the path and up the porch steps. "Leah, you got one from Emma." A smile brightened her eyes as she handed Liz Ann her mail. "One from Rachel's brother; one from Eli Beiler."

Liz Ann's heart gave a sudden thrust, then began to

beat rapidly. She longed for up-to-date information about Rachel, but she had to know what Eli had in mind. Her fingers trembling, she ripped open the envelope and unfolded the paper. Leah was motionless. She was probably holding her breath, too.

"*Vell*?" She began to bounce. "*Wass* he say?"

Joy fountained within Liz Ann. She felt as though a mountain of soapsuds were inside, frothing to get out. "Eli sold his car! He says he's joining the Church, and he wants me to come home."

Tears welled in Leah's eyes. "I'm so happy for you." Her voice choked. "If only Peter would sell his car and . . ." She blinked and a tear rolled down her cheek. "Are you going home?"

"Oh, *ja*!"

Leah glanced over her shoulder at Samuel. "My dear brother won't be happy to hear that."

"Wait!" Liz Ann flipped the paper over, read the next sentence, and laughed. "Read this for yourself."

Accepting the paper, Leah read where Liz Ann pointed. "Peter John is writing to Leah to tell her that he sold his Trans Am. We pray you both start to pack."

Liz Ann met Leah's tear-filled gaze with blurred vision. "We're both going home." She swiped at a happy tear. "I warned Samuel that I was praying for this to happen. Do you think Amos will be devastated over your leaving?"

Leah shook her head. "I convinced him that his heart was really pining for Elsie Miller. After seeing her a few times, he agreed with me."

When Liz Ann thought about Rachel, she sobered. "I wish my cousin could be as happy as we are."

"Read her brother's letter."

The news included Rachel's latest prognosis. Her leg and arm were healing nicely, but they would scar, and she might have a slight limp. It was her face that concerned her family. Her left cheek wasn't healing as quickly as the doctor had hoped. The burn on her face would probably leave a scar, but they hadn't told Rachel as yet. Liz Ann's heart ached. How could she enjoy her renewed relationship with Eli when her beloved cousin was suffering so drastically?

Ohio. Rachel touched her face. Even though they continued treatment, the surface skin felt as dry and cracked as old leather. Why weren't they talking to her about it? She was in a semi-private room and hated the way her roommate stared at her.

"You should look at your face," the woman said.

"Amish aren't permitted mirrors," Rachel explained quietly.

The woman shrugged. "You don't have to own a mirror. There's one in the bathroom."

The nurses had been helping Rachel to walk with crutches. The left one hurt her arm a bit, but she was learning to cope. Every time she went into the bathroom, she kept her eyes downcast. The nurses always accompanied her and seemed to be watching closely. Perhaps they wondered if she would give in and use the mirror that had been forbidden by her church. It was becoming more and more difficult to battle her curiosity.

Her roommate continued to sow seeds of temptation. "Why don't you just sneak a peak. No one will know."

My Lord will know, Rachel thought. *And so will I.*

Her intentions were honorable; however, the next time she needed to visit the bathroom, she didn't summon the nurse. Entering alone, her gaze traveled slowly upward. Someone had covered the mirror with a towel. Rosy had been in for a visit. Had she been the one to drape the looking-glass? Was she afraid Rachel would look at herself? Was it disobedience that concerned Rosy? *Or was she afraid I'd see my face?*

Reaching with trembling fingers, she grasped the towel

and pulled gently. She expected to meet her own gray eyes, but the material snagged. Rachel felt relieved to have been stopped. Then, as though playing a fiendish trick, the towel dropped. Her reflection loomed before her. She screamed and lost her grip on her crutches. They cracked against the wall and clattered onto the floor. Her knees weakened, and she seized the edge of the sink for support.

A nurse came running. "Oh, Rachel!" Supporting her, she helped her back to bed. "You rest, dear. I'll get the doctor."

Rachel watched her go. Tears stung her eyes, then rolled down her face. There was no way she would ask Michael to sit at the table with a woman who looked as she did. Besides, the *Kinder* would be frightened of her. Why was she worried? The decision wasn't hers. Michael would not want her, now.

Peggy, a teenage volunteer, swept into the room, her pink skirt swishing. Smiling, she waved a letter. "Another one from Michael Zook," she said, her voice melodious.

"Put it with the others." Rachel Kay fought more tears.

Peggy's smile faded and she placed a hand on Rachel's arm. "Is there something I can do?"

Rachel studied the girl's pretty round face. Her long auburn hair shimmered and concern filled her light-blue eyes. Her compassion comforted Rachel, but the girl's beauty reminded Rachel that she had lost hers.

"Maybe it will help if I read your mail to you."

Rachel shook her head. "Thank you, but just put it with the rest."

Frowning, Peggy placed the letter on the neatly stacked pile on the stand, then left quietly.

Every day another letter arrived and joined the rest. Rachel soaked in warm baths, then the doctors worked with her skin. Pain was her companion—except when she slept. Even then, misery was her pillow and anguish her coverlet. She wondered if she would ever know joy again.

Exhausted from another soaking ordeal, she lay on her bed staring at the ceiling. Her phone in the hospital room rang. She was closer to it than Edna, her roommate, but she refused to pick it up. She noticed the woman's struggle to reach the instrument, yet she didn't offer to help. Shame flew at her like sinister bats. She cringed.

Edna finally managed to grasp the phone. "Hello . . . Yes. She's here." The woman proffered the receiver, her brown eyes challenging. "It's Michael Zook."

Rachel's eyes widened, then stung with tears that she forbade, and her stomach cramped from struggling to control sobs. Her heart throbbed with wanting but she clenched her fingers, refusing to reach for the phone. She wouldn't be marrying him. How could she bear hearing his voice? How could she stand his pity?

Edna sighed. "Rachel can't talk to you right now, Mr. Zook." She put the receiver back and peered at Rachel. "You're a real dope. That man cares about you."

"He . . . hasn't seen me."

Edna looked pensive. "You should look like me." She laughed. "A burn would probably make me look better."

It wasn't true, but Rachel appreciated the woman's effort to try to lift her spirit. Each day dragged by. The pain of the burns lessened, but the anguish in Rachel's heart mounted.

Michael called frequently. Each time, Rachel refused to speak with him. She knew she would burst into tears, and she couldn't stand to humiliate herself or Michael.

Several more days crawled by, pushing heartache and dragging misery.

A nurse stopped near her bed. "You have a visitor, Rachel."

She eyed her closed door and swallowed. "Who?" Her voice was a choked whisper.

"Michael Zook."

She turned her head. "I can't see him."

"He has flowers."

Blinking fast to disperse the sudden tears, she swallowed hard. "Please tell him to go away."

"Rachel?" he called through the door.

Her throat tightened; her stomach cramped and she felt as though she were strangling on the inside. She opened her mouth to tell him to go away, but no sound came.

"Rachel, please let me come in."

The rich timbre of his voice vibrated her core, and the earnestness of his plea gripped her heart. Still, she shook her head. The nurse quietly retreated.

For three days, Michael tried to talk to her through the closed door, but her throat constricted around sobs and she couldn't answer him. Apparently taking her silence as a rebuff, he left. Grief settled on Rachel like a huge suffocating claw. She prayed and believed the Lord would give her strength to cope with losing Michael. She couldn't understand why she'd been asked to suffer so, but it wasn't for her to question the Lord. He and He alone would decide her destiny. She must accept it, adjust, and continue to praise and adore Him.

"I will be faithful to *der gut* Man until the end of my life on Earth, no matter what He asks me to bear," she murmured, but prayed for Him to lighten her burden.

One sunny morning in early April, Dr. Joy Commings entered her room. "This is discharge day for you, Rachel."

"Oh." A sword of fear pierced her heart. *How will my little girls react to my unsightly face?*

Rosy and Sara Kate came to help Rachel pack her few belongings. Rosy folded the robe and put it in Rachel's case.

Sara Kate opened the stand drawer and withdrew the packet of letters from Michael. "*Ach!* They aren't opened!"

She glanced at Rachel's bandaged left hand. "We should've opened your mail for you."

Rachel battled her aching heart. "I chose to leave them sealed."

"*Fer wass?*"

Sara Kate studied Rachel's face and seemed to realize her dilemma. Sadness shadowed the girl's expression as she turned away.

The rented car turned up the lane that passed Rachel's property. Looking out the window to see how much damage her cottage had sustained, she gasped. Blackened foundation stones, the remains of burned timbers and gray ash were all that remained. Scraggly weeds grew where her flowers had once bloomed. Tears burned her eyes.

I still have Annie and Susan, she thought, *at least until they see my face.*

When the car stopped at Wayne's farmhouse, he came to help her inside. Getting ready to leave the hospital and the trip home had taken a lot out of her and she slumped into the recliner in the living room. Prissy leaped to the arm of the chair and peered curiously at her, then jumped down and walked slowly away. Was even the cat going to reject her, now?

"Annie!" Sara Kate called up the stairway. "Your *Mem's* home."

"*Mem?*" Little footsteps resounded on the stairs.

With each little thump, Rachel's heart throbbed more violently. She thought about running, but she would not be able to get very far. She longed to cover her face, but, sooner or later, she would have to get used to her little girl's reaction. Gripping the arm of the chair with her good hand, she waited, barely breathing.

Annie appeared in the doorway, paused, and stared; then slowly moved forward to climb into Rachel's lap. Her gray eyes filled with question and compassion, she gently touched the burned side of Rachel's face. "Does it hurt, *Mem*?"

"Not any more, unless I bump it."

"Will it git all better?"

"I . . . don't know."

Annie continued to study the burn, then she smiled. "It looks like a big prune, *Mem*."

Rachel smothered a gasp. The child couldn't have known how her description would gouge Rachel's heart.

Little arms went around Rachel's neck and Annie laid her head on her shoulder. "I love you, *Mem*."

The lump in Rachel's throat seemed to grow as large as a basketball. "Does my face bother you?" she asked, then instantly regretted it. A child told the truth. Was she ready to hear it?

Pushing away slightly, Annie peered at the burn, again. "Oh, *Mem*." She smiled. "Jesus will make it all better."

Rachel hugged her. How wonderful was the faith of a child.

Michael's letters continued to pile up on Rachel's dresser. Still, she refused to open them. She would not answer the door, and unable to abide the pity she knew would be in the eyes of the ladies in her district, she hid in an upstairs bedroom when company came. Her face slowly healed, but she knew she looked horrid. She used an old Indian remedy that had helped a friend. Each morning she fried two slices of bacon and saved the drippings. After washing her burn with Absorbine Junior, she applied the cooled grease. If it worked, she would declare it a miracle and praise the Lord.

Holding the bowl of grease, she stared at the particle of bacon that floated on top.

Sara Kate stopped near her. "Let me help you cover your burn."

Sighing, Rachel proffered the bowl.

Rosy waved a card as she entered the room. "Rachel,

we got an invitation to a wedding in November."

The announcement created painful echoes in Rachel's heart, for she and Michael would have been married in November. "Who's getting married?"

"Liz Ann Lapp and Eli Beiler."

"*Un wonderbar!*" Some time ago, when Liz Ann was praying for Eli to settle down, the girl had asked Rachel to be one of her sidesitters. She had joyously agreed. Now, her situation would warrant her absence.

Supper was served and the family had just taken seats around the table when a rap resounded on the door.

"I'll get it," Wayne said.

Before he got to the door, it swung open. Rachel gasped.

Twelve-year-old Lydia Zook rushed into the kitchen, her eyes darting from one family member to another. Covering her face, Rachel jumped up and fled to the downstairs bedroom. Closing the door, she leaned against it, her heart pounding. What was the girl doing here?

"Rachel?" Lydia called, tapping on the bedroom door. "Rachel!"

CHAPTER TWENTY

Rachel's heart fluttered wildly. What could Lydia want? She gasped. Had Michael come, too? *Fer wass?*

The light rapping continued. "Rachel," Lydia called softly. "Please let me in."

There was a catch in the girl's voice. Was she crying? Had something happened to her father? Concern for Michael encouraged her to open the door; however, she kept her face averted. Prissy slipped into the room and took a seat in the chair by the window.

Lydia closed the door softly and rested her hand on Rachel's arm. "*Es speid mich es ich sel gedu had* (I'm sorry that I did that)."

"Did *wass?*"

"It's my fault. Oh, Rachel, your burns are my fault!" Her voice continued to rise as she spoke. Then she burst into sobs.

Forgetting the embarrassment of the huge prune on the side of her face, Rachel turned to her. "Lydia, *wass* are you talking about?"

The girl flung herself into Rachel's arms, nearly knocking her over, for she hadn't yet regained all her strength, and at twelve years, Lydia was already five inches taller. "I hated you for caring for Papa. I was afraid you'd ruin our life. I wished for something to happen to your pretty face so that Papa wouldn't want you anymore."

"*Vell* . . . I guess you got your wish."

"No!" Lydia wailed. "Can you ever forgive me?"

"*Ach*. The fire wasn't your doing. While I was away,

Mark lit lamps to make my cottage look lived in. Since he needed to fill my lamps, he kept a can of fuel handy. Expecting to return that evening, he set it under a fabric-covered box on the hearth. His infant son developed a fever, and Mark forgot about the hidden fuel. It was a bit damp and cool for the girls. Not knowing about the kerosene, I lit the logs I had piled in the fireplace. The heat caused the fuel to explode, and the flames were fed by escaping gas through broken lines."

Lydia clung to Rachel's good arm. "I feel so terrible! Please come back to us."

"I'm afraid I can't do that. Your Papa wouldn't want me, now, and I won't embarrass him by making him tell me so."

Lydia studied Rachel's face. "The burn looks bad, but your sweetness shines through. I'm so ashamed. If you *kom* back to us, I'll do everything I can to make you happy." More tears rilled down her young cheeks. "Please *kom* home to *Pap*."

The door behind Rachel opened quietly, then closed. Prissy flicked her ears and blinked.

"I want my face to heal," Rachel murmured, "then we'll see."

Lydia glanced over Rachel's shoulder and nodded slightly. Slipping away, she left the room. Strong hands rested on Rachel's shoulders. They were too large to be Rosy's and not large enough for Wayne or Henry. Rachel swallowed. The hands tried to turn her around. She resisted. Prissy switched her tail in satisfaction and cocked her head at a curious angle.

"I love you," Michael whispered in Rachel's ear.

She gasped. "But you haven't seen my face."

"Anything that hurts you grieves me, but whether or not your face is marred has nothing to do with my love for you."

"I'm ugly."

"You're beautiful."

"I have a horrid scar!"

"I will remember you the way you were and forget the marks when I look at you."

"You can't!"

"*Ja*, I can. That's what real love is, Rachel." Turning her around he pulled her into his arms. "I would love you if you had no face at all."

She rested her forehead against his blue shirt. This man was one in a million, and he loved her. How long would it take her to forget her looks and be able to face him without wincing? "Maybe I could fix something to cover my cheek."

His warm lips rested on her forehead. "A face doesn't make a woman any more than blossoms make a tree." His embrace tightened. "Have you not heard that it is when a flower's petals are crushed that the sweetest essence flows from it?"

"*Ja*, but this is different."

"We will face it together. Some may see a scar when they look at you, but I see love that surpasses your saving your own life."

"*Wass* do you mean?"

"You were outside. You reentered the flaming house to rescue Annie. She would have died, had you not sacrificed to go after her."

"*Wass* else would a mother do?"

"Love sometimes calls us to sacrifice. You have been asked to give more than most. You were willing."

Jesus gave his all, she thought as she rested her head against Michael's chest.

His arms tightened. "You gave the years of your youth to raise your siblings, then you were willing to risk your life to save Annie. Now, I'm asking you to give more. Will you?"

"*Ja*." Her heart overflowed with adoration for this man;

she wanted to give the rest of her life to him. "You have a particular need?"

"Oh, I do." Chuckling, he placed two fingers under her chin and tilted her face upward. "I need *you*, Rachel. I want you to be my wife and the mother of my *Kinder*." He grinned. "Those that are here—and those that are to *kom*."

How could she have doubted the depth and earnestness of his affection? Loving him with all her heart, she gazed into his sparkling eyes. It was the first time she had faced anyone squarely since being burned.

Michael stared at her cheek, his smile fading. Her heart convulsed as his expression changed. Bending closer to her face, he squinted. Jerking free, she whirled away.

"Wait!" Gripping her good arm, he coaxed her to face him. "Let me see that."

"No." The word squeaked through her constricted throat.

"Rachel." Gently, for it wasn't in him to force his will, he held her and tilted her face to the light. "How long has it been since your doctor examined your burn?"

"About three weeks. I didn't go back when I was supposed to. She always says the same thing, and I didn't want to hear it, again."

"The damaged skin on the surface is dark and scaly, but at the edges, it is loosening and pealing away. Underneath, the new skin is soft and white." He grinned. "It looks as smooth as a baby's bottom."

Since there were no mirrors in her home, she hadn't seen her face since the day at the hospital. She bit her lower lip.

Michael touched her unaffected cheek. "Darling, I've seen many burns, and my guess is that your face won't scar much."

The old Indian remedy must be working—with the Lord's help. She smiled. "I'll pray harder."

"We both will. *Wass* ever *der gut* Man sends us we will

accept and adjust to. We will pray and believe He will do *wass* is best for us."

After much pleading on Lydia's part, and Michael's quiet encouragement, Rachel agreed to go back to Lancaster County with them. Rosy said she would come for the November wedding—even if there were ten feet of snow.

It didn't take long for Rachel to pack, for her belongings had been burned—except for her quilts. Rosy had made her two dresses. Sara Kate had practiced her sewing skills by making clothing for Annie and baby Susan.

Because of Jack, Michael hired a van instead of a car. Lydia already loved the huge dog, and she said she knew her siblings would accept him on sight.

As Lydia explained how Jack was going to become a member of their family, Annie listened intently. Moisture collected in the little girl's eyes, making them shimmer like liquid silver. "Jack's my doggie." Her lower lip quivered, and a tear trailed a wet ribbon down her cheek.

"Ach!" Lydia knelt to hug her. "Of course he's your doggie. You and *Mem* Rachel are going to live with us, too."

Annie's questioning eyes sought Rachel's, and Rachel swept the little girl into her arms. There had been too much fast talking for Annie to comprehend everything. "Remember me telling you that soon we were going to live at Miriam's house with Lydia, Andrew, and Moses?"

Annie nodded, sending another tear down her cheek. Smiling, she swiped it away. "And Jack, too, *Mem, gel*?"

"*Ja.* Jack will live where we do."

Satisfied, Annie wiggled to get down. Going to the porch, she hugged Jack and explained, in a two-year-old fashion, how he was going to love his new home.

Rachel's nearby siblings came to send her off with hugs and best wishes. After many tearful waves, the hired van headed eastward. As the vehicle rounded a curve, Rachel glanced back. Prissy sat on the gate post, watching the vanishing van.

When they were well on their way, Rachel rested her head against the back of her seat and smiled. She would be able to help Liz Ann with her wedding. Her smile broadened. *Then she can help me with mine.*

Michael had told the driver to go to Lapps' first, because he wanted to help Rachel carry her bags into the house. When the van stopped, Jack bounded out the open door before Rachel could unbuckle her seat belt. Martha had been sweeping the porch. Her broom stopped in mid-swing, and her eyes widened. She blinked as though she wondered if the huge dog were real. He stopped several feet from her and wagged his tail. She timidly reached a hand to him. He sniffed it. She petted him.

The Lapp family greeted Rachel with smiles and welcoming hugs. Rachel's attempt to hide her face was futile; however, no one commented about the mark. After the van left to take Michael and Lydia to their home, Liz Ann led Rachel to the bedroom they were to share with Annie and Susan. Liz Ann was bubbling with happiness. Rachel listened to her explanation of how Eli had sold his Buick and joined the church. Leah Miller was overjoyed that Peter John had sold his vehicle at the same time and also joined the church. Both couples were to be married in November.

Liz Ann giggled. I thought I'd found sunshine with Eli; but it turned cloudy when he stubbornly continued his *rumspringe*. Her smile made her face radiant. When we're married, it will be glorious!"

Rachel shared her cousin's joy. "Leah Miller's ecstatic, too. Are she and Peter John serious about moving to Kentucky?"

"Oh, *Ja*. Peter John already has a lead on a farm, and they're excited about going."

As the days passed, more and more of the damaged skin peeled from Rachel's face. She continued the treatment with bacon grease and Absorbine Jr. She hated smelling like a cured ham and feeling like a greased piglet, but if the remedy worked, it would be worth the humiliation.

When the old skin had pealed off, Rachel's face felt new and tender. How she longed to study her reflection in a mirror, but she continued to be obedient to the rules of the district. If her face looked like her arm or her leg . . . The burns on her extremities had been more severe. She had used the old remedy, but the muscles under her skin had been somewhat damaged. Sighing, she went to the kitchen to help with supper, her limp hardly noticeable.

The Lapp men were still at the barn; Naomi hadn't returned from an afternoon visit to Zimmermans'. Martha was gathering the eggs, and Ella was in the room playing with Annie. After setting the table, Anna Ruth vanished up the stairway, leaving Rachel alone with Liz Ann. Again, Rachel sighed.

Liz Ann peered curiously at her. "*Was is letz?*"

Rachel pleaded with her eyes. "Please tell me about my face—and be completely honest. *Wass* does it look like to you, and *wass* are people saying?"

Liz Ann looked pensive, then she slowly said, "*Vell*, most of your left cheek is whiter than the rest of your face, but the summer sun will probably blend your skin tone." Compassion brimmed in her green eyes. "There's a mark on your cheekbone that probably won't go away."

A stabbing pain shot through Rachel's middle and her heart cramped. "How big is the scar?"

"It's an inch and a half long and about a half inch wide."

Rachel swallowed a persistent lump in her throat. "Is it purple?"

"It's white—with a slight tinge of pink."

Tears smarted the backs of Rachel's eyes, but she forbade them to flow. A light-pink scar wasn't as bad as purple or a brownish hue, still . . . She turned to the sink to finish peeling the potatoes. "*Gross Dank* for being honest."

Liz Ann hugged her. "Once people get to know you, they don't notice the mark." She laughed softly. "Ella says it looks like you bumped into the edge of a door frame."

Rachel was a bit relieved. She thought about riding in a carriage with Michael and was thankful her scar was on the side where it would not show when he glanced her way. Was it prideful to want to hide the mark?

The sun was still fairly high when Michael's carriage stopped at Lapps's gate. Due to exercise, Rachel's limp was only slightly noticeable. Joy effervesced within her as she hurried to meet Michael. Luke whinnied a welcome and she petted him.

Michael returned her generous smile. "Let's go for a walk."

They strolled down the path toward the peach trees. Pausing, Rachel peered at the clear light-blue sky. The scent of fresh green growth and blossoms sweetly scented the air. A robin left her nest in the nearby apple tree and fluttered to the grass several feet away. Michael's eyes took in the scenery, but invariably returned to Rachel's face. She tried to ignore the desire to screen the mark on her cheek, but Michael seemed to be studying her scar. Her heart ached. How long would it be until she could accept being marred and go on with life as though nothing had happened? She supposed that was too much to hope for. She would learn to accept it, though, and praise the Lord for her blessings.

The early evening sun sent fingers of brilliant rays through the leaves that made lacy patterns on the ground. The dapples of light played on them as they strolled along the path. A slight breeze moved Rachel's blue skirt and toyed with Michael's beard.

Stopping, he turned to her and took her hands in his. Adoration shone in his light-brown eyes. "We don't get to spend enough time together," he murmured. "I wish we could marry before fall."

Rachel felt framed in peach blossoms as she smiled up at him. "The time will come, although the days seem to pass so slowly."

He peered intently at her scar. She had stopped wincing and turning away, but when anyone stared at the blemish, she became self-conscious and wanted to flee.

"When I look at your scar, I see love," he said softly. "It's a symbol of your caring. Has anyone told you that your scar is shaped like half of a heart?"

The thought made her laugh softly. "No."

"*Vell*, it is. The top rounds to the right." His smile broadened. "I have a birthmark on my shoulder shaped exactly like that, only mine rounds to the left at the top." His eyes twinkled. "When we're married, our marks will form a complete heart."

His arms gently encircled her and she rested her head against his light-blue shirt. A warm and wonderful feeling encompassed her, and she felt protected in a cocoon of love and loyalty. She had much to thank the Lord for. She had been blessed. She thanked the Lord for His grace and mercy. It seemed as though her love for Michael would consume her. "I wish we could be married right away."

"*Ja.*" His embrace tightened. "We will ask the Bishop. Maybe he will give us special permission."

Two weeks later, in spite of the busy season of farm work, Michael and Rachel were married in his home. Rachel had attended many weddings and had envisioned how she would feel at her own, but her ecstasy greatly surpassed her expectations. Amid the festivities, Michael's eyes met hers. She knew the love that shimmered in their depths matched her own.

When they were finally alone, he took her in his arms. "My dearest Rachel, and now we are one."

Nestling within his embrace, she envisioned his four

Kinder and her two. She laughed softly. "And now we are eight!"

"*Vell, ja* . . . yet."

"Oh, Michael, I prayed for love, my own special Eden. I found it with you; then after I was burned, I assumed I'd lost my chance for happiness."

"You were the dawn of a new Eden for me, but my life turned to shadows when you refused to see me." His arms tightened, pulling her closer. "We have been blessed, darling Rachel."

"*Ja.* It's the dawn of Eden for both of us."

"*Un wonderbar.*"

She reveled within his warm embrace. "*Un wonderbar a hundret muhl!*"

The End

Other Books to Enjoy From *Barbara Michel's Eden Series* . . .

Ensnared by a web of guilt, Rebecca searches for true meaning in her life.

Faced with adversity, Elizabeth hunts for answers.

Any Eden Series book is $9.95.
1-800-358-0777

Wholesome Drama From Our Historical Novel Series*

*All are available with free study guides for home schoolers.

This true-life mascot is a "pet" for those who love to reenact Civil War adventure.

Waves sweep John Howland from off the deck of The Mayflower — he is rescued only to face adversity at Plymouth Colony the following year.

Intrigue surrounds the mysterious stranger named Adam — the one-armed soldier from the Civil War.

Any of the above $9.95 from